M000033062

Also by Rosalie T. Turner

*My Very Own Book of the Lord's Prayer*
published by Abingdon Press

*Going to the Mountain: Lessons for Life's Journey*
published by WinePress

# Freedom Bound

### A Novel

### Rosalie Turner

*For Joan —
Hope you enjoy this —
Rosalie Turner*

Copyright © 2006 by Rosalie Turner

All Rights Reserved. No part of this book may be reproduced
in any form or by any electronic or mechanical means, including
information storage and retrieval systems, without permission in
writing from the publisher, except by a reviewer who may quote brief
passages in a review

ISBN 978-0-9679483-3-1

Library of Congress Control Number: 2006921993

This is a work of fiction inspired by the life of Anna Kingsley.
Names, characters, places and events are the products of the
author's imagination.

Cover and Text design by Darron Moore,
**MOORE OR LESS DESIGN**

Printed in the United States of America

First Edition

Season of Harvest Publications
Campbell, Texas 75422

Dr. Fred Tarpley, Senior Editor

## Dedication

With love and gratitude to
Willonet Cable
and
Dr. Fred Tarpley,
Mentors *extraordinaire*

## Acknowledgments

This book could not have been written without the excellent research of the main authority on Anna Kingsley, Dr. Daniel L. Schafer in his book, *Anna Madgigine Jai Kingsley: African Princess, Florida Slave, Plantation Slaveowner.*

I am grateful to so many friends and critiquers, especially Gerald and Carol Ashmore, Jim and Serene Johnson, my Birmingham, AL Book Club, and the Moreno Valley (NM) Writers Group.

Thanks also to the Park Rangers at Kingsley Plantation, Roger & Carol Clark, for help with my research.

To the Embassy of Senegal Cultural Counselor, Fatoumata BNDAO, for research help.

To Caroylyn Huickley for all your help, encouragement, and for your friendship.

Deep thanks go to my editor, Jim Ainsworth, at Season of Harvest. You have taught me so much.

Most of all, thanks to my husband, Frank Kile Turner, for love, support, patience and encouragement. I couldn't have done it without you.

# Freedom Bound

A Novel

Rosalie Turner

# Chapter One

*Yang Yang*
*Wolof state, Senegal, Africa*
*May 1806*

Rough hands on her shoulder jerked Anta awake.

"Anta! Get up!"

Groggily, she tried to make sense of her father's tense voice and the screams in the background.

*What was happening?*

Anta struggled away from her dreams, confused, as if she were swimming deep under water in the river and broke onto the surface but couldn't yet get her bearings.

"Anta! Bolanile! Urbi! Get up!" Her father's voice sounded more urgent.

He pulled away her light cover. "Anta. Come. Now."

She had never heard that tone of voice from her father, that urgency, that...terror. His face finally came into focus for her, and what she saw there filled her with panic. Her father's usually calm brown eyes darkened with dread, his face set in a mask of anger and fear. Anta's mother pulled her two sisters from their mats.

"What...?" Anta started.

"It is the tyeddo warriors! Run!...Scatter! Try to get away!"

With her father pushing them, Anta, her mother, and her two sisters, Bolanile and Urbi, burst out the door of their mud hut into chaos. People ran in every direction. Screaming. Calling out. A dust cloud engulfed the entire village.

The vicious attackers swooped down on the townspeople, cutting off escape and shooting some of the men on sight. Anta screamed at the sight of the warriors, their long hair in one braid, their faces covered with cloth to protect them from the dust, their eyes slits of violence.

On their sturdy horses, yelling as they came, they were worse than any nightmare. The riders loomed as huge monsters, some with swords slashing through the air, others with guns spitting fire. Some threw their torches onto the thatched roofs of the huts or inside, and the leaping flames silhouetted the warriors in a grisly light. Sparks surrounded Anta. She choked on the smoke and dust.

She turned to grab her sister, but where was she? Where was Mama? Terrified, she looked right and left for them. "Mama! Papa!" The dust swirling in the air choked the words in her throat.

Instinct told her she had to act.

Anta ran. She ran with all the strength in her lean thirteen-year-old body. She darted this way and that around huts, pushing between people, tears streaking through the dust and soot on her ebony cheeks, leaving her face painted as if for war. Anta ran through the village with no sense of where she was going.

She jumped around a pile of rags in her path, only realizing as she ran on that she passed the lifeless body of an old woman, a neighbor. "Mama!" Anta screamed, desperate in her need for her mother to make sense of the chaos.

More and more huts burned. She felt the searing heat from the flames. Sparks burned her arms and face like some evil beast nipping at her as she ran. Her sobs tore at her throat. She stumbled as she glanced behind her. The dust clogged her mouth and nose, stung her eyes. Her breath came in gasps.

Where could she run? There were no woods nearby for hiding. Through the half-light from the fires, she saw the baobab tree on the other side of the millet field. If she could reach it, she could hide in its branches. She raced on.

The burning huts cast an eerie light over the destruction. Anta ran with the speed she had developed living in that harsh land. Gasping, she clutched her chest to keep it from bursting. She ran through the millet field. The stubble from the dried stalks slapped and cut her bare legs, the stinging pain making her cry out. She saw the large baobab tree just ahead. With no leaves, it offered little protection, but perhaps....

Anta neared the edge of the village, but still the noise overwhelmed her, a loud, rushing roar, the whoosh of the thatched roofs burning; the yells of the tyeddo; the screams of the people; the final blasts of muskets. Anta wanted to put her hands over her ears, but she had to run.

Even above the wave of noise from the village, Anta heard the terrifying clopping of hoof beats behind her. She pushed herself harder than she ever had before. She must get away. She must.

A massive, sweaty arm swooped, lifted her up and threw her across the saddle. The horse had not even slowed as the rider grabbed her. She heard the throaty, evil laugh from behind the scarf over the warrior's face, a sound of cruel victory. The horse and rider whipped around with Anta, a sack of meal in the rider's lap. Her face hung down, but the thick dust swirled so that she couldn't see the ground flashing by. Anta felt a terror beyond anything she could have imagined. Her ragged breath tore at her throat.

At the town center, the rider shoved Anta to the ground. Her shoulder smacked against the hard earth, and she cried out in pain. Another warrior grabbed her arm and shoved her into the group of villagers being massed together. Anta became part of the moaning and crying that rose up like a hopeless prayer around her.

She looked around for her family. *Where are they?* She shivered so violently she couldn't do anything, couldn't call out, couldn't seek her father's strong arms to protect her. Rooted to one spot, she stared out at the horrendous sights around her. The thatched roofs of the huts burned completely. The night shimmered as bright as day in the firelight. Bodies of some of the men lay scattered about like dead, fallen leaves.

Anta wrapped her arms around her body, trying to still the shaking. She sensed an arm around her shoulder and looked up into the face of her older half-brother, Madu. Anta felt her legs start to crumble, but her brother held her up and pulled her closer. Although he was the son of Efia, the other of their father's co-wives, Anta had always been close to him. She welcomed the strength of his broad shoulders, thick neck, and firm voice. She slipped her delicate hand into his large one and looked into his well-chiseled face, the high cheek bones, full lips and his large, dark eyes.

"Madu." Smoke and dust made Anta's voice hoarse. "What is happening? What will happen to us?"

"Be still, Anta. We will get through this. We will be all right."

"But Papa and Mama....where are they?"

Her brother held her closer and did not answer.

"Tell me. You must tell me." She feared the answer.

Her brother paused. "I thought they would take Father prisoner since he is of royal lineage, but,...but I saw him fighting back, and then they shot him. I saw him fall." His voice broke, and he buried his head against Anta's hair.

Anta winced as though she had been shot. "No! Nooo!"

Scarcely daring to hear any more, Anta asked, "And my mother?"

"Your mother ran to him, bent over him. I saw that."

"And then?"

"A horseman raced by, I saw the hoof flash out. It struck her in the head. She fell over Father's body."

Anta could no longer speak, and the tears came in great, racking sobs. Sorrow overwhelmed her. The primal keening wail of grief tore from the deepest part of her. It screamed in protest against the terror.

\* \* \*

Hours passed, and still the tyeddo kept the villagers gathered, tossed together like a pile of scraps. The gentle gray of dawn showed the bruised remains of the village. Anta held tight to Madu's arm as if it were a lifeline holding her up. Among the mass of misery, they had found her sisters, Bolanile and Urbi, as well as Madu's mother, Efia. This sad remnant of the family clung together, weeping, shivering.

The mood of the village changed from panic and terror to one of despair. The sounds were no longer horrified screams, but more of a subdued sobbing. Grief beyond grief. This sounded as chilling to Anta.

"What will happen to us now?" she again asked Madu, as she watched the victors flourishing their guns and swords, circling the captives.

"You have heard about these raids, little sister. You know what will happen. We will be sold as slaves on the coast." His voice carried his bitterness.

"But... but we are in the royal line. We cannot be slaves." Bolanile's words came out as a wail.

"Ha." Madu spat out the words. "Being descendants of Njaajaan Ndiaya will not matter now. We will all be made slaves, any who live."

"Madu." Anta needed Madu to be strong, like Papa. Her eyes implored him to tell her something encouraging, some hope she could cling to, but he lowered his gaze and put his arms around his three sisters.

5

His mother spoke for the first time. "We should not have been surprised by this raid. These raids have happened all around us for years. We should have been prepared."

Anta turned to her. "Then why? Why did this happen?"

Efia shook her head and looked completely defeated. "We are like people everywhere. We did not think bad things would happen to us."

The tyeddo warriors shouted orders, pulling and pushing the villagers. Anta tried to make sense of what was going on. The horsemen lined up the captives, put wooden yokes around their necks, and tied their hands together. A chain ran from yoke to yoke. Anta held tighter to Madu's arm. *I will not be yoked like an animal.*

Anta did not see the captor approach them. She let out a startled scream as the stocky man grabbed Madu and pulled him away. Anta held tighter to Madu's arm, sobbing. "No. No." With his free arm, the man raised his rifle as if to strike Anta with it.

"Anta," Madu spoke quickly. "Stop. Do not fight them. That only makes it worse. Do not be afraid. I will be watching over you."

Bolanile and Urbi each held one of Anta's arms. Anta could no longer reach Madu, but she strained her whole body towards him. "Madu. Madu." As Madu walked away, she kept repeating his name, softer and softer each time as hopelessness filled her.

The three sisters held each other and watched as a captor chained their brother to one of the carts heaped with carvings, drums, colorful fabrics, all the spoils of war the tyeddo collected. Madu would have the added burden of pushing the weight of that cart as they all were marched to the coast.

Anta looked at Madu's mother. If Efia had been her own mother, Anta knew she could find some strength and comfort there. Efia, though, seemed beaten down and destroyed. She stared vacantly ahead, as if her soul had already left her body.

It was the three sisters' turn to be added to the chain of captives. Two warriors grabbed the girls by their arms and jerked them up, then paused, talking with excitement to each other in their dialect. Anta could not understand what they were saying, but it sounded cruel and evil to her. Laughing, one warrior dragged Bolanile while one pulled Urbi to a separate group of young women and girls and roughly threw them into the heap.

"What are they doing?" Anta asked Madu's mother, her voice full of fear.

Efia looked over at the collection of girls. "Those are the ones the tyeddo are keeping for themselves."

Anta started forward. "No."

Madu's mother grabbed her. "You cannot help them. And they might be better off than we are anyway."

Anta drew back in horror. *What could be worse than being a slave mistress to the tyeddo?* She sank back to her knees. In the space of a few dark hours, she had lost both her parents, and her half-brother had been pulled from her side. Now she had lost her sisters. Efia, with her spirit beaten, might as well be lost to her, too. It was too much. She could not bear it. Collapsing and weeping, Anta felt that she could not endure another minute of this agony.

\* \* \*

Anta, numbed by grief, winced at the weight of the wooden yoke as it settled on her young shoulders. The heaviness bit into her tender skin when the clanking chain passed through the yoke.

The people of Yang Yang were lined up. The heavy metal chain connected each to the other as if they were livestock to be herded to market. The young men chained to the carts were forced to the rear of the line of march. Anta tried to find Madu, but she could not easily turn her head with the wooden yoke around her shoulders.

The mounted tyeddo warriors moved up and down the line. They kept their guns and swords close to them, but now brought out whips that whistled through the air as they lashed out at the line of captives.

A masked warrior chained Anta behind an older man, a friend of her father's, and in front of a large women named Isis. With a crack of a whip, the captors gave the signal for the agonizing journey to begin. The column of tragedy moved westward. All around them lay the remains of their homes and the bodies of some of the men and women of the village, flies already beginning their terrible infestation.

As the chained line reached the edge of the village, each managed to turn for a look, a glance trying to gather in a lifetime of memories.

With desperation in her soul, Anta slowly turned her head. She gasped to see the destroyed village, the skeletal remains of the round mud huts that had been security for all of her life. Her eyes took in the stark outline of the leafless baobab tree that she had hoped would save her, now a silhouette against the gray smoke rising from the burned-out village. The grisly scene seared into her memory, and with it came an anger beyond any she had ever known.

# Chapter Two

*March to the Coast*
*May 1806*

Anta jolted awake as the tyeddo yelled and cursed at the captives, slashing their whips in the air, urging the prisoners into
the morning. With no chance for privacy, Anta squatted to
relieve herself, as most of the others were doing. She could
not believe that a whole day had passed since the nightmare
began. During that first day, Anta had been too numb to take
in the reality.

Later, the piercing blue of the midday sky sent the harsh
sunlight's shimmering heat in waves beating on her bruised
and cut body. The westward trek continued through the
savannah grasses and shrubs. The salt of her sweat burned
into the open sores caused by the yoke rubbing her narrow
shoulders and neck. The raw places on her legs from running
through the millet field made her long for the soothing salve
of the gum acacia tree her mother used. Flies and gnats
buzzed at her wounds. Anta whimpered in pain as she set
one dusty foot in front of the other. She remained barefooted
and wore only the thin cotton shift she had been sleeping in
before the raid.

The tyeddo rested the captives from time to time, giving
them water and food twice a day. Anta wanted to believe they
could be kind, but Isis set her straight on that. "The only reason
they give us food is because they do not want us to die off. Each

of us will bring them money or goods from the slave trade."

Anta kept her sisters' group in view throughout the morning. After the noon meal, that band of young women branched off in another direction. As she saw the separation happening, Anta screamed out for her sisters. "Bolanile! Urbi!" Her tears flowed again. A warrior slashed his whip at her and yelled something she could not understand. The tip of the whip sharply cut into her upper arm, and Anta screamed. She looked down at the thin welt across her arm, droplets of blood seeping from the cut.

"Anta. Anta. No," Isis urged her from behind. "Do not yell out or fight against them. It will only be harder for you."

During the day, Anta could see only the bent form of her father's friend scuffling along in front of her. When they stopped for the night, Anta doubted that she could sleep although she was beyond exhaustion. Even with her hands tied in front of her body, she managed to eat the dried meat and bread the men passed out to the captives sitting on the dusty ground. The tyeddo slapped or whipped those who dared to talk to each other.

As they rested for the night, they were not kept in their rigid lines, and Anta looked around at the faces of those she had known all her life. Already, they began to seem like strangers to her, gaunt, unseeing. Anta, who always lived with an unstated sense of privilege, recoiled at being no one. Her life had turned upside down, and she couldn't make sense of it.

"Anta," whispered Isis. "Come lean against me and try to sleep."

Anta hesitated, and, when the guards were not looking, eased her weary body against the generously padded one of Isis. Tears pricked the corner of her eyes as she allowed herself this comfort, one often found in her mother's embrace. Anta dozed fitfully throughout the dark night. Between her restless times of sleep, she stared into the blackness around her. *Why did this happen? What will happen to me now?*

Anta tried to remember the harsh lessons she had learned the day before as the westward walk began again. Today, she would try not to cry out. Her body ached as she took her first uncertain steps. She felt pain everywhere. Her head throbbed; she had cuts and bruises all over her body; her muscles screamed in protest against what they had endured; her stomach called out for food, and her abdomen hurt with the threat of dysentery. The hot breath of Sahara Desert winds seared into her.

The captors used their long guns to nudge everyone up and straighten the lines. The defeated people dragged on, occasionally stopping for some water, a few morsels of food, and rest in the hottest part of the day. A pack of wild dogs, their shaggy fur with splotches of brown and white, followed the sad parade for some distance, but gave up for fresher possibilities.

Late in the morning of the third day, the man in front of Anta stumbled and fell. Anta could not react quickly enough, and she tumbled over his body. As she pushed herself up, her eyes swept over the man's face. She screamed and drew back. His eyes were open and staring, sightless, into nothingness. A warrior jumped off his horse and knelt by the man.

Anta watched in horror as the warrior removed the man from the chains and yoke, dragged the body off to the side, and kicked it farther out of the way. He mounted his horse and signaled the line to move on.

Anta could not stop looking at the discarded body. The man had been a friend of her father's. Minutes before, he was a living being, stumbling along in front of her. Now, he was nothing. As she passed him and moved on, a shivering started in her that she could not still. She couldn't breathe. She turned her face forward and tried to take deep breaths. She could hear Isis whispering to her from behind, "Just keep going, Anta. Do not think." She did not believe she could go on, but she had no choice. The line kept moving. Slowly, step by dusty step, Anta kept moving westward.

All afternoon, as she trudged numbly on, the empty yoke hung in front of her. The weight of the yoke and chain pulled against her, tearing at her own flesh where her yoke rubbed and tearing at her heart with its new layers of grief. She tried to hold the chain and yoke up to keep them from brutalizing her skin any more.

By the end of that afternoon, several more had died. Each time, they were tossed to the side, like trash. Anta knew it would not be long before the sun and the scavengers left nothing but bleached bones. Now, when a death occurred, she no longer shivered; she simply stumbled on. She had used up all her emotions. Her ability to care about others shut down. She almost wished that she, too, could lie down and feel nothing. Almost.

She tried not to notice the deaths that occurred, not to see her parents' faces in her mind. She tried not to think. She could not bear considering what the next day might bring. Tomorrow loomed, an unknown agony which stalked closely like a wild dog waiting to attack.

* * *

Anta sensed a subtle change in the air, perhaps a soft wind from the coast - something. The flat Senegalese countryside, with its thick savannah grasses, taller elephant grass, shrubs, and jackelberry trees along the creek beds, had not changed much from the land around Yang Yang as she and the weary band of captives trudged on.

The sun caught the amber of the dried grass, making the afternoon scene appear honey-coated, but Anta saw none of it. She didn't notice the small herds of zebus with large, fleshy humps and droopy ears similar to the oxen around her village, or the white cattle egrets pecking for their nourishment. Before, she would have delighted in seeing the western antelope lounging under the shade of an acacia tree, but now, in her painful stupor, she didn't care. She did feel the swirling dust as it gritted in her hair and eyes. Because it was spring, it had been months since the last rain.

Toward afternoon, Anta began to make out the outline of a town ahead. "There is the market town, Rufisque," Isis whispered to her. Anta had heard of the coastal town before. Her father had traveled there, but now the name barely registered in her tired mind. The single thought that came to her was that they might finally be able to rest. She ached with tiredness, and she felt that it took all her strength to drag one dirty and blistered foot in front of the other.

As the bedraggled group entered the town, Anta began to look around. She had never seen a place larger than her own village of Yang Yang. Compared to that, Rufisque appeared huge and reverberating with activity. In her weakened state, the scene was almost more than Anta could take in. Instead of round mud huts with thatched roofs, square buildings of stucco surrounded and hemmed her in. The closeness of the houses to each other made Anta wonder how one knew where the boundary of a family unit began or ended. It all seemed to jumble together.

The tyeddo pushed and prodded Anta and the others through the town to the market place. The noise and activity there grated against Anta's ears, making her feel queasy. It swirled around her as the dust along the trek had done, but instead of the red, gritty dirt, colors, smells, and sounds assaulted her and left her dizzy. Out of the corners of her eyes, she watched the people they passed on their way to the town's center. Many of the people looked very much like the people of Yang Yang, the same burnished ebony skin, the same colorful clothing. Some had skin like the brown bark of a manketti tree. A few had the pale white skin of the missionaries who came through Yang Yang. All of them hurried from place to place and talked in loud, strident voices. Very few of the people stared at them; most just glanced, then went back to their own business.

*Does no one care about us? Isn't there anyone who will come to our rescue?* Anta's shoulders slumped further. In Yang Yang, if a child were hurt, some mother could be counted on to pick her up and kiss away the pain. Anta had never before been around people who didn't care. That realization added another wound to her aching heart.

The tyeddo yelled at the captives, indicating with their ruthless, biting whips that the line should stop. They were in a cleared area in the center of the market. Anta glanced around at the stalls of pots, pans, and flour sieves, of prayer mats and drums, of *bukina*, the loose-fitting dresses made of all patterns of cotton. Her gaze took in the dried fish, tamarind seeds and pods, rice and maize and millet. Her stomach ached at the sight of the food, and a moan escaped her lips.

Men, important-looking men whose skin shone almost as dark as her own, walked through the lines of the beaten people of Yang Yang. They squeezed the arm or leg of this one or that one. She watched with anguish as they forced open the mouths of some, peering at this private place with no shame. She recoiled as they pulled the ragged tops of the women's garments to stare at their exposed breasts.

The men came down the line toward Anta. She already felt as though she were an object, no more than a mango or yam to be poked and prodded, as she had seen her mother do when selecting food for the family's meals. The thought of her mother swept through her with a sharp sadness. She took a deep breath and tried to make her mind go numb again.

The first of the men came to Anta. Even though she stared straight ahead, she could see him look her up and down. She wanted to slap away his judgmental touch as he put one hand around her upper arm and used his other hand to tilt back her head. She longed to run away and hide, but she could not move. She stared straight ahead until she could see nothing, feel nothing.

"This one, also," said a male voice as he poked her shoulder.

A guard unchained Ante: the yoke was finally removed. As they led her away, she looked back at Isis with desperation. Her eyes pleaded. *Isis, come with me. I don't want to be alone. I'm scared.* Anta began whimpering, feeling the terror take over her mind again. *Where are they taking me? What will happen to me?*

Anta feared, with her heart breaking, that Isis would be taken to another group, and she would never see her again. Efia was already lost to her, a lifeless form left by the side of the road that morning. Anta also had passed the bodies of Sowande, Mawali, Ebun, names that used to be neighbors.

The large black man leading Anta away cuffed her face with the back of his hand and yelled something at her in his own dialect. Anta stumbled at the blow. He raised his hand as though to hit her again, but jerked her upright and moved her to another group. With her hands still tied, the rope burns leaving bracelets of raw flesh on her wrists, a thick rope around her waist tied her to a line of women, strangers in front of her, strangers behind.

After some time, Anta and the others were marched to the shore where long, narrow wooden canoes were waiting. They reminded Anta of the pirogues the fishermen used on the river near them, but she had never been in one. She looked around for Isis, but couldn't find her. Anta had prayed that Isis would be brought to the same grouping, but that hadn't happened. *No one stays with me.* Bitter, bitter thoughts.

The ocean lay before her for the first time, its icy blue force rushing toward her in waves just as her father had once described. When her father told her about the ocean and the great ships that sailed on it, it sounded wonderful. Seeing it now filled Anta with dread.

Anta and the others waited on the sandy shore. The white foam rolled in; then the water retreated. She watched with amazement. *What kind of force controls this?* The wind and ocean's roar was constant and terrifying to her ears.

The men herded the lines of prisoners to the canoes, men in one line, women and children in another. As the canoe breached the foaming water, Anta could see in the distance a small, dark rock of an island. From the shore of Rufisque, the island looked like a tiny, granite-colored mysterious shroud rising up from the wideness of the ocean. She gripped the narrow side of the canoe with hands still tied and feared what lay ahead for her.

# Chapter Three

*Gorée Island, Senegal*
*May – June 1806*

During the short trip between Rufisque and the island, Anta stared at the small, rocky atoll ahead. *Why are we going there? I will be trapped on that rocky place, with nothing but water all around.* The isolation of the island terrified Anta.

She wondered where she might end up. She had always heard talk about the slave ships, but never paid much attention. After all, she was descended from royal blood. She would not be a slave. Now, she tried to remember all she had heard. Some said the slaves were taken to countries far across the ocean and made to work day and night in the fields. Others said no; that's what they wanted you to think. Really, they took you to a place called Europe, where everyone was a cannibal who fed on the captured Africans. Anta shivered. She could not imagine a fate so horrible.

She looked back at the land behind her. Her eyes swept past the market town on the coast and searched for the way back to Yang Yang, the way home. *Will I never find my way back again?* A sob shuddered in her throat. "Mama, Papa," she wanted to cry out. Her fists clenched tighter on the sides of the canoe as anger, fear, desperation swirled within her. Her breaths came in gasps.

The view of the rocky place ahead blurred as her eyes filled with tears. The moans and cries around her mixed with her own and became a lament echoing across the water. As she looked over her shoulder, Anta thought she saw Madu being herded to the beach with a group of young men. A whisper of hope rose within her.

Anta felt the unsteady rocking of the canoe. Her glance darted to the sides and ahead, willing the vessel to stay afloat. She could see that the island, a hard, narrow rock, did not stretch far. Flat at one end, it rose a little at the other. The craggy island looked dark, cold, and filled with loneliness.

The canoes beached on the thin, sandy area at the base of the island. The burly guards jerked Anta and the others from the canoes and pushed them forward. Anta noticed the slight elevation of the island as the men now herding them marched them up through the streets. *Who are these strong black men controlling us? Are they the slave traders I had heard about? Are they just guards? Would they be kinder than the cruel tyeddo?*

Steep stone walls of large buildings lined the narrow streets, throwing them in dark shadows. The putrid smells that eked out of them told of death and despair. Anta had never seen such large buildings. Her mind swirled with questions. *What could be in such massive places? Were they walled enclaves for homes? Did giants live in them?* Anta shuddered, wondering what more horrors she would have to endure. She wanted to cry and run away, or fall down in a heap of despair, but she had to keep going forward, her body numb.

As they turned into a walled courtyard, Anta gasped at the sight of a huge and beautiful home. The whitewashed walls of the house shimmered in the sunlight, and cobalt-blue shutters framed the many large windows. Anta blinked against the glare. Cool, gray flagstone paved the courtyard, and groupings of potted trees cast their shade over orange, red, and yellow blooming plants. In the walls around the courtyard were heavy wooden doors, but Anta saw only the main house. She felt a stirring inside, a longing for the peacefulness of such a beautiful place. Anta never imagined such wealth existed. *Who would live in this place? He must be some kind of a god.*

A twin staircase bordered by pots of overflowing bougainvillea curved at the center of the house. A tall, stately woman stood regally at the top of the balustrade, her ebony skin shining in the sunlight. Soft folds of a saffron-colored toga-like garment draped around her. Anta's breath caught in her throat. Awed, she felt that they should kneel in the presence of such a royal personage. She had never heard of a queen such as this one, living in splendor beyond reality. Anta's spirits lifted. Perhaps, this woman would show kindness and look after them. Perhaps, here....

The guard closest to her opened one of the massive oak doors along the sides of the walls. "Get in there." He pushed Anta and the other prisoners into a darkened cell. Anta stumbled in the dimness but caught herself before she fell. The smell of human waste rose up to gag her. With the light from the open doorway, her quick glance showed her that the room was about twelve feet square. Chains attached to the walls already held several women; pails set next to each for their urine and excrement. Anta sensed the overwhelming despair.

The guard roughly untied their bindings, replacing them with manacles fastened to a length of chain cemented to the wall. The chains were long enough to reach the pails.

The heavy door slammed shut, and the metal bolt clanged into place. Ante's sense of terror returned. She felt her stomach knot, felt the bile rising up in her throat. Her hands clenched and unclenched.

This dungeon had no windows, just slits high in the walls for ventilation, cloaking the room in the dimness of a starless evening. Anta put her hand against the rough stone wall to steady herself and recoiled at the clammy coldness she felt there.

She jumped as a voice next to her hissed, "Did you see

any ships out there?"

"Ships?"

"Yes, ships. From Europe. The slave traders come by ship. It is our only hope to get out of here before we die."

"Die?" Anta repeated. Even though she saw death during her horrifying journey, she never allowed herself to think that she, Anta Majigeen Ndaiye, might die.

"Are you senseless, girl?" the scratchy voice asked.

"Leave her alone," said another voice in the darkness. "She just got here. Let her get her bearings."

Anta's eyes were becoming accustomed to the grayness. Although the dimness made it hard to see, Anta sensed the shapes of people chained all around the walls. She tried to think back to the canoe trip. *Had I seen ships, those strange vessels my father had described, at anchor around the island?*

"Yes," she finally replied. "Yes, I did see ships. Three, I think."

"Ah, you are lucky, then," came another voice, a gentler voice. "You may not have to wait long in this place."

Anta heard a woman from across the room speaking what sounded like a question, but she could not understand the dialect. She had so many questions herself, she did not know where to begin. "I saw a woman looking at us as we arrived. Won't she....Will she look out for us?"

"Ha." spit out the voice on her right. "We've been here long enough to learn all about her. She is a *signare*, the so-called wife of one of those European traders. She runs the "canoe company" that brought you here. She does not care for us. It's the money she cares about."

Anta's heart sank at that news. She tried to hold the sobs back. Grief and fear overwhelmed her. If she started to cry, she might never stop. "But what...what will happen to us now?"

"We'll rot and die in this hole," the voice next to her grated out, "Or, we'll be sold as slaves and die a worse death on the slave ships, that's what." The bitterness and defeat in the voice were like hot oil, dripping over and suffocating all around it.

"Stop that." came the other voice. Then she continued in a softer voice, "I am called Bella. *Nanga tudd?*"

"*Ma ngui tudd* Anta." Anta replied. "Anta Majigeen Ndiaye. From Yang Yang."

"Anta, we have been picked by one of the slave traders. They will take us from this island, Gorée Island, to the slave ships."

"And where do the slave ships go?" asked Anta.

A pause. "I do not know."

Anta sank back on her heels, resting her back against the cold slab of stone wall. She had a chance to stop and think about all that had befallen her. She did not want to think of it, did not want to remember awakening to the panic, the smell of smoke, the wrenching away from loved ones. *Will I see Madu again, or even Isis on the slave ship? Will I ever see any of my family again?*

As she sat in the darkness, the oppressiveness of the odors seemed to push her farther to the ground. The blackness of the room enveloped and crushed her. She heard rustling, chains clanking, as people shifted positions. This dungeon, truly, was a place of death.

Anta hugged her arms around herself and tried to remember the comfort of her mother's embrace, the strength of Madu's arm on her shoulder, even the feeling of leaning against Isis' padded body, but she felt nothing. *I have lost everything. There is nothing left for me.* She began to rock back and forth; the silent screams inside her poured out as a low keening moan.

"There, there, now, little one. Hush now," came the soothing voice of Bella. "Reach your hand out to me. Come, now, reach out. Feel my finger tips reaching yours?"

Anta stopped rocking and turned toward the voice, even

21

though she couldn't see the person. Slowly, she stretched out her hand, leaned her whole body toward the comforting sound.

"That's right, little Anta," murmured Bella. "There. Feel my fingers touching yours?"

Anta felt the warmth of Bella's fingers, stroking her own.

"See? You are not alone. Try to be strong. We will help each other."

They sat in silence for several moments while Anta luxuriated in the warm touch of another human being. The monstrous ache inside her began to recede. She sighed.

"Thank you," she whispered.

Anta drew back her hand, lowered her head to rest on arms crossed over her knees. When she closed her eyes, she used the force of her will with the new strength Bella had conveyed to her to keep herself from absorbing the smells. Her mind told her that she might be any place. She might be home on her own mat in their hut, her mother rising in the early morning to stir the fire up and start their meal. Her mother even might be humming the tune she loved so well. *Yes, I can almost hear her. I can almost smell the wood smoke from her cooking. I will put myself there, back in that safe place. Not here.* Anta felt that first sliver of strength inside her rising up, rising over the ashes of what were now the ruins of Yang Yang, rising above the pain in her body, rising above the threat of death around her. She would find that strong place inside her. She would.

The guards brought the evening meal, porridge and bread. Anta used the dim light from the open doorway to look at Bella. She had expected a small, gentle woman, like her mother, but Bella did not match the quietness of her voice at all. She appeared as a very large woman, even taller than Anta's father. Her skin glowed dusky in the evening light, not as dark as Anta's. A bright-colored red and yellow *bukina* dress covered Bella's ample body, large, meaty arms pushing out of the sleeves. A turban wrapped her head with some multi-colored fabric, making her head look even larger. Bella's eyes were her most dramatic feature, wide set and striking with almost black irises in coconut white, which lit up her whole face. Her nose was broad, her lips thick and full, all the features together giving the image of strength and power.

\* \* \*

Three days later, Anta jolted awake at the grating sound of the heavy door being opened. She had learned to look out when the guards opened the door to bring food and water. She could tell if it was morning or evening by the way the light reflected outside the door. Anta had lost so much of what grounded her; she could not bear to lose sense of time, too. The guards brought the same meal of millet or maize porridge and bread twice a day, along with blessed cups of cool water.

Not long after they finished their scant serving, the guards came again. Their captors yelled at them to stand and unchained them, then tied them in a line to each other. With shouts and shoves, the guards marched them through the streets to a large center area, much like the marketplace at Rufisque but without the colorful stalls. This time, instead of Africans, foreign-looking men, white-skinned men with sharp, beak-like noses, piercing eyes, and thin, cruel mouths, stood around watching.

Anta stood perfectly still as the men circled among the captives, sometimes approaching her and touching her, treating her as if she were some inhuman object. She quickly learned to use her mind to put herself somewhere else, or to shut down her thoughts. Men's hands were all over her body, arms, legs, face, breasts.

Her light shift, torn and filthy, still covered her body. Anta stood rigid and still while writhing with anger inside. She imagined her hands clawing the men's ugly pale faces until her scraping nails drew blood. She wanted to hurt them, hurt them with a violence, as they were doing to her very soul. Instead, she stood straight and tall, like the African princess that she was, and in her mind she returned to Yang Yang, back to the time before terror snatched her away.

The white-skinned men talked to the slave traders in a language Anta couldn't understand. She watched, without appearing to see anything, as the traders divided the captives into three groups. With yells, curses, and shoves, they moved the groups to the beach where Anta saw many other captives already waiting. Her eyes searched incessantly for Madu. *Is that him? No, Madu is much taller. Oh, please, please, brother, be with me again.* Bella was tied next to Anta, and there was some small comfort in that. She did not see Isis in any of the groups, and now Anta knew that she never would see her again.

As more and more captives were brought to the beach, Anta continued to search for Madu. *What had happened to him? Had he already gone on a slave ship? Maybe he had escaped. Maybe...maybe he was dead. No.* Anta would not let herself think that.

# Chapter Four

*The Middle Passage*
*June – July 1806*

Sitting on the sand in the heat of the day was difficult for Anta. The sand scratched her legs where her gown rode up to her thighs. Perspiration streamed from her brow, burning her eyes. She wanted to run, but there was nowhere to go.

Bella would occasionally say, "Anta, relax. We can do nothing but sit and wait. Be still."

Time passed, and still no sight of Madu. Anta felt her sense of hope slipping away. A new group struggled onto the beach, and Anta studied each one. *That one. That is Madu, I'm sure.* His dark brown body was covered with dust, making him look almost gray, but there was no mistaking him. It was Madu. She wanted to run to him, but ropes held her back. She longed to call out to him, but fear of the menacing guards kept her from uttering a sound.

Instead, she willed him with her eyes to look at her, to recognize her. *Please, Madu, see me.* At last, he glanced her way, and their eyes met. They held each other with their gaze, and Anta felt a strength come into her body again. She had family. She wasn't alone.

\* \* \*

Many hours later, the blazing sun crossed the sky, sending its blistering hot rays on them as they sat on the shore. With little interest, Anta watched the progress of the white slave traders as they divided the slaves into groups and yelled at workers. Instead, her eyes connected and reconnected with Madu. It was almost as if they were talking to each other.

"Be brave, little sister," his eyes told her.

"I will try," hers replied. "Are you all right?"

"I will be all right."

Midday, they were given water and a roasted yam. All during the day, the canoes went back and forth to the ships, carrying the boxes and baskets that Bella said were supplies for the journey. Anta eyed the menacing ships bobbing at anchor. She wanted to be away from the dark, foul dungeons, but she had never been on such a contraption, and could not imagine that thing staying on top of the water. The ships, their sails wrapped around tall masts, did not appear to be very large, and she saw there were hundreds of captives in each group. *Surely, just the weight of all of us would send the ship deep under the water. And, once at sea, how would the ships ever find their way to land again?* With each rising fear, Anta looked to Madu, and he sent her a message of strength with his glance.

As the softer shades of gold and rose settled in the dusky sky, the slaves went in canoes to the ships. Their voices rose with pleas, cries, screams of fear. Several tried to break away from the guards, jump from the canoes. The guards slammed their rifles into those trying to get away or lashed at them with whips. The sound of their distress reverberated over the ocean.

Anta became more and more terrified as they approached the strange, wooden vessels, the slave ships she had heard horrifying stories about. Even Bella found no reassuring words for Anta. The canoes bounced dizzily in the waves as they pulled alongside the ships. The guards untied the women and children, and with shoves, whips, and curses, forced their trembling victims to climb the netting over the side of the ship. More white men on the deck shouted at the captives in their strange language. The crew made their orders known with pushes, jabs, and slaps.

Anta saw Madu and the men, still chained in pairs, taken to another area of the ship. Others of the crew shoved Anta and the women and children toward an opening in the deck. As she got nearer to that opening, it looked like a huge mouth about to eat her, and all she could see inside was darkness.

Anta and the others, many dozens in number, were shoved through that gaping hole and made to go below the deck of the ship. Her feet hit against a rough ladder and she struggled down. Those below her crowded together, and those above forced Anta down the steps. She had to keep moving into the darkness below although every fiber of her being wanted to fight against it. She began to have trouble breathing, as if she was suffocating, each breath tearing from her trembling chest.

"Just keep moving, Anta." The sound of Bella's voice kept Anta from collapsing in despair.

As her eyes accustomed to the dim light from the few openings high in the sides of the ship and with her hands feeling the way, Anta understood that the narrow, wooden planks along the walls were their beds.

"Grab one, quickly," urged Bella's voice from behind her. Knowing that Bella was near helped Anta calm her breathing. Anta reached an empty shelf and pulled herself onto it. She gripped the sides as the ship rose and fell with the waves. Drawing herself up into the smallest ball possible, she tried to remember what her mother's face looked like. She could not imagine, would not let herself consider, what might lie ahead.

\* \* \*

Anta woke to the rocking of the ship, feeling the hardness of her wooden bed pushing against the sharp points of her shoulder, hip, and knee. The dim light of early morning came sifting through the openings. The wooden shelves that were their bunks lined the walls of the ship on both sides, two high. Anta, on a top bunk, peered over the edge to be sure Bella was still below. Bella's large body filled the bunk and spilled over the side. Anta reached her hand down to touch Bella's firm arm, and the warmth she felt there eased her trembling.

Anta tried to sit up, but the ceiling was too close, so she slid off the bed to the floor, standing as tall as she could and stretching her aching body. She made her way past sleeping bodies to the wooden vat for their excretion and relieved herself. There were only three large vats for all the women and children, two feet wide at the bottom and one foot wide at the top. Already the smell made Anta gag, and she quickly went back to her bunk.

The captives stirred as children cried with hunger. Anta rubbed her concave abdomen and tried not to think of breakfasts in Yang Yang. Light burst into the hold from sailors opening the trap door. A tremor of fear shuddered through the group. All eyes looked toward the opening. Two sailors shouted and gestured. Anta couldn't understand their guttural language, but from their expressions and gestures, she was sure they were yelling, "Come up. Come on you filthy beasts. Don't make us come down and get you."

Slowly, the frightened group moved toward the ladder and the sunshine. Anta got behind Bella, her hand on Bella's back for reassurance. Anta blinked in the bright daylight. The sky was already a soft blue with a few wispy clouds.

"Are they going to let us walk free, no chains or ropes?" Anta asked, her voice full of amazement.

"I think so. But why not? Where could we escape?" Her voice was bitter.

"Where are the men? I want to find Madu. He's my
brother. I saw him on the beach when we came to the ship."
Bella shook her head. "You will not get to see him. Don't
you see that wooden wall down the center of the ship? The
men and boys will be kept on the other side. They will be
tied because the men slaves will bring the best prices, and this
captain doesn't want to lose any of them."

"How do you know all this?"

Bella laughed, her deep, throaty laugh. "We do not speak
this white man's language, but somehow, one learns things
and passes that information around. I have learned this is a
Danish ship called the *Sally*."

"Do you know where we are going?"

"Not yet, but I am sure I will hear that some time."
Anta's thoughts returned to her half-brother. "But Madu...I
want to see Madu."

"I know, little one, but there is so much we might want
that we can't have. To keep from dying of a broken heart, we
must look for what is good. I have heard that this ship has a
"loose captain." That means he did not pack us in so closely
that we could only be lying tightly against each other with no
room to move at all. He knows we are an investment for him,
so he will treat us better."

"So he will not put us back in chains?"

"They say that we will not be chained again, but the men
are linked together in pairs by ankle shackles."

A commotion several yards away caught Anta's attention.
Sailors dragged out big buckets of gray-looking porridge and
dumped a pile of wooden spoons. The women and children
scrambled for them, and Anta and Bella quickly joined them.
There was much shoving and pushing, and Bella grabbed
Anta's hand, pulling her into the fray. Anta felt someone
try to slap her away, but she stayed firm until she grasped a
spoon and shoved it into the porridge. The sailors brought
out another bucket of the same, and soon everyone found a

place to eat. The sound of wooden spoons frantically scraping against the empty wooden bucket made Anta want to cry. She longed for a banana, the sweet taste of the millet cakes her mother used to make, the warmth of fresh fried bread filling her mouth.

As she turned sadly away, the two women next to her began yelling at each other, hitting and yanking hair. "You ate my share." One's fingernails slashed at the other's face. Anta moved back quickly as two sailors grabbed the women and threw them aside. Another sailor tore the ragged garment from one and began whipping her bare back with a leather thong.

Anta drew back in horror. The slaps of the whip made bands of red across the woman's back, and she screamed in pain with each lashing.

Bella's large arm went around Anta and turned her away from the agony. Together, they stumbled off to another part of the deck, Anta with her hands over her ears to hide the sound.

"You said he was a good captain," wept Anta, leaning against Bella's ample breasts. "You said...."

"We will still get beatings. No matter what, we will still be beaten because we are slaves now. We are not people anymore." She spat the words out and held Anta more tightly.

Anta wept.

* * *

Anta gagged and her stomach churned violently as the cramped hold full of defeated captives became stifling in the heat of day, the fetid smells overpowering. Fortunately, the late summer weather was good to them the first weeks. Each morning the women and children struggled up the ladder to the brightness of the deck. Anta gulped the fresh air as she pushed her way into the sunshine. Not being chained to a wall or tied to another person helped her spirits a little.

She looked out at the vastness of sea and sky before her. *Where are we going? How can this be happening to me? I cannot be a slave.* A hundred times a day these thoughts tumbled through her mind. Her fists clenched with her unconscious desire to fight back against the unseen force trying to destroy her.

On deck, Anta stayed close to Bella and carefully watched the crew. Those white men with their yellow hair looked so strange to her. They yelled often and laughed among themselves in a loud, raucous way that sent chills of fear down Anta's back.

Anta cringed as one of the sailors grabbed a woman and slammed her against the wall. He pushed his body against her again and again as several other members of the crew gathered around and cheered him on. When he was finished with the victim, she fell to the deck, like a discarded pile of rags.

Anta leaned her head against Bella. "They like to hurt the women."

"Oh, yes," was Bella's bitter response.

"I will die if they do that to me."

"You must stay very quiet and out of their way."

Each day Anta saw one or more of the women violated in the same way. Several of those women tried to jump overboard to what, Anta knew, would be certain death. Only one made it. The others were caught by sailors before they could jump, and they were stripped and flogged. Anta winced with every vicious stroke and tried not to weep when she saw the cruel, bleeding welts on someone's back. With each flogging, she remembered the feel of the tyeddo warrior's cutting whip on her arm.

Bella tried to hide a lot of what was happening from Anta, but that was impossible. Anta rarely spoke, but she watched everything very carefully. She was horrified as illnesses seeped through the captive population. Those who were sick lay where they fell until they died.

Every morning after the captives were brought on deck, some sailors went into the holds and dragged out the bodies of those who died during the night. Anta's glance followed the sailors as they unceremoniously hauled the bodies to the end of the ship and tossed them into the water like refuse. A greedy group of sharp-finned giant fish - Bella told her they were called sharks - now followed in the ship's wake. Anta would not let herself imagine what happened to the bodies once they were thrown overboard. The first time Anta witnessed the removal of the corpses she wanted to scream, but fearing what the sailors might do to her, she remained silent. Screams upon screams had formed silently inside her. She feared that if she ever opened her mouth, the screams would hurtle out until she filled the whole world with cries.

# Chapter Five

*The Middle Passage*
*July – August 1806*

Anta felt there must be a way to find Madu. She walked slowly along the eight-foot-high wall dividing the decks, searching for an opening of some kind. One doorway cut through the wall, but an armed sailor stood guard there. Whenever the sailor glanced her way, Anta melted into nothingness. Finally, she found a few slits in the wood.

"Look. There are these little spaces in the wall. I can see through to find Madu."

Bella ran her hand around the rectangle opening. "I think these gaps are so the sailors can shoot into the men's side if there is a riot."

"Don't tell me that. I do not want to think of such a thing. I'm just glad I discovered a way to look for Madu." Finally, one day, he was there.

"Madu." she whispered the name to herself. A warmth of joy spread through her body. Her fingers tingled to reach through the wooden barrier and touch Madu's strong arm again. *Madu.* She held his name in her mind like a precious gem. Madu was alive and on the same slave ship. She still had family. That was all that mattered.

The days were endless, but the nights were worse. The hold reeked of human misery. It was like being in a tomb-dark, dank and hot. There was never silence, always the tortured sounds of misery cutting through the air; the moans of pain; sobs of grief; cries of despair; the protesting of a people believing that God and Allah had deserted them.

Two babies whimpered their way into the world. Anta was familiar with the cries of a woman in labor, but the wailings from those mothers' mouths were different. There was more than the sound of physical pain. Even though it was in different dialects, Anta understood these tragic mothers were begging the gods to keep from bringing a child into that world of hell. Anta thought maybe the mothers' pleas had been heard after all. The babies died within days.

Anta wanted to stay against the wall watching Madu whenever she saw him, but she did not dare take the chance of calling attention to herself. With the women and children milling around the deck, she felt that she could make herself invisible to the sailors. She moved to be by Bella among a group of about thirty, trying to catch the best of a breeze.

Anta loved the feeling of the wind in her hair, and she lifted her face to the sun's warmth. The sailors had put out a vat of vinegar again, so the women could wash themselves. Anta always felt so clean when she had a turn using one of the rags they all shared. Sometimes the sailors would haul up buckets of seawater and throw it over the captives. It was refreshing at first, but in the heat of the day, the salt dried and seemed to cake their bodies.

As she leaned back, she realized there was a stickiness between her legs. She looked down and saw the slight line of blood easing down her thigh. "Oh, Bella," she moaned. "I did not think about this. In Yang Yang I have the rags Mama prepared for me when my moon time comes, but here I have nothing. What will I do?"

"There is not much we can do. It is a problem for all of us. Rip the end off your garment and make a strip. Tie that around you as best you can." She paused, looking at Anta's skimpy shift. "My gown is long and full. I will tear a strip off mine for you. Whenever they bring out the vinegar, wash the rag and yourself. I am sorry. That is all you can do."

Anta looked at Bella, the tears pooling in her eyes. "Why is everything so hard? Why are we being punished like this?"

Bella simply shook her head. She had no answer.

* * *

The days dragged on into weeks. Anta was sure it had been at least five weeks since they left Gorée Island. Bella made a scratch mark with her long fingernail on the bunk as each day ended. Anta had been able to speak with a few women from Yang Yang. Hearing the familiar dialect touched a place deep inside her. Perhaps even in the new land, wherever she might end up, perhaps even there, she would have some roots of home.

Deaths occurred every day. Anta was numb to them now. She learned that there were things worse than death: like being raped by the sailors; like watching your children die; or seeing your husband's lifeless body thrown to the sharks. Some tried to take their own lives rather than live as slaves. Only one more had been successful in jumping overboard. The sounds of the screams as sharks tore into the woman still ricocheted around Anta's brain.

Twice daily, the sailors brought out wooden tubs of porridge, yams, or, rarely, dried meat or fish. Bella always tried to push open a place for Anta to squeeze in. The porridge did not taste like that her mother made, even though made with millet. This gruel was cold and full of lumps, but Anta, aching with hunger, was glad for whatever there was to eat. By now, at least a third had lost their spoons, so they used their hands or tried to steal another's spoon. They were given water to drink three or four times a day, and the cool, clear liquid made Anta feel better each time she drank.

"Bella, look." Anta was horrified to see a sailor hold a

shovel with hot coals by the lips of one of the women whose baby had died. "What are they doing?"

Bella shook her head sadly. "She only wants to die, too, so she is trying to starve herself. They threaten to make her swallow the coals if she doesn't eat."

Anta could not take her eyes off the woman. *You must eat. Do not let them put those burning things in your mouth.* The tension was almost a visible force between the woman and the sailor. Finally, the bereft mother began weeping and scooped up some porridge. The sailor laughed cruelly at his perverted victory.

"You watch," said Bella. "From now on she will only pretend to eat. Soon she will be with her baby. Those who need to escape by death will find a way to do it."

* * *

Anta endured the life she couldn't escape. In good weather, she and the others could be out in the fresh air. She came to think of the hold as a place of death. She could occasionally catch a glimpse of Madu. Anta liked to find a comfortable place to sit among a large group and then use her imagination to go someplace else; to go back to Yang Yang; to be with her mother and sisters again; to be safe.

When the weather turned stormy, life became a living hell. Confined to the small space below the deck, Anta was sure the heat, smells, and sickness conspired to kill them. There were a few openings from the deck that were usually ajar, but during bad weather they were closed against the rain. When they were kept in the hold, Anta curled up on her ridge of wood and gripped the sides tightly as the ship bolted upward, then slammed down. Besides the usual stench, almost everyone was seasick. Many could not get to the waste vats in time, making the hold treacherous to walk through.

After two days in the hold, Anta could not stand it

anymore. Even if it was storming, she yearned to be outside. Finally, the hold door was opened, revealing a clear sky. Anta could not get up the ladder fast enough. She sucked in the cleaner air and shook her head a few times to clear it. Slowly, she sidled over to the wall to see if Madu was all right.

The men were chained together, as always, and Anta's eyes went down the line to where Madu usually was. With relief, she noted that he was in his place. The man shackled to Madu, appeared very ill. He was leaning over, as if he had no strength.

*Madu, get away from him. Do not let his illness spread to you.* Anta could not take her eyes off them, as if willing Madu to safety. Bella came to her and took her by the arm.

"You have been at the wall too long. I can see that something is wrong. Come with me." She pulled Anta to a place where they could sit.

"That man by Madu....He is very sick....We must get Madu away from him."

"You know we can do nothing. You cannot help your brother."

"But, he's my brother. He's all I have left." Anta felt the hysteria rising within her.

"You have yourself. That is what is important, Anta. You have yourself."

Anta fiercely shook her head, but she had no more words.

\* \* \*

Anta was at the wall the next day, watching through the slit, as they unchained the man's limp body from her brother, dragged him to the railing and threw him to the sharks. She trembled as she carefully watched Madu. *Is he showing any signs of the sickness, too?* She could not tell.

On the following day, Anta thought she would die from fear over what was happening to Madu. She no longer cared

37

how long she stood watching through the slit in the high fence. Danger to herself didn't matter: only Madu. She did not doubt that Madu had the sickness. His color had paled to that of cold ashes. He appeared disoriented, and his body glistened with sweat. Anta watched with fists clenched and a moan in her throat. In her mind, she knew that she could do nothing to help Madu, but in her heart she could not accept that. She had to save him.

She watched as Madu slumped over; as the sailor came to him and kicked his prone body; as Madu tried to rise up and fell flat again. Anta watched as her brother was unchained and dragged to the edge of the ship. She screamed and strained against the wooden wall separating her from the last of her family. It was too much. She could not bear this agony. With a heavy kick, the sailor pushed the body of Madu into the foam.

"Madu!" screamed Anta, her head thrown back and the name bursting from her heart. "No. Not Madu." Her nails tore at the wooden wall between them in a frantic effort to reach Madu. Jagged splinters of wood cut into her hands.

Bella ran toward Anta, but a sailor got there first. He pulled off Anta's filthy rag of a garment and, screaming obscenities at her, threw her to the deck. He slashed her back with a cat-o-nine-tails. Anta, screaming Madu's name, tried to get away, to reach toward the last place where Madu had been. The sailor yanked her back and whipped her again. The pain of losing Madu even more than the pain of the beating was too much for Anta, and she slipped into the oblivion of unconsciousness.

# Chapter Six

*The Middle Passage*
*August – September 1806*

Bella and another woman carried Anta to her plank bed. For two days and nights she raged in her delirium, raged against the tyeddo warriors, against the slave traders, against a world that would take her family from her, one by one. Her voice was hoarse, her throat raw.

"No!" she screamed over and over. Her arms thrashed against the enemy in her mind, the enemy that chained her and bound her and beat her. "Mama. Papa."

"Madu, come back." she called, tossing and turning violently on her narrow bed.

"Why can't I just die? I have no reason to live."

After two days, she began coming back to the real world. She didn't want to live in a world where she had no one left, no one who knew who she was, no one who loved her. She could not live in a world where she was a slave, where she could be beaten, chained, raped. There was nothing to live for.

"I want to die. I want to die," Anta murmured over and over as she came back to consciousness.

Anta opened her eyes to find Bella standing by her, using part of her moistened bright turban to sooth Anta's fevered head.

"Bella," she began. Her lips felt dry and caked, and her

back burned with pain. "Madu....He's gone....I cannot go on...."

"Turn over. I will tend your sores."

Anta neither knew nor cared how Bella found a cloth and cool water to soothe the raw, bleeding welts across her back. Two days had passed since she had seen the unbear- able– Madu torn away from her. Now she knew she was truly, completely alone, and she wished only for death.

Bella's gentle hand smoothed the blistered, oozing wounds on Anta's back. With each touch, Anta shuddered from the pain.

"They are getting better. You are healing," Bella told her.

"I will never get better. I am all alone now. I want to die."

"I know, little Anta, but you are too strong. You will not die."

Anta turned until her gaze met Bella's. "I have no reason to live, nothing to live for."

"You think that now, but you are wrong. I have told you before. You have yourself, your strong and victorious soul."

"I have nothing."

"You have you, and the truth is our own soul is all any of us really have. Even if you were back in your beloved Yang Yang that you have told me about, even if your mama and papa, and your sisters and brother still lived, it wouldn't matter. It would still be you, yourself, who made your life."

"I don't understand."

"All any of us have is ourselves, to think our thoughts, to make our decisions, to live our life. Within each of us is the strength to make a life. You still have that inside you. No one can take that away. Whatever they might do to you on the outside, only you can touch your own soul. You can use your mind and your imagination to live through anything."

Anta closed her eyes and let Bella's words sink deep. She could not deal with them now. Her mind was too full of pain and anguish. *Madu.* She wept silently. *Madu, my brother.*

*Mama. Papa. Bolanile. Urbi.* Over and over she called the litany of names, names which could never again respond. Finally, she escaped into sleep.

\* \* \*

"Come. It is a beautiful, clear morning. You must come up out of this hole. You will die if you stay down here."

"I want to die." Anta turned her back on Bella.

"Ah, no you don't. Come, now. Come with me."

Anta motioned for Bella to go away.

"No, I won't go away. Now you listen to me, Anta Majigeen Ndiaya. You say you are descended from royalty, but look at you. You cower like a weakling. Get up, now."

Anta turned to look at Bella and was startled by the anger she saw in Bella's face.

"But I...."

"No excuses." Bella's eyes seemed to spit fire.

"But, Bella...."

"Are you a coward? Are you only a sniveling little girl?"

Anta burned with indignation at the insults. Bella had never spoken to her so sharply before. No one had. *I am not a coward.* "No...I....all right, I'll come."

Anta raised her bruised and aching body to a sitting position. She slipped her ragged shift back up over her shoulders, and looked up at the opening to the deck. A clear blue sky beckoned her. She was surprised that she felt herself wanting to go up, to be part of the world again.

"That's right. Come now." Bella's voice softened as she helped Anta to stand.

For a moment, Anta was dizzy and reached back to the bed to get her balance. Her back still burned from the wounds of the cat-o-nine tails, but her legs became steadier. She worked her way up the ladder and along the deck. She could not, would not, look at the long, center wooden wall, no longer caring who might be on the other side. She eased herself to her favorite place, a pile of rope on the forward deck. Her eyes scanned the horizon. There was nothing but endless blue ocean meeting blue sky. In the warmth from the sun, Anta took in some deep breaths. She felt the rough texture of the ropes against her legs, the gentle breeze lifting her hair.

*I'm alive. I am all alone, but I am still alive. I will show them I am not a weakling, not a coward.* She kept hearing Bella's words in her mind and in her heart. *Could what Bella told me be true? Is my soul really strong and victorious? I have already survived more than I would ever have believed possible.* It was too much for Anta to take in. She closed her eyes and let the sun work its healing on her.

\* \* \*

For two months, the *Sally* sliced its way through the ocean waters. Anta felt herself becoming stronger. Bella no longer needed to push open a place for Anta at the feeding tubs. Anta forced a space for herself. She made sure she got some food and water, but she still always ached with hunger. She walked around the small space of deck as much as she could.

Anta kept to herself. She did not want to form ties, only to lose the connection again. Scar tissue formed over the hurting places in her heart and the wounds on her back. She listened to Bella's counsel, yet she would not let herself love Bella. Not yet fourteen years old, she had left her childhood and youth behind.

Anta knew that something inside her had died that night of the tyeddo raid, something she would never get back. More died when Madu was shoved into the water. Yet, within her, there was a steeling, a hard, sharp edge forming. This strength was forged with anger and bitterness, but it gave birth to a determination, a determination to survive; even more, a determination to be free again.

* * *

The ship's lulling motion made Anta realize they must
be stopped. A slight hump of land rose on the horizon.
Excitement ran though the slaves in the hold. Where were
they? What was this place?

"It is a place called Havana, Cuba," the word was passed
down. "We will be kept away from others on shore for awhile,
and during that time we will be given fruits and vegetables
again to make us appear healthy. We will get to wash, and
they will give us oil to rub on our skin. They want us to look
good so we will bring a high price at the market."

Anta took in this information quietly. *So this was the
deciding time.* She had survived the tyeddo raid, survived the
walk to Rufisque, survived the prison at Gorée Island, and
even survived the "Middle Passage" as she had learned the
trip from Africa was called. She had lost every one of her
family. Whatever happened in this new place called Havana,
Cuba, would seal her destiny.

Anta stood a little taller. *What could be worse than what I
already lived through? I can win over any terrible thing that comes
my way now. I will be strong, and I will not let anyone destroy me. I
am Anta Majigeen Ndiaye from the royal line of Njajaan Ndiaya.*
She raised her head higher on her long, slender neck.

* * *

The days of quarantine passed slowly for Anta. The extra
food, especially the mangoes, papayas, bananas, and fresh
yams, tasted so good to her, yet still her stomach ached with
hunger as if she could never make up for the many weeks of
deprivation. Each day the tension aboard ship rose higher
and higher. Those captives who still had family knew it
would not be long until they might be sold apart, never to see
each other again. Anta knew her time with Bella was short.

The white men yelled some instructions at them and gestured for them to line up. Anta trembled as her turn came to climb over the side of the ship to the small boats bobbing below. She and Bella were the last to settle in their boat, and the sailors pushed off and rowed to the port. On land, white men led Anta and the others to a wide, open area.

Anta reached out to Bella to steady herself. "Your legs are used to the ship's movement," Bella said. "I counted the marks on my bunk. We've been at sea for seventy-four days."

Walking on firm land seemed very strange to Anta as her feet scudded through the dust. The noise of the busy port was loud in her ears: so many people shouting, moving about. The odors that filled her nostrils carried her back in time to her home; fish sizzling in a pan, bread baking. Anta put her hands on either side of her face as a desperate attempt for grounding.

White men mingled around, looking her over. She knew they were taking in her straight, tall body; her slender, strong limbs; her long neck; and the firm tilt of her head. She willed herself to go somewhere else in her mind. She could see the mud huts of Yang Yang, heard her sisters laughing as they climbed the baobab tree to swing from its branches. Her mother knelt in front of their hut, grinding the millet into powder. Her father....Where might her father be? Her father was squatted in front of Mawali's hut as they talked about herding the zebus to market. And, herself?...Anywhere but at a market place in Havana, Cuba, waiting to be sold as someone's slave.

* * *

Anta stood immobile as two men approached. A slight-built, dark-haired man circled her, looking, but refraining from poking and prodding. His brown eyes didn't have that evil glint Anta noticed in so many of the men. Out of the corner of her eye, she watched the two men talk briefly together.

"I think there is some fire in this one," Zephaniah
Kingsley said, smiling slightly. "Look at the defiant way she
holds herself. She is young, a teenager. That would be good.
I could train her the way I want."

The other man chuckled.

"Buy this one, Henry, and load her on the *Esther*. I'm
going to see what I can find out about taking on a load of
rum. I'll meet you this evening." With one last look at Anta,
he hurried off. The other man went to the *Sally's* captain
and, after some discussion and pointing at Anta, money and
papers were exchanged.

*Does this mean I have been purchased? Am I now someone's
slave?* Anta's heart beat fast. She cringed as the man came
back and took her arm. "Come along. You belong to Master
Kingsley now," he said as he propelled her forward.

From the way that he held her, it was obvious that she
was his property. Anta's eyes sought out her dear friend.
Bella meant so much to her, taught her so much. "Bella," she
uttered as tears sprang to her eyes. "*Be beneen yon,* good-bye."
Anta knew this moment would come, but that did not make
it any easier. Bella raised her hand, as Anta gulped several
times to keep her sobs inside as she moved along with the
stranger.

# Chapter Seven

The *Esther*
*September –October 1806*

Anta was relieved that the man leading her did not put her in chains or ropes. He held tightly to her arm and marched her along to the pier. Without a word, he put her in a small boat, climbed in, and rowed out to a ship like the *Sally*.

*Not another ship. I can not bear those horrors again.* She whimpered and shivered as she was pushed up the webbed rope on the side of the wooden vessel. The rope felt rough and oily in her hands.

On the deck, Anta looked for other slaves. Only a few black sailors worked around the sails and ropes. Looming ahead of her on the deck was the dark opening. The hold. Anta trembled with terror.

The man pulled her past the dreaded opening. They entered a hallway and passed two doorways. He stopped at the third door, opened it, and pushed her inside.

Anta looked around the small room. There were no chains on the walls. Four small wooden bunks protruded from the walls. Burlap bags were spread on them for padding. Two large buckets sat in the corner. There was no one else in the room. Anta looked at the man who brought her, her eyes widening in fear.

"You'll be all right," he said, patting her arm. He turned and left the room, shutting and locking the door behind him.

Each breath came out with a cry of fear as Anta put a hand to her throat. She rushed to the door and tried to open it, but it was securely locked.

"No! No!" she cried out. Anta, in all her life, had never been completely alone. In Yang Yang, her mother and sisters were always around. Even during all the horrors she had endured since the raid, she was never alone. Now, there was no one.

Her heartbeat sped, her breath came in shallow gasps, and her whole body trembled. Nothing she had lived through was as frightening as this. She ran to the small opening in the window and managed to push it open. It was too small to crawl through. "Mama. Papa."

She backed away from the opening until her back was against the opposite wall. She eased down the wall, sliding to the floor, knees drawn up, hugging herself. The sobs started then, sobs she had held in since the night her parents were killed.

Anta rocked back and forth, weeping. Her whole body shouted out the grief that overwhelmed her. The afternoon sun moved across the sky, and still Anta wept and rocked. She called out the names of those lost to her. *Mama. Papa. Madu. Bolanile. Urbi. Bella.* No one came to comfort her. Loss and loneliness filled her soul, and she could not bear it. Her eyes were swollen from weeping. Her throat sore from sobs.

As the sky was filled with the golden-edged clouds turning rose, she sat in silence, all her energies spent. The quiet surrounded her. She felt a vacuum pushing against her, just as she had felt the misery and darkness of the dungeon on Gorée Island. As the gentler light of dusk seeped into the lonely room, Anta heard the door being unlocked. Her breath caught in her throat as the door opened. A large black man entered with a wooden plate of food and a small bucket of water. "Here. Eat this." His voice was deep and strong. It was not her dialect, but it was the Wolof language.

Anta's face lit up with relief at the familiar sounds.

"Where are you from?"

His laugh was balm to her hurting spirit. "I be from Jolof, but long time ago."

"Please tell me, who has bought me and where are we going?"

"Our Massa be called Zephaniah Kingsley. He be a good massa. We goin' home to his plantation, Laurel Grove."

"Our Massa? Are you a slave, too?"

"I be a slave and a sailor, but I be workin' to earn my freedom."

"Earn freedom? How can you do that?"

"In Spanish East Florida, where Massa Kingsley gots his plantation, we can buys our freedom when we done earned enough money to pay for half our value."

The first sliver of hope surged through Anta. She got up from the floor and came to take the plate. "I will do that. I will earn my freedom." She smiled at the sailor, her first smile in months.

The big sailor laughed again. "That not be easy for a girl," he said. He left, shutting and locking the door again.

Anta stood still for a moment, staring after him. "I will be free again." She took her plate and sat on the wooden bunk. "Rice and fish. This is a feast." She ate greedily, savoring the food and the new information.

\* \* \*

The next forty-eight hours were the strangest two days Anta had ever experienced. She was alone in the little room, but she learned not to fear the solitude. Twice a day, one of the black crew members brought her a meal. Porridge, bread, and fruit in the morning, and rice or potato and fish or dried beef in the evening. Sometime during the morning, one of the sailors took her on deck to empty her slops bucket. For the first time, she allowed herself to acknowledge that she was a slave, bought as property. *But, I can become free again.* That thought sustained her, gave her strength. *I will remember what Bella taught me.*

Two days later, Anta was startled by the turning of the door handle. It was too early for the evening meal. She let out a gasp of relief as two girls near her age were pushed through. The younger one looked terrified, the older almost calm, resigned, at least. The younger girl was small and thin, colored like rich mahogany. Her features were sharp and bird-like. She reminded Anta of a tiny dove that might flit away. The other girl was short and solidly built, her skin slightly lighter than Anta's. Her clear, dark eyes had a calmness and friendliness about them which went straight to Anta's heart.

"I am Anta Majigeen Ndiaya. I am from the village of Yang Yang in the Wolof states," she announced after the door had closed again.

"I am also from the Wolof states," said the older one. "I am Sophidya Chidgigine Cissé." The younger girl sat in the corner and wept. When she began to speak, Anta realized it was a different language. *How will we be able to talk?*

Sophidya went to the girl and put an arm around her, murmuring soft words of comfort. Anta realized that there are ways of communicating beyond language, and she held this new knowledge close to her heart.

Anta cleared her throat. "Do you know anything about Master Kingsley?"

"No, not yet."

Anta hesitated, then spoke. A seed of an idea had been germinating in her mind, an idea for freedom. "I think this Master Kingsley is not a harsh man. My hope is that when he learns my father is a descendant of Njaajaan Ndyaie, the royal line, he will give me my freedom."

Sophidya's voice was gentle. "That may matter in Jolof, or

any of the Wolof states, but it does not matter here."

Anta wanted to argue. "But,...." She had no words. "But, I can't be a slave," she finished weakly, tears in her eyes. "I want to be back in Yang Yang."

Sophidya took Anta's hands in her own. "You know you will never see Yang Yang again. You must accept that and let it go."

Anta hung her head as tears fell from her eyes. "I don't want to."

The younger girl watched them, trying to understand what they were saying.

Sophidya spoke firmly. "I have been here quite a while and I have learned a lot. At first, I felt as you do, but that only made it harder. We can not change what has happened. Let go of your roots. Those ties can not help you now."

Anta took a deep breath. "I know. But, I have learned that in Spanish East Florida we can buy our freedom."

"I have heard that also, but that is true for the men. We women have no way to earn the money we need to buy our freedom."

Anta's heart skipped a beat at the bad news. "But, what can we do? I will do anything to be free again."

Sophidya dropped Anta's hands. "There is one thing." She paused, as if weighing the wisdom of telling Anta. "It is a hard thing, but it is all we can do. We must try to get Master Kingsley to care for us, to take us to his bed. If we have his children, he might someday set us free."

Anta drew back sharply. "But, I have never....I do not want to....It is only since last year that I began the women's bleeding. I...."

"I know what to do. I will teach you."

"But, he is a white man. He is our master."

"Exactly."

Anta wrapped her arms around herself and felt the anger and bitterness rising like bile in her throat. *I do not want to do that.* A stronger thought followed. *I must be free again.*

\* \* \*

During the days waiting for the journey to begin, no one bothered them, only entering the cabin to bring food or take the girls on deck to empty slop pails. Anta and Sophidya began to call the younger girl "Ampah," the closest they could come to what she said her name was. The sores from the yoke around Anta's neck healed, but left scars, as did the wounds from the cat-o-nine-tails beating. The scars from the yoke were pale half-moons, etched forever through her skin to her very soul.

The day came when the *Esther* set sail with a shuddering that made Anta grasp the edge of her narrow wooden cot. That night, the door opened. The captain, Henry Wright, who had brought Anta to the ship, stepped into their small space. All three girls drew back. He carried a pail of water and a rag with him. Slowly, he looked over the three. "You," he bellowed, pointing at Sophidya. "Wash yourself and come with me. Master Kingsley wants you."

Sophidya stared stonily ahead as they left. Anta trembled. She wanted to be chosen to get her freedom, but the prospect of going to the master's bed terrified her. She lay awake that night, staring into the dark. She knew about the coupling of men and women, knew that someday that coupling would be part of her life. But this. The idea of a white man fondling her, touching her most private places, forcing his ugliness into her was too horrible. Every fiber of her body silently screamed against the violation.

When Sophidya returned, she was strangely quiet. She reported only that Master Kingsley insisted her name was now "Sophie" and that he was not cruel.

\* \* \*

The next night, the captain came again with his water and

his rag. He pointed at Anta this time. Without a word, he shoved the pail and cloth at her and leaned against the door frame as Anta's trembling hands tried to wash herself. She had known this time would come, had tried to prepare for it. Now that it was actually happening, she wanted to scream and run away.

A short way down the hall, Captain Wright opened a cabin door and pushed Anta inside. "Wait here." He gestured that Anta should stay and left, shutting the door behind him.

Anta looked slowly around the empty cabin, gasping at the beauty of the rich things. On a table, she saw papers finer than she could imagine. There were all kinds of black markings on them, words, she supposed. There was a small glass holder with a feather sticking out of it. Very slowly and carefully, she lifted out the feather. The end had been filed sharp and was covered with black. *That must be how those marks are made.*

Spread across much of the table was a large drawing. Most of the picture was blue, with odd-shaped areas throughout. On this drawing lay some kind of instrument, oddly formed with sections of glass. Anta could not imagine what it was for.

At the edge of the table was a flat plate, shaped the same as the wooden ones she was familiar with, but all similarity ended there. This plate was a creamy color, smooth. And ringed with a narrow gold band. It was the most beautiful thing Anta had ever seen. Trembling, she tenderly touched it, marveling at its smoothness. On the plate were several small, round objects, brown in color. Anta could not imagine what they were. She picked one up and smelled it. It had a wonderful, strange, sweet aroma, a little like the cocoa they sometimes had in Yang Yang. She gently set it back down and moved farther into the room.

A cabinet of drawers was against the wall. Anta's glance

moved to the shiny, square object on top. She almost screamed and jumped back. Someone was there. But when she moved, the person moved, too. Anta peered closer. She had seen herself only in the water at Yang Yang, but now she realized she was looking at a reflection of herself.

She eased her way closer and gazed with amazement at the face before her. The chin was narrow and strong, the lips full. Her high cheek bones seemed to accent large, clear eyes above them. Her eyebrows were full and arched. Her forehead was smooth, and her thick, black hair was tugged into the braids she had made some days ago. She smiled, and the face smiled back. Her shoulders were broad for her slender body, rounded gently into her firm, long arms. Two tiny mounds of flesh rose tenderly on her thin chest, giving promise to her womanhood. She wanted to laugh but didn't dare make a sound, so she continued her inspection.

There was a chair near the bed, honey-colored with a curved seat. The back, too, was curved, with round posts from top to seat. The chair had wooden braces on the sides where Master Kingsley could rest his arms. Anta longed to try it out, but she was afraid.

A small nightstand stood next to the bed. A light made of glass and filled with liquid sat on the nightstand. A thin, fiber ribbon was stuck though the top. A pile of books lay beside the lamp. Anta touched the books gently, lifted one, and opened it. She had seen a book before, when the missionaries visited Yang Yang, but had never held one. She knew it was full of words, and she wished she could read the words. It was like a mystery waiting to be solved, a secret to be learned. She set the book back on the stand.

The bed itself looked so soft to Anta. There was deep padding on the wooden bunk and at the head of the bed a soft cloud of something. Anta imagined sinking gently into the softness. A beautiful and intriguing fabric covered the bed. The pattern repeated multi-colored squares, and each square was like a picture, but so was the whole fabric. Anta reached out her hand to touch it and smiled at the texture. She drew the fabric close to her face, smoothing the softness against her cheek.

"So you like my quilt, do you?" came a voice from the doorway.

Anta whirled around, dropping the fabric as if it were on fire.

Master Kingsley laughed a deep, friendly laugh, not at all like the one the tyeddo warrior had uttered when he captured her. He walked into the cabin and closed the door. His brown, wavy hair contrasted the whiteness of his skin. His brown eyes were deep-set above a long, thin nose. His sharp chin jutted out, giving an air of confidence. He was not a tall man, not much taller than Anta, and his wiry body was slim but strong-looking. Anta sensed his aura of power and control.

"Here," he said, picking up the fabric and draping it around her shoulders. "See how it feels."

Anta stared at him, uncertain what to do.

"Now, now. Don't be afraid. It's just a quilt."

Anta drew the fabric close around her, luxuriating in the feel of it. "Kilt," she repeated.

"No, Anna. Quilt." He said it slowly. "Quilt."

*He called me Anna, not Anta. How can I make him understand my name?*

She pointed at herself. "Anta."

"Oh, I know what the papers say, but I am going to call you Anna. You are Anna from now on."

Anta felt anger rising inside. Who was he to tell her what her name was? She jabbed a finger at herself. "Anta."

A cold, icy look came into Master Kingsley's eyes, and it sent a shiver down her back.

"You are my property now, and I say your name in Anna."

Anta looked at him, confused. He knew her right name,

but he was calling her Anna. Anna must be the way her name was said in his language. With a flash of insight, Anta knew that it would not do to make him angry. If he said her name was Anna, it would be Anna.

She pointed at herself again. "Anna."

He laughed his deep laugh. "That's right. But I confess, I like a girl with spunk." He removed his jacket and folded it carefully on the chair. The casual way he began to undress made Anna tense with anticipation. She feared what lay ahead. *Perhaps I can delay him.*

She pulled at his sleeve. His laughter made her bold. She pulled him toward the table and pointed at each of the objects there, then made her face look puzzled, as if asking a question.

"So you want to learn things. Good. Shows some intelligence."

He began pointing to each object as he said the names. She repeated each name. "Ship's log. Quill and ink. Inkwell. Map of the world. Sextant. China plate. Chocolates...here, eat one. They're good."

Anna backed away.

"Come on. Try one. You'll like it." He put one in his mouth and gestured that she should do the same.

Anna placed the small, brown thing in her mouth and bit down. She was stunned by the creamy sweetness, the exotic flavor. It was like nothing she had ever tasted. She wanted to close her eyes and savor it.

Master Kingsley laughed again. "See, I told you you'd like it."

After Anna finished the chocolate, the taste lingered in her mouth. She wished it would last forever.

"Later, you can have another." He moved toward her. "I have other things to teach you." He reached out and stroked her arm. Anna shivered and her fear showed in her eyes. Her heart beat faster.

"There is nothing to be afraid of. Take off that filthy rag

and climb into bed."

Anna stared, unsure of what he was telling her.

Master Kingsley turned and walked to the bed. He pulled back the covers revealing the soft, cotton sheets. Holding a hand toward Anna, he said, "Come."

Anna slowly approached the bed. She touched the sheets, amazed at their softness. She tried to concentrate on the bed itself as her master's hands pulled her shift off her shoulders and arms until it slid to the floor.

He pointed to the bed and pushed her forward.

She climbed onto the bunk, biting her lip to hold back her tears. She stretched out on her back and closed her eyes. She heard him drop one boot on the floor, then the other. His clothing rustled as he removed garments and placed them on the chair. Even with her eyes closed, she could see his every move. She tried to still her trembling. She felt the coolness of the air touching her naked skin and felt the goose bumps rise. Finally, she felt him ease his body onto the bed, and she turned her face to the wall as her nostrils caught his sweaty scent. Her breathing became a gasp as he moved his heaviness on top of her. Anna tried to use her mind to put herself someplace else.

# Chapter Eight

Anna woke slowly, not wanting to come away from the safety
of sleep. She touched the wooden hardness of her own bunk
and found comfort in the deep breathing sounds of Ampah
and Sophie. Memories came flooding back in a rush, his
gentle words, his insistent thrusting, the pain, her tears. She
knew she would never forget the smell of the lamp oil as it
burned beside the bed, the rocking motion of the sea, the
sound of water lapping against the wooden sides of the ship,
the weight of his body on hers. She shook her head to remove
the distasteful recollection, but she couldn't. Those memories
were seared as painfully into her mind as the vision of the
lone baobab tree silhouetted against the smoke of Yang Yang.

The ultimate violation of her body was done. She remembered her mother's words. Only the first time would be
painful. At least she had been spared the agonizing mutila-
tion girls had gone through in their womanhood ritual of
years past. *Now there is nothing more anyone can do to me. I know
that I can endure this.* Anna turned over and drifted back into
a restless sleep.

When Captain Wright came to their room that evening,
Anna barely glanced at him, knowing that Ampah would be
ordered to Master Kingsley's room. Ampah, at eleven years
old was the youngest by far. She had spent the day huddled on
her bunk, whimpering in anticipation.

"Anna, he wants you again," Captain Wright barked at her. Anna jumped slightly at hearing her name. She looked up at the captain, confused.

"Yeah, you, Anna. Come on."

Anna took the washrag from his hand. After washing herself, she followed Captain Wright out the door, turning to look at Sophie with a puzzled expression.

"Anna, come in," Master Kingsley greeted her warmly. Taking her arm, he led her to the table. "Let's see if you remember the new words." He pointed to the sharpened feather. "What is this?" He lifted his eyebrows with the asking so Anna understood that he was questioning her.

Anna looked at him in surprise. This experience was not what she expected. She urged her mind back to the words he had said last night. *What had he called that?Ink?...No, it had a funny sound....*

"Quill" she said, finally.

"Excellent. I knew you would be a good student. Let's go over everything again." For the next half hour, he walked Anna around the room, pointing to things, naming them, having her repeat them.

At the bedside, he removed the quilt and draped it over her shoulders.

"Quilt," said Anna, again savoring the softness of the fabric against her skin.

"Yes, quilt. And on you, it looks like a royal robe. I bought you because of that regal air you have. You look like a proud African princess." He smiled at her, not knowing the truth he had uttered, and urged her onto the bed.

\* \* \*

A pattern emerged. She was taken to Master Kingsley's room each night and given an English language lesson. Soon, he brought her to his cabin during the day to teach her new words. He delighted in her learning.

Now that they were at sea, the young women's cabin was not locked. They were allowed to come on deck as they wished.

"Of course, we could not go anywhere, except overboard," Sophie said.

Anna tossed her head and let the wind cool her neck. "I don't care. I'm glad for any sense of freedom we have."

"You're right, of course. Look, even Ampah has stopped her tears."

Anna smiled at the younger girl, and then she sighed. *Life is incredibly better than the past few months have been, but I never forget for a minute that I am the property of someone else, that I lost my childhood, my life at Yang Yang.*

The three girls sat together on the deck as they braided each other's hair. Sophie stopped her braiding. "Anna, you look so sad.

"I was just thinking of my sisters," Anna replied. "It was not so long ago that we sat together, doing each other's hair like this. I miss them so much."

Sophie nodded her head. "I, too, miss my family. But you are the lucky one. Master Kingsley chooses you every night. You are sure to start a baby, and so you might get your freedom. What hope is there for me, or for Ampah?"

Anna leaned back and watched the clouds floating overhead. One looked like a horse jumping and one like a fish. She felt the warmth of the sun on her body. The heat radiated from the smooth wooden boards of the deck,

"It is so strange to me. We have been sailing for eight days, and I have stayed with him for seven nights. He is so kind to me. When he sends for me during the day, he teaches me his language, even how to write it. I think he enjoys the teaching as much as I want the learning."

Sophie finished doing Ampah's braid and sat cross-legged on the warm boards of the deck. "He does seem to be a kind master," she commented.

Ampah tried to be part of the conversation. "Massa Kingsley...good."

Just then he came around the corner himself.

"Anna, come. I want to show you something." Master Kingsley indicated that she should follow him to his cabin. Anna jumped up and eagerly and followed. *What will he teach me this time?*

Inside the cabin, he pulled out the chair by his table and sat down. "Look at these, Anna." He pulled more maps out on his work table. "These are plats of my plantation in Florida, Laurel Grove. This is where you will be living."

Anna looked over his shoulder at the markings, the sketch of trees, a river, buildings. She could tell the largest square was probably his house, but there were many others. She pointed to a grouping of small squares, and said, "What is?"

"Those are the slaves' houses. For slaves. And behind each house is a place for a garden. Garden." With his hands gestured plants growing and being eaten. "Each family grows some of the food it needs."

Anna moved her finger up and down the row of markings for the slaves' houses.

"What is...for Anna?"

Master Kingsley pushed back from the table and pulled Anna onto his lap. "No slave house for you, my dear. Those are for the field slaves. You will be at the Big House. I want you to stay near to me. Do you understand?" His hand gently rubbed her arm.

Anna looked at the plat of Laurel Grove. She pointed to the large square. "Anna?"

"Yes. Anna will stay in the Big House."

Anna thought about all she had learned of Zephaniah Kingsley in the week she had been with him. She had learned that he could be gentle and caring, and that he could be cold and hard. He was not a mean man, but it would not do to

go against his wishes. He was old enough to be her father.
At times, he acted like a father; teaching her; instructing
her how to eat like a lady at his table; how to greet someone
when introduced. Other times, he enjoyed her as a lover, and
sometimes like a husband, just having her near. Anna really
did not know what to make of the change in her status from
being marched as a chained captive across Senegal to whatever her position was with Master Kingsley. But there was one
piece of knowledge she held tightly. She knew she was doing
the one thing that might someday make freedom possible.

\* \* \*

The weather remained pleasant, without storms. They had
been sailing for almost two weeks, following the coastline
whenever possible.

"Soon we be... Laurel Grove?" Anna and Master Kingsley
stood at the railing, watching a settlement come into view.
He smiled at her attempt to speak English. "You mean 'Will
we soon be at Laurel Grove?' Say the whole sentence, Anna."

"Will we soon be at Laurel Grove?"

"We still have quite a way to go. This is Charleston. I will
unload and sell the rum and molasses I bought in Cuba; then
we will sail back toward Florida."

Captain Wright navigated the ship alongside a pier, and
the black sailors tied the *Esther* tightly with thick ropes and
lowered the gangplank. One of the crew came to Anna and
the two other girls watching the landing.

"You gots to go to your cabin, now. Captain Wright done
tol' me to lock you all in."

Anna bristled, but Master Kingsley was already down the
gangplank, so she could not appeal to him. *No matter how good
the master is to me, I am still just a slave.*

That evening Master Kingsley sent Captain Wright
to bring Anna to his cabin. "I brought you something, a

present." He handed her a bundle wrapped in plain paper and tied with a string.

Anna smiled at him shyly. She was awed by him, by the things he did. Slowly, savoring the joy of having a gift, she untied the string. The paper rustled as she opened the parcel. Anna drew in a sharp breath as she unwrapped a powder blue cotton scarf and a brush and comb set with silver handles. She touched the soft, luxurious fabric gently and marveled at the good things that were happening to her. This thoughtful act touched a place inside her, and tears came to her eyes. She murmured, "Thank you." Her voice trembled with emotion. Anna wondered at her strong feelings. *His kindnesses unsettle me so.*

\* \* \*

Anna loved standing at the rail enjoying the autumn sunshine. *If this were Senegal, we would be starting the drought time.* She searched for similarities between this strange new land and Senegal. She longed for something that might look like home to her, but there was not much so far, other than the flatness of the land. The trees were tall with a burst of fan-like leaves at the top. Master Kingsley called them palm trees. She didn't want to lose the memories of her life back in Yang Yang, of the games she and her sisters played, of her parents, the songs her mother sang, the stories her father told. When she tried to see it in her mind, she simply saw that stark silhouette of the baobab tree, reaching with its leafless, gnarled fingers into the smoke-filled sky. The vision of its barrenness reminded her of despair, loss, and death.

Master Kingsley came up behind her and laid his hand gently on her shoulder.

"Look, Anna, we are getting closer to home. Tomorrow we will dock at St. Augustine, and I will go ashore to register you three *bozales*. You will be official in Spanish East Florida then."

Anna looked at him quizzically. "*Bozales?* What is it?"

"That just means someone new from Africa. You," he pointed at Anna, "from Africa."

Anna nodded her understanding. Master Kingsley talked to her a lot, and most of what he said she did not understand. But she was learning words, and he was a good teacher. She knew she would need the language to get along in the new world. Still, she was glad to have Sophie to talk to in her own dialect.

It seemed to Anna that the kinder Zephaniah Kingsley was to her, the more terrifying the past months became. She had not allowed herself to feel and respond to the terror while she was going through it. Now that she was feeling safer, she could let down her guard. One night, in the darkness of dreaming, the terror came back to her. She awoke with silent screams muffled in her throat and tears coursing down her cheeks.

"Anna, Anna, it's all right now." Master Kingsley's voice soothed her as he held her close to him. "You were just having a bad dream."

Anna's racing heart began to settle. "Home...," she said, remembering the word. "Mama...."

"I know. I know, little one. You have seen terrors I cannot imagine. But you are safe now. I will look out for you. You are safe. Safe." His gentle hands calmed her.

She did not understand the word, but sensed it was a good thing. "Safe," she whispered to herself.

# Chapter Nine

*Laurel Grove*
*October – November 1806*

Two weeks after leaving Havana, the *Esther* rocked in the gentle swells off St. Augustine. Master Kingsley lowered himself into the small dinghy and was rowed to shore. Anna, Sophie, and Ampah stood at the rail, watching, wondering what life was like in that land of Florida. From what she could see of St. Augustine, Anna thought it was a bustling city. There was a large fortress near the pier where Master Kingsley had left his rowboat. Anna noticed a number of men dressed in uniform.

Master Kingsley brought several parcels with him when he returned. He handed one of the bundles to Sophie and one to Ampah. "To wear when we get to Laurel Grove. Throw away those rags you have been wearing." The two girls looked to Anna for explanation. She looked to their master.

He took back the package he had given Sophie and opened it, revealing a homespun cotton dress. He held it up to Sophie, indicating that what she was wearing should be thrown away. All the girls smiled.

"Anna, come with me." He led the way to his cabin. Inside, he gave her a package. "I got this especially for you, Anna. I think you will look lovely in it, with your height and slimness. I want to see it on you."

Anna took out a muslin dress, simple in lines, a soft

dusty-rose color. Ecru lace trimmed the collar and cuffs. She held it to her bosom, her eyes sparkling with pleasure.

"You are so pretty," he said.

"So pretty." She smoothed the folds of the dress.

"Put it on. Let me see. Then I have another gift for you."

Anna pulled off what was left of the garment she had worn for weeks and dropped it on the floor. She pulled the new dress over her head and let it fall gently around her. She felt like a princess again. She laughed with delight and spun around, the skirt flaring around her.

Master Kingsley sat smiling. He opened another small package. "Now close your eyes and hold out your hands." She looked at him, not understanding what he wanted.

"Close your eyes," he repeated, covering her eyes with his hand, "and put out your hands." He opened her hands in front of her.

For just a moment, Anna felt so vulnerable that she did not think she could stand. She felt him put a small object in her outstretched hands.

She opened her eyes and looked. A chocolate. Her mouth began to water as she anticipated the amazing taste and texture. She wanted to pop it in her mouth, but she dared not. She looked at him for permission.

He laughed. "Yes, Anna, for you. Eat it. Go on. Enjoy."

\* \* \*

The schooner sailed toward their final destination the next day, skirting the coast. After some miles, they turned into the mouth of a river. Anna sensed a growing excitement in Master Kingsley. He pointed out more and more to her. The land was low and flat. He told her the river was called the St. Johns River. As they passed areas of short, green grassy plants, sometimes with pockets of water around them, he told her, "Marsh." She tried the new word, and he nodded.

They passed settlements and fields with amber colored stalks drying in the sunlight as they had in Senegal, and smaller plants with wisps of white still visible. "Corn," he told her. "Cotton." Mostly, they passed tall slender trees, with sharp green needles instead of leaves. "Pine trees. Very good for timber."

As they passed a small settlement on the banks of the river, he said, "It is called Cowford. We come here to trade." He seemed to want her to learn everything about the new land, but she felt that her mind had been crowded with too many new words already.

Master Kingsley stood at the rail, as if wishing himself already home. Anna watched him as he leaned into the wind. His frame was slight, his height not much more than Anna's. He always dressed neatly, presenting himself as a successful trader and plantation owner. He stuck his clean-shaven chin slightly forward, perhaps asserting himself to make up for what he lacked in stature. His brown hair was long, worn tied in the back. His brown eyes could twinkle with merriment or slice into her with a cold hardness. He was a complicated man, but she felt an increasing sense of trust in him and, surprisingly, a growing fondness.

"Anna, come look," he called her to him.

Anna's gaze took in the acreage on the west side of the river. On a slight incline above the dock stood a two-story house, white with a porch around it. It looked huge to Anna.

"You...your...house?" she gasped. She remembered the home of the *signare* on Gorée Island and thinking that a god must live in such a place. *Could it be true that I will live in such a home myself?*

"It is beautiful, isn't it? Yes, that is where I live, and that is where you will live also. And look there. Those are my orange trees, and those fields hold the Sea Island cotton we plant here, and those fields are the sugarcane...." His excitement was infectious as Anna took in the plantation before her.

She wanted to say that it was beautiful, and she was glad she would be a part of it, but she did not have the words. She took his arm, and as he turned toward her, she smiled and looked deeply into his eyes. She hoped her expression would convey what was in her heart.

"Anna," was all he said as he gently stroked her cheek. She knew, then, that they could share without the words. She would work very hard to learn the words, but in the mean-time, this would be enough.

* * *

The schooner was still being secured to the dock with thick ropes when Master Kingsley jumped off. He greeted a large, muscular black man who was ordering all the workers to their tasks. Their conversation was animated, and Anna was amazed when they laughed together. The man joined Master Kingsley as they boarded the ship and approached Anna.

"Anna, this is Abraham. Abraham Hannahan. He is my overseer. He is in charge of everything when I am away. If I am gone and you have a problem, go to Abraham."

He turned to the overseer. "Abraham, this is Anna. She is one of the three *bozales*. Find a place for the other two in the slave quarters, but bring Anna to the Big House. She will be one of the house slaves. I want her to be near me."

Abraham looked at Anna, appraising her. She instinc-tively reacted to the judgment in his eyes, and she drew herself up tall, like the princess she was, and gave him an aloof stare. The moment was charged with a kind of electricity. Anna took a quick measure of Abraham, noting his tall stature, his muscular arms. His black hair curled slightly over the wide forehead which dominated his face, making his eyes deep set and hard to read. All his features were broad: his nose, lips, and chin. Everything about him gave the appearance of a solid rock.

"I get my things." She turned and went to the cabin. She used her new blue scarf to bundle up her comb and brush set and her old garment that she had torn into rags for her bleeding time.

Abraham directed another slave to take Ampah and Sophie to their quarters. The three friends shared their fears about a new place with their eyes but said nothing in farewell. Anna realized that the time on board the ship had been only an interlude before a scary unknown.

She followed Abraham to the back of the Big House and into the kitchen. He turned her over to the three kitchen slaves. Celia, obviously in charge, looked Anna over carefully. Celia reminded Anna of the fat green lizards abundant in Senegal. She was short and squat, her features thick in her broad face. Her hair was hidden under her green head rag, making her large eyes even more prominent. Although she was probably about the same age Anna's mother had been, Celia's dry, leathery skin made her appear older. She squinted her eyes as she appraised Anna, just as a lizard would do as it watched its prey.

"So, Massa want you in the Big House. I don't knows what good a thin little chile like you can do with the housework, but come on. Dis other room here can be fo' you."

She led Anna to a small room off one side of the kitchen.

"This be your room now. Later you see de house. Tomorrow, you start helpin' in the kitchen." She turned abruptly, the ring of keys hanging from her waist jangling authoritatively, and left Anna to look about the tiny space.

The room was barely six feet square with a sloping ceiling. A narrow cot was on one side, covered with one of the beautiful patterned blankets Anna had come to know as quilts. A bucket for relieving herself sat next to the cot. Anna was pleased to know that she would not have to go out in the night. On the opposite wall was a small, wooden washstand with a china washbowl and pitcher. Anna ran her hand over the smooth, creamy white surface. She laid the comb and brush Master Kingsley had bought her next to the bowl and stood back. She was settled. After all she had been through since that fateful, terrifying night in April, it was a good feeling.

Anna jumped when she heard a tapping at her door, even though it was a soft noise. Opening the door, she faced a young woman only a few years older than she. Anna vaguely remembered seeing the girl in the kitchen when Abraham brought her to the house. She was slim, not very tall, and dressed in a brown homespun dress with a white bib apron covering much of it. Her coloring was not as dark as Anna's, and her black hair was pulled back under a blue and brown colored scarf wound around her head several times. The girl's brown eyes glanced about quickly, and her whole demeanor reminded Anna of a nervous rabbit. Anna noticed how the girl stared at Anna's dress, and she felt uncomfortable that her gown was so much finer.

"I be Mariah. Celia tell me show you de house."

"I am Anna." Mariah had already turned and started through the kitchen. As they walked through, Anna took in more of the room. One end wall was filled with a huge stone fireplace, tall enough for Anna to stand upright in. Several metal brackets, blackened with soot, were positioned in it along with a large metal box with two doors on the front, many black cast iron skillets, pots, and two large kettles.

As the two girls passed through the kitchen, Celia never looked up from her work rolling out flour dough on a center table. Nearby was a large wooden bowl filled with apples ready for the pie. The pungent smell of fruit and cinnamon sent a hunger pang to Anna's stomach. She wondered if she would ever get over the deprivation she suffered on the trip from Yang Yang to Havana.

Mariah led the way through the kitchen into a small hallway lined with cupboards.

"This be the butler's pantry."

"What is ... but...buters ...pansy?"

Mariah stopped and turned. "What is it? Don't you know nothin', girl?"

"I...." Anna began, searching her mind for the right words. "I do not know... house," she tried to explain. "I never....This first...I go to house."

"You ain't never been in a house?" Mariah eyes were wide in amazement.

Anna shook her head.

Mariah sighed as if realizing the enormity of the responsibility before her. "This be the butler's pantry," she started again. "All de china, crystal, and de silver be here. You don't touch it. Only Charles and Celia."

"Who is Charles?"

"Charles be in charge of de whole house. He make sure everytin' be right. He de only one can go in Massa's study to talk to him. He tell Celia what to do, and Celia tell us. We do whatever Celia tell us do. You'd best learn that mighty quick."

They walked through the massive dining room with its heavy mahogany furniture. Between the gleam of the furniture and the shine from the chandelier and mirror on the wall, Anna felt the room glittered in its beauty.

"Massa eat here. You don't touch nothin'."

Anna nodded her understanding.

"This be the parlor," Mariah said as they entered a room more beautiful and richly furnished than anything Anna could imagine.

"Parlor," she repeated as she gazed around. On the front and one side wall, windows reached all the way to the floor. Heavy gold drapes bordered the windows from top to bottom, pooling against the gleaming hardwood planks. Two black stiff sofas faced each other in the center of the room, with matching chairs along the side. The wall on the far end of the room held two enormous mirrors with gold frames. A heavy-looking mahogany table was against the remaining wall with several glass decanters on it and a large landscape painting mounted over it. Anna could not imagine what people used this room for. She wanted to stay and gaze at herself in her new dress in the full-length mirror, but Mariah was already on her way to the next room. As Anna caught up with Mariah in the hall, she could only gasp at the sight of the curving staircase to the second floor.

They crossed the hall to a room on the other side. Anna could not believe her eyes. Shelves filled with books lined each wall. Another sofa sat in the center, and a large table and chair sat on the side.

Anna stared at the books lining the walls. "So many."

"Dis be de libr'y."

Anna turned in a circle trying to take it all in. She stopped at a strange, round object in the corner. She recognized that it was like the maps Master Kingsley had shown her in his cabin.

"Dat be a globe of de whole world," Mariah said, obviously proud of her knowledge.

Anna already felt dizzy by all she had seen. She held tightly to the smooth, polished wood of the railing as Mariah led the way to the second floor. *I'll never find my way around the house.* Anna tried to keep up with Mariah's words, but there was too much to take in. The tour took them through many bedrooms, but Anna could not keep them straight. Mariah paused at one closed door.

"This be Massa's room." She started to say more, then flicked a knowing look at Anna before she started down the hall.

It was so fleeting, Anna wondered if she imagined it. *Why are you judging me? I was captured, purchased, and brought here against my will. He chose me, and now I am only trying to regain my freedom.* Anna wanted to explain but knew it wouldn't matter. She followed Mariah down the hall.

"Where is it...you sleep?" Anna asked. She had seen
Celia had another room off the kitchen, but there were no
rooms there for Mariah and the other house slaves.
Mariah opened another door revealing stairs to a third floor.
"Up dere," she pointed. "We gots rooms at de top of de house.
Dere is six of us house slaves in two of de rooms, and Charles,
he gots a room up dere, too."

They went down another staircase into the kitchen. Anna
wanted to lay her head down on her bed and put everything
out of her mind. There was simply too much.

"Dis be Portia and dis be Lily," Mariah introduced the
other two women in the kitchen. Portia was probably in her
mid-thirties, guessed Anna. She was almost Anna's height,
but outweighed her by at least fifty pounds. The extra weight
made her face round and full.

Portia put her hands on her broad hips and said in a raspy
voice, "And who be you?"

"I am Anna. Anta Majigeen Ndiaye...from Senegal."

"Well. Ain't you somebody," she snorted derisively and
turned back to her work at the fireplace.

Lily, nearer Anna's age, was tall and thin, her bones
jutting out at her shoulders, elbows, and hips, making her
seem like all sharp angles. Even her nose was pointed in her
long, thin face. She said nothing to Anna, but looked her up
and down slowly, her thin lips drawn in a scowl.

"We all has been with de Kingsley's since we was borned,"
Mariah said, as if that explained the haughty attitudes.

Anna had to get to her room. Her head was spinning
for all she seen throughout the house, and her feelings were
bruised from the aloofness of the other slaves. Since she
couldn't be with Sophie, she longed for solitude.

# Chapter Ten

*Laurel Grove*
*November 1806*

On her first morning at Laurel Grove, the silvery dawn was
barely slipping into the sky when Celia threw open her door.

"Get up, girl. Your job is to gets the fire goin' so I can get
Massa his breakfast. Hurry up now."

Anna quickly put on her dress and splashed cold water
from her pitcher on her face. She rushed to the fireplace and
began to stir up the coals.

Celia carried a kettle over to the fireplace and hung it on
one of the brackets. She looked at Anna with a frown on her
face. "Dat dress...." she began.

Anna put her hand protectively against her chest.
"Dress?"

"Where you get dat dress, girl?"

Anna shook her head in confusion. "Master Kingsley
gave dress."

Celia's eyes narrowed. She grabbed Anna's sleeve. "Dat's
not a workin' dress for a slave."

Anna felt tears of confusion come to her eyes. *This is my
only dress. What does she want me to do?* The sound of Mariah,
Portia, and Lily arriving drew Celia's attention away from
Anna.

*I cannot let her make me cry. I must stay out of her way.*

Anna learned Master Kingsley's routine by watching

through a crack in the dining room door. He rose early and expected his precious coffee to be ready. Then he breakfasted on bacon and biscuits and gravy while he met with Abraham to go over the day's plans. As she watched, she wondered, *Will he call for me? Has he forgotten all about me?* She wanted to carry his food out to him, but Celia scowled at her and told her to stay in the kitchen. Mariah was allowed to carry the food to the table.

A tall, gray-haired and stern-looking man stood at attention behind Master Kingsley making sure everything was served correctly. *Must be the Charles Mariah told me about. Something about him reminds me of Papa. If this were a village in Africa, he would be the headman.*

When Anna finally tumbled into bed that night, she thought she would fall asleep immediately. She was tired and her head ached. Her mind couldn't rest, though. *That Celia is like a senior wife. She is so bossy. She always yells at Mariah, too. Mariah acts scared of Celia. I won't act like that. Lily and Portia are plain arrogant. They think they're better than everyone because they're house slaves not field slaves. I hope Master Kingsley does not forget about me. I can't keep being a slave here. I need to see Sophie again. How will I find her? I've got to stop thinking and sleep.*

Anna made herself take deep, slow breaths as she tried to empty her mind. Sleep finally rescued her from more fearful thoughts about what tomorrow might bring.

* * *

On the third night, there was a soft knock on Anna's door.

"Massa sent fo' you. He want you in his room," said Mariah. "Follow me. I show you de way."

"I....thank you," was all Anna could think to say.

There was no conversation as Mariah led her through the long hallways to Master Kingsley's room. Anna was sure she would never find her way back on her own and hoped she could stay with Master Kingsley throughout the night.

He was sitting at his writing desk, the light from the oil lamp flickering as he wrote. Anna stood silently, waiting. He laid down his quill, slapped shut the book he was writing in, and turned to Anna with a smile.

"And how do you like my Laurel Grove, Anna?" he gestured widely.

Anna could understand so much of what he said, not from the words which were still strange to her, but simply from watching the whole of him, his eyes, his mouth, the way he moved his arms.

"Laurel Grove...is...good." She saw her answer pleased him.

"Yes." He laughed. "It is good, and it will be a good place for you. You'll see. Tomorrow I will take you with me as I ride over the plantation. I will teach you all about it."

Anna smiled to herself. She felt safe here with Master Kingsley, and she knew that by going to his bed, she was traveling the road that would bring her back to freedom. It was a road she was willing to travel.

\* \* \*

After breakfast, Master Kingsley sent Abraham to bring Anna to the stables. Anna had many questions she wanted to ask the overseer, but his long strides put too much distance between them for her to have any conversation.

It was Anna's first chance to look around the plantation. She noted the washhouse where two slaves were stirring huge black caldrons over an open fire. Wet bed linens snapped in the slight breeze as they hung on ropes strung between two trees. She could see the lines of slaves' houses in the distance. *I wonder where Sophie is.*

Master Kingsley was waiting with three horses by the barn. He was dressed in riding breeches, high black boots, and a tweed jacket over a white shirt. Anna thought he looked very handsome with his brown hair glistening in the morning sunshine.

"Have you ever ridden a horse?" Master Kingsley asked her, gesturing to the black mount next to him.

Anna remembered the terrifying few minutes she had been on the tyeddo warrior's horse, thrown over the saddle like baggage. She did not think that counted as riding. "No."

"Well, it is perfectly safe. You will enjoy riding my gaited horses. They are smooth and easy. All you have to do is sit on them."

Abraham boosted Anna up into the saddle of a short, sorrel mare, and the two men mounted their horses. Anna's heart began beating faster as she looked down from this new height. She clutched at the saddle rim with one hand and the horse's mane with the other.

"Anna." Master Kingsley laughed gently. "Do not be afraid. Look," he nudged his horse next to hers. "Take these in your hands. These are reins. Reins. Hold them like this."

She repeated the words he emphasized. "Reins," she said and took them in both hands.

"Good. Now, relax. Your horse will follow mine. Just sit there and enjoy the ride."

Anna looked at him, wanting to trust the large animal under her, but a trace of fear kept her uneasy. As they clattered out of the lane in front of the Big House, Anna began to relax to the swaying motion of her horse. She felt so tall, as if she could see forever from this high vantage point.

Anna finally stopped concentrating on holding tight to the reins and looked around her. The plantation was huge. Master Kingsley told her it was a thousand acres. She could not imagine how much a thousand acres was. She tried to listen closely and understand.

He pointed out the two areas of slaves' cabins. "One is called Shipyard, and one is called Springfield." As they rode past Springfield, he explained that a slave named Peter was in charge of all that area. There were cabins with plots of land behind them for gardens, poultry coops, a mill house for grinding the corn and grain, a carpentry and blacksmith shop, and a barn for the livestock.

The field slaves did not look up at Master Kingsley, but Anna was very much aware of their eyes studying her. She was studying them, too.

"Anna, this field of cotton where the slaves are working has been picked once. They are going through for the second time."

Men, women, and children five or six years and older were doing the picking. Long bags trailed behind them as they shuffled slowly along, their hands deftly removing the last of the white fluff. Their clothes were basic brown, but not ragged. Most wore head coverings of some kind. Occasionally, one would call out to another. Sometimes, a soft laugh could be heard.

"You see all these workers?" He spread his arm widely. "They are all Africans like you although many were born on my family's plantation in Charleston. They live as you did in Africa, doing the field work. They work for me from about dawn until two o'clock in the afternoon. When they finish their work, I let them have time for their own crops or fishing or hunting. Life is good for them here." He turned to look at her. "It will be good for you, too."

He moved on, and Abraham and Anna followed. "That hedge around my Mandarin orange trees is two thousand feet of other kinds of orange trees. They grow well here.... Those acres are planted in Sea Island cotton....This is the sugarcane we grow....Here are my fields of potatoes, corn, and beans, which I grow for all the workers to eat. I feed my slaves well, Anna, and if there is extra, I sell it at market....I have a store over there." He pointed to a long, low building. "I sell to my neighbors as well as to my slaves."

By the end of the morning, Anna was glad to get off the horse. When Abraham helped her slide off the horse, her legs felt wobbly, like the feeling when she first walked on shore after the long Middle Passage. Out of the corner of her eye, she caught a glimpse of the quick smirk that passed over his face. As she started walking toward the Big House, she winced from a stiffness in her legs and back. She had enjoyed the ride, though. There was such a sense of freedom to be able to ride along, above the heads of everyone as they toiled in the fields.

When Anna walked into the kitchen, Celia scowled at her.

"Humph. You be off ridin' with Massa like you somebody, and here dere be work to be done. After we do de noon meal and clean up, you go with Portia and Lily to do the dustin' and polishin'." Celia abruptly turned back to the metal box in the fireplace, pulled out a pan of biscuits, and slapped them noisily on the table top.

Anna was confused. *What was Celia so angry with me about? After all, Master Kingsley sent for me. I had no choice but to go. Who does she think she is, looking at me with those mean eyes?* Anna wanted to turn her back on Celia and storm off to her room, but reason prevailed. *I can't to that. I have to do what Celia says. I am a slave. A slave.* Anna felt an old bitterness creep back into her heart.

She spent the afternoon on her hands and knees in front of the fireplaces, cleaning out the soot and polishing the brass andirons. Almost in tears, she looked at the black grime on her dress as she finished her job. Lily glanced over from where she was dusting books on a library shelf. "Maybe now you won't think you so special when you gots to work like de rest of us."

Anna glared at her. She wanted to protest, to deny that she was a slave like them, but it was the bitter truth. She drew herself up as tall as she could and reminded herself that she had a plan. *Someday, freedom will be mine. When I have Master Kingsley's baby, he will give me my freedom. Then they'll have to sing a different song.*

The next morning, Anna woke early. *I can't let Celia have an excuse to scold me.* She got up and quickly washed in her bowl on the washstand. She luxuriated in the feeling of being able to stay clean, something she had taken for granted in Yang Yang. As she slipped into her dress, that feeling diminished. Even though she had scrubbed her dress with water from her wash bowl, the smudges of soot stood out like exclamations.

Hurrying into the kitchen, Anna was glad to see Celia was not there. She brought the fire to life in the fireplace, filled the kettle with water, and hung it as Celia had. She wondered if Master Kingsley would take her for a ride again today. She began to feel light-headed and slightly sick to her stomach. *Was that a reaction to riding the horse yesterday?*

Celia came up behind her. "What is it, girl? You sick?"

Anna swallowed the bile rising in her throat. She was almost never sick. What could be wrong? "No...I don't know..."

Celia snorted. "You already gots a baby comin'. I knows that look."

*A baby?* Anna was stunned. *A baby already?* It was what she had hoped for, what she wanted. A baby was her way to freedom. And yet...?

# Chapter Eleven

*Laurel Grove*
*November – December, 1806*

Anna was queasy when she first got up for the next several mornings. She began to believe that she might be pregnant. Her emotions flew up and down, from elation that the dream of freedom might become a reality; to despair that she didn't know how to care for a baby and that her own mother was a lifetime away and could never help her. She wished she could talk to Sophie again. Sophie seemed so much older and able to understand so much. But Sophie was out somewhere with the field slaves. She saw Celia the most, but she was always cross. The other house slaves, Portia, Lily, and even Mariah sometimes, followed Celia's example.

*I'll just show them. I don't need their friendship. After all, I have Sophie's...and Master Kingsley's...at least, some of the time.* She frowned, remembering the times his eyes turned to ice, and his voice cut through her coldly. She needed to count on him...but could she?

* * *

Each evening Anna tried to clean her one dress with water in her washbowl, but she was not very successful. Celia grabbed her arm one day as she was finishing scrubbing the pots. "Look at you, girl. You a disgrace to dis house. You gots to have a work dress and some undergarments. Come wid me to de storeroom."

Upstairs, Celia took one of the keys from her ring and un-locked a door along the back hallway. Anna was amazed to see shelves along all four walls with jars of fruits and vegetables, linens, cloths for the table, silver candlesticks, bowls of glass and silver, and bolts of fabric. Celia marched to the shelves with brown homespun fabric. The fabric matched the other house slaves' dresses. Celia picked up a bolt of cloth, dumped it in Anna's arms, and then took one of white fabric for an apron.

"I tell Harriet to make you up what you need," Celia said.

"Harriet?"

"She de seamstress for all de plantation."

"Seamstress?"

Celia stopped and turned to Anna. She shook her head in disgust. "Humph. African. Don't know nothin'." She made the gesture of sewing. "She make you de clothes you need." She turned on her heel and walked down the hall muttering to herself.

Anna hurried to catch up. *Someone to make clothes for me? That is such a good thing. Why does Celia have to spoil it by acting mad at me?*

* * *

Anna was washing the big cast iron pots used to prepare dinner when Charles scurried into the kitchen.

"Quick," he said. "The Massa want you come eat wid him. Clean yourself up fast, girl, and get in dere."

Celia gave her usual snort of displeasure as Anna tidied her hair and followed Charles.

"Anna." Master Kingsley sat at the head of the table. "It seemed lonely to dine by myself tonight. Come and join me." He gestured to the place next to him. Anna had eaten with him a few times in his cabin aboard the schooner, but this formal dining room was overwhelming. The large mahogany table stretched out before them with chairs for twelve around it. In the center was a large candelabrum with at least a dozen candles spilling their soft light over the arrangement of flowers and fruit. Portraits of stern-looking people hung around the walls in ornate gilt frames.

Charles stood directly behind Master Kingsley. He tried to signal something to Anna with his eyes.

*What is he trying to tell me?* She looked at Charles, her eyes pleading for help. Master Kingsley was busy talking about something, something to do with Laurel Grove, of course.

As Mariah brought in the first course, Charles quietly slipped over to Anna and removed the linen napkin from her plate, gesturing to her to put it on her lap. Anna looked up gratefully. She stared at the steaming bowl of soup before her and at the array of three spoons by her plate. She looked to Master Kingsley to see which spoon he would use, but he was busy buttering a slice of bread. Her eyes went to Charles. He nodded almost imperceptibly to his right. Anna looked to her right, but she still didn't know which of the three spoons. Slowly she placed her fingers on the nearest one and looked up at Charles. He shook his head, no. She moved her fingers to the next. Still no. She smiled, picked up the outside spoon, and began eating.

As they finished their meal, Master Kingsley put his hand over Anna's. "Come with me to my room this evening, dear Anna. I will show you how I keep my records. You are learning everything so fast."

Anna, feeling more full than she ever had, followed him from the dining room. At the threshold, she turned back to Charles and gave him a smile of gratitude. His return smile warmed a lonely place inside her. This gesture was the first token of kindness she had felt from the slaves, and she cherished it.

* * *

In the weeks that followed, Master Kingsley often took Anna with him as he roamed his plantation, sometimes on horseback, sometimes just walking. She listened and watched closely, learning as much as she could about this new land.

"Owning property, Anna, is the key to power and influence. If you have the land, you can open doors. You see how I have divided the land. The cultivated land has been cleared of pine and oaks, and the uncleared land is being held for foresting. Later, when that land is cleared, it will be used for cultivation while the first-used fields are rested."

Anna realized that was the way millet farming was done in Senegal. She visualized the fields of corn and millet on the edges of Yang Yang. Perhaps the two worlds were not so different after all. A wave of yearning swept over her, and she felt a lump in her throat. She could almost see the men of her village working in the fields. Those Africans in this field might have been Sowande or Mawali...or even ...Madu. *Madu*, a voice within her cried with longing. She was filled with an aching for what used to be. *No.* she told herself. *I must not let myself think these thoughts. Tonight, in my own room, I can remember.... And I can weep in my pillow.*

She saw Sophie several times, and when they had free time in the afternoon, they were able to visit together. Sometimes Abraham would be with Sophie when Anna arrived, but when he saw her he would walk quickly away.

"Why doesn't Abraham like me?" she asked as they sat on Sophie's front step.

Sophie smiled. "Anna, honey, just look at yourself from his eyes. You, just barely more than a chile, come in here from nowhere, and you're always at the massa's right hand. That was Abraham's place."

"But I can't take Abraham's place."

"I know that and you know that. Maybe you need to find

a way to let Abraham know that, hmm?"

"Oh, Sophie. It is so hard here." Anna sighed and leaned her head on Sophie's strong shoulder, finding the little comfort that was there.

When Anna felt sure she was pregnant, she went to Sophie's cabin. She was relieved to see that Abraham wasn't there.

"I think I am with child. How do I get my freedom?"

"You must wait until the child is born. Once it is a living thing, Master Kingsley will probably say you can be free. Have you told him yet?"

"Oh, no. I want to be sure."

Sophie laughed. "I think you can be sure. You are with him more and more. I see you with him all the time."

Anna smiled. "He is teaching me all about Laurel Grove, and he almost always calls me to dine with him now. Lately, in the evenings, he works with me to learn the language, to read and write it."

Sophie's dark eyes were serious. "You are more than fortunate, my little friend. Do not take that for granted."

"No, I do not take it for granted. I try to learn everything I can. I will need it when I am free." She hesitated. "And, Sophie, I no longer want only to be free. I want to own some land myself."

Sophie's rich laugh burst from her mouth. "This time, I think you want too much, Anta."

"Perhaps.... Perhaps not."

\* \* \*

December brought a softness to the air. The heat of Florida no longer beat on them so strongly. Crops had been processed and put up; fields had been prepared for new crops. There was a lull in the work. This morning, as she wound her way down from Master Kingsley's room, she noticed the house slaves bustling about more than usual. Portia, Lily, and Mariah were placing garlands of pine boughs and the large, shiny magnolia leaves around the hall and parlor.

"What are you doing?" asked Anna.

"Decorating for Christmas," Portia replied.

"What is...Christmas?"

"You thinks you so smart, but you don't know nothin', girl."

Anna ignored the derision.

Mariah explained, "Christmas was when de baby Jesus was borned. We celebrate him on December 25. It be a wonderful day – no work and we gets special gifts."

"What gifts?" asked Anna, delighted by the prospect.

"We get oranges and nuts, and we be 'llowed to travel to see family, and..." began Portia.

"Oranges and nuts. Why I get those now. Maybe I will get another gift," Anna said.

Celia came into the room and stood with her hands on her hips. "You get 'tirely too many gifts now, you ask me."

Anna raised her head higher, reminding herself that she was a princess.

Celia moved closer. "You be one uppity negra." She shook her finger in Anna's face. "You think dat just cuz de massa beds you, you de woman of dis house. Well, it t'ain't so. You jus' a slave like all of us."

"I don't care about being woman of the house. I am of royal blood and anyway, someday - I am going to be free again."

"Ha. Dis ain't Senegal. Don' you be forgettin' dat."

"This may not be Senegal, but I will be free again. I have a way to that freedom, and you know it. A child already grows inside me. Massa's child. He will give me my freedom when the child is born."

Mariah, Portia, and Lily closed around Anna at the news, the excitement of a new baby overriding their disdain of Anna.

"Are you sure?"

"Have you told Massa?"

"No, not yet." Anna hesitated. "But I will tell him at Christmas. It will be my present to him." She smiled regally, turned, and walked to her room.

* * *

The Christmas season brought a sense of excitement. Anna felt the anticipation among the slaves, and even in Master Kingsley. He went to dinners and balls at nearby plantations. If couples stopped by at Laurel Grove when Master Kingsley was with Anna, he introduced her to his friends. It confused Anna even more about her status.

"Anna, I am having guests for dinner on Saturday night. I want you to join us," he told her as they dined together.

Her eyes widened in fright. "Oh, no, Master."

He looked at her in surprise. "And why not?"

Her mind raced with a dozen responses. *Because I am a slave. Because I don't know your language that well. Because they will snub me.*

"Because...because I don't have a good dress to wear," she replied weakly.

"I already thought of that, and I have told Celia to have a good dress made for you."

*Now Celia will really hate me.*

"Please, Master. I do not want to...I..."

"Anna." his voice was full of sharp edges that cut into her. "I want you to join us for dinner on Saturday. There will be no more discussion."

Anna looked down at her hands clasped tightly in her lap, her appetite gone, her mind swirling with silent protests.

Saturday arrived too soon for her. She stood in the parlor before the guests arrived and viewed herself in the huge mirror. The black silk dress fit perfectly. The collar was high

on her slender neck. Tiny glass buttons lined the bodice to
her slender waist. The simple white lace at her throat comple-
mented her ebony coloring. The sleeves ended with a point
at her wrists, emphasizing her long, graceful fingers. She had
on not only her new petticoat, but also two of Mariah's that
shaped the long skirt into a gentle, stylish bell. Sophie had
slipped up to the big house and helped Anna wrap her blue
scarf into an elegant turban covering her hair, leaving the oval
of her face dramatic in its simplicity.

"You look lovely, Anna dear."

She gave her master a shaky smile as she heard Charles
open the front door to the guests. Master Kingsley went into
the hall and welcomed his friends, ushering them into the
parlor where Anna waited, wishing she could be somewhere
else.

"This is Anna," he announced comfortably. "Anna,
meet John and Elizabeth Matthews, and Jose and Esmeralda
Sanchez." Anna did a slight curtsy and nodded her head
toward the guests as Master Kingsley had instructed. He
appeared oblivious to the slight gasp the two couples gave as
they saw Anna, but it was not lost on her. Anna's legs felt a
little weak. "Come sit down. Have some wine."

Charles entered the room bearing a silver tray with five
wine glasses on it. Everyone but Anna took a glass and settled
on the sofas and chairs. Anna sat on the edge of a chair,
silent and feeling as alone as if she were back in her own
room.

It was difficult for Anna to follow all the words of the
conversation, especially when both the Sanchez' spoke with
their different accent. No one looked at her as they talked
of people Anna did not know or subjects Anna could not
comprehend. Elizabeth Matthew's shrill laugh cut through
now and then although Anna did not understand what was
amusing.

Charles soon announced, "Dinner is served."

The three couples proceeded into the dining room. Master Kingsley sat at the head of the table, the two women on his right and left. Anna seated herself at the foot, as she had been instructed. *Master Kingsley looks so far away.*

With six at the table, both Mariah and Lily were serving tonight. Anna tried to catch Mariah's eye and smile, but Mariah wouldn't look at her. Throughout the soup and main course, a spirited conversation went on among the five others, leaving Anna to eat in silence.

"It is true that more and more Americans are moving into Florida," John Matthews said.

Jose Sanchez looked troubled. "And that does not bode well for us."

His wife frowned. "Because there are not enough of us Spaniards here. We huddle together in St. Augustine. We are losing our power elsewhere."

"I have observed that to be true," said Master Kingsley.

Anna's glance went from one speaker to the other, trying to keep up with what they were saying. She finally gave up and concentrated on her meal. *I'm glad I met with Charles this afternoon to practice what spoon or fork to use.*

"Have you been in our country long?" asked Senor Sanchez, startling Anna from her solitude.

Her glance flew to Master Kingsley. *What do I say? Help me.* She begged with her eyes.

"I brought Anna back on my last trip. We arrived back in October. She is learning English very quickly." He smiled at Anna.

"Jose," interjected Elizabeth Matthews, "Have you been on any trips lately? She looked down the table at Anna with an expression that clearly said, "We do not wish to have any conversation with you."

Anna felt as though she had been slapped. She wanted to bolt from the table in tears, but instead she told herself over and over, *I am Anta Majigeen Ndiaye. I am an African princess. I am Anta Majigeen Ndiaye. I have a strong spirit. No one, not even this pale, yellow-haired ugly woman with a laugh like a hyena, can touch my soul. I am Anta Majigeen Ndiaye.*

After saying good night to his guests, Master Kingsley took Anna's hand and led her to his bedroom. "You did very well, my dear. Everything went nicely."

Anna spun around. "It did not go 'nicely'. They hate me. They treat me like dirt under their feet. Do not make me do that again."

"You are being too sensitive." He began to undress, ignoring her.

"I do not know the word 'sensitive,' but I know I am right. I will not do that again."

He crossed the few steps between them and grasped her shoulders in each hand. "You will do whatever I say you will do." His hands bit into her tender flesh, but his words hurt her more than his physical strength.

Anna trembled with the desire to fight him, but she knew she could not. She dared not look at him. If he saw the anger in her eyes, he might actually strike her. She was as close to hating him as she had ever been. In bed, he took her with a violence that felt like the wounding from the tyeddo warrior's whip. She turned her face to the wall and wept silent tears.

# Chapter Twelve

*Christmas 1806 – March 1807*

A special guest arrived on Christmas Eve.

Master Kingsley introduced the short, swarthy-looking man in the black cassock. "Anna, this is our priest, Father Mendez." Anna took in his dark hair and brown, piercing eyes. They seemed to look deep inside her, without judgment. "He will give us all a special blessing tonight."

Anna smiled at the priest and appreciated the kind acceptance that appeared in his expression. She knew of his religion from the missionaries and had heard about priests before. The religious visitors to Yang Yang all tried to introduce a different way of religion from the Muslim way she had learned. It was from them she first heard the name of Jesus.

"Come, let us have our dinner first, Father Mendez. Anna will join us. She is learning a lot of our ways. I think she will be a big help to me with things here when I am traveling."

Father Mendez looked at Anna again. "I'm sure she will be helpful." He sat down and drew his linen napkin into his lap. "Will your sisters and their husbands be joining you this Christmas?" he inquired of Zephaniah Kingsley.

"No. Isabelle and George won't be making the trip. She will soon be having a baby, and the trip is too long. Martha and Daniel will come in the spring."

Anna looked up with interest. She had not considered that Master Kingsley would have family. *I wonder what they will think of me?*

After a feast of ham and turkey, sweet potatoes, squash, corn, biscuits with honey, and dried apple pie, the three stood to leave the table. "Charles," Master Kingsley instructed, "call all the house slaves together on the front veranda and tell Abraham to bring the field slaves to the front of the house."

Anna looked at him, puzzled.

"It is time for the blessing from Father Mendez. Come along. We will wait on the porch."

As all the slaves gathered in the dusk, Anna was surprised at the large number. She had seen them in the house or in the fields, but never had seen them all together. *There are so many.* Her eyes searched for and found Sophie, and the two exchanged smiles.

The household slaves stood on the large veranda on one side, Charles and Celia in the front. The field slaves gathered in front of the steps. Abraham demonstrated his position of rank by mounting the steps halfway to the porch. Anna was acutely aware of her unusual position since Master Kingsley kept her between himself and Father Mendez.

*He must care for me.*

As the full moon climbed the night sky, Master Kingsley stepped forward, raising his hand for quiet. "You have done a good job this year. I thank you. Tomorrow, there will be gifts for all of you. Now, Father Mendez will give you a Christmas blessing. Father Mendez."

Anna marveled at the utter silence as the priest lifted his hand and in a deep, rolling voice, eyes closed in prayer, said some special words over the group. She felt goose bumps on her arms. They were not from the cool evening but from a mystical sense that filled her heart. She felt the first glimmer of an inner peace since the night of the tyeddo raid. *This Father Mendez must have some special powers. Someday, I will talk to him more about his religion.*

Later, Anna and Master Kingsley sat together in his room

while he had his last glass of whiskey. "I like your Father Mendez. What do you call his religion?"

"He is Roman Catholic. That is the official religion of Spain and so, of course, it must also be ours here in the Spanish colonies. It is required of us if we are to be residents here."

Anna absorbed this knowledge.

Zephaniah set down his glass and went to his mahogany highboy. "Anna, I have a Christmas gift for you." He handed her a package tied with a red ribbon. "Merry Christmas, my dear."

Anna untied the ribbon. She smiled as she unwrapped a dress of blue sateen. Delicate lace outlined the scoop neck and the cuffs.. Anna stood, the paper and ribbon falling to the floor, and held the dress up to her. She had never seen such luxurious material. Its soft sheen shimmered in the light.

"It is...beautiful."

"I thought it would look lovely on you. Now that you share my dining table with company, you should have a dress like that."

Anna gently wrapped the dress again to take to her room. "I have Christmas for you," she said.

"You have a gift for me?"

"Yes, a gift." She urged him back into his wing chair and stood in front of him, wondering at the words she should use.

"I..." she faltered. "I give you a child." She held her breath, wondering what his reaction would be.

"A child? You are going to have a child?"

Anna nodded, smiling.

"Well," he said, shaking his head in wonder. "Well, isn't that something? A child. I never thought about your having a child."

"It is...good?" she asked.

"Good? Why, I guess so. I would be glad to have a son to

teach about the plantation." He laughed, a big, hearty laugh. "Well, well. That is quite a Christmas surprise."

Anna's thoughts went to his first reaction. "You never thought about a child?" Her eyes narrowed with irritation.

Master Kingsley laughed again. "Anna, you are feisty. That is why I first chose you, but, honestly, this is too much. Don't worry. I'll provide for any child of yours." He turned and began removing his jacket.

"This is not just a child of mine. It is your child, too." She hissed the words at him.

He paused in the midst of folding his jacket and turned slowly back to her. The anger in his eyes made Anna take a step backward.

"Do not forget your place," he said slowly, emphasizing each word. "You are a slave. My slave. Now, leave me, Anna. I do not want you tonight."

Anna snatched up her gift, gave Master Kingsley a last look full of her confusion, anger, and fear, and stormed out the door. She paced the small area of her room, slapping a fist into her open palm as she walked back and forth. "I cannot be a slave. I cannot be a slave."

Finally, her heart stopped racing, and her indignation subsided. She undressed and crawled into bed in her white shift. *I cannot bear to think of it, but I am a slave. I know I must behave like one until Master Kingsley sets me free. I cannot afford to have him angry with me.* She sat up in bed. *I should go to him and say I am sorry.* She rose and slipped through the quiet house.

Anna knocked softly on Master Kingsley's door and opened it. He was standing at the window, gazing out. He turned toward her. Before he could speak, she rushed across the room and took his hands in hers.

"I am sorry, Master Kingsley. You have been good to me, and I should not get angry. It's just....It's just ...so hard...so hard to be a slave."

His eyes softened at once. "Anna, my dear. Come to bed."

* * *

Spring eased its way into the world of Laurel Grove, teasing Anna with its warm presence one day and cool, biting winds the next. Anna had never felt better in her life, her growing pregnancy agreed with her. She often walked around the plantation without her master. She knew her interest in everything pleased him. He now had her plan the meals and work with Celia to keep the kitchen supplied.

"Anna, you need to tread carefully around Celia," Sophie warned her one afternoon as they worked together planting lettuce and peas in Sophie's garden.

Anna paused. "What do you mean?"

"Celia thinks you're a threat. She thinks you want to be head of the kitchen, or even the whole house. Maybe she'd have to go back to being a field slave."

Anna laughed at the thought. "There is no way I would become the main kitchen slave. I'm going to be free. No, I am no threat to Celia."

Sophie shook her head. "Listen to me, girl. Until you're really free, you're just a slave like the rest of us. Don't you be forgettin' that. You best be tryin' to make Celia a friend."

Anna's shoulders slumped. The spring air didn't seem as full of promise now. "I guess you're right, Sophie."

* * *

"I have a lot of work to do this evening, Anna." Master Kingsley stood after the evening meal.

Anna sighed and went to her little room off the kitchen. Master Kingsley had been inviting her less and less to his room, and she wondered if he were thinking about marrying one of the white women he had met at a Christmas ball. She missed that time with him. She missed learning the language, but she also missed his gentle, loving, and strong embrace.

Anna slipped out the kitchen door into the cool evening. She walked slowly to the river and out on the pier. Watching the sliver of a new moon rising slowly over the water, Anna tried not to think of evenings in Yang Yang. She walked toward the grove of Mandarin orange trees. She could see the soft green buds of the new growth. The tender beginnings of the new crop reminded her of her own vulnerability. She shivered. She rubbed her arms briskly to change the feeling and returned to the Big House.

The kitchen was quiet and empty, a fire banked in the huge fireplace. Anna walked through the silence to her quarters. She paced around the tiny room, straightening her brush and comb set next to the wash bowl, smoothing the wrinkles out of her dresses hanging against the wall from a nail. Settling on a corner of the bed, she picked up some needlework she had started. Some of the older women had shown her how to make little sacques for the new baby, and she had been trying to make a supply of them. After sewing for awhile, she set down her work and looked around. She fingered the latest books Master Kingsley had lent her and selected one to read.

She soon put the book down in exasperation. *There are still so many words I do not know.* She picked up another book then set it down and went back to the original one.

"I will ask Master to help me." She jumped up and marched resolutely to his room.

Anna knocked softly and pushed the door open. The Master was not at his desk as she had expected. Her eyes flew to the bed. Munsilna, a field slave, looked at her with wide, surprised eyes. Master Kingsley lay beside her. "Later, Anna." His voice was sharp.

Anna felt a wave of shock over her entire body as her hand went to her mouth. She quickly shut the door, hoping to block the view of what she had seen, hoping to make it not real. Her legs were shaking, and for a few moments she stood, rooted to the floor. With a shuddering sob, she fled back to the sanctuary of her room.

Her thoughts were jumbled together. She had thought... But, what had she thought... that she was his wife? ...that she was mistress of Laurel Grove? Of course not. Yet, she had let herself begin to feel that way. Even in Senegal, a man did not have only one wife. Why had she thought her master would be any different? And why had she thought she was that one wife? But he was always so loving towards her. She had believed she was important to him. If there were others he cared for, would he not give her the freedom she longed for?

# Chapter Thirteen

*Laurel Grove*
*March – June 1807*

The next evening, Anna busied herself in the kitchen and did not enter the dining room for the evening meal. Charles came looking for her.

He took her arm as if to shake her. "He ask if you be sick. What you doin', girl? You gots to come eat wid him."

Anna bit her lower lip and followed Charles to her usual place. She sat down quietly, eyes downcast.

"Anna, did you see how much clearing has been done this week? I am very pleased with it." Zephaniah spoke between spoonfuls of split pea soup.

"Yes." Anna listlessly moved her spoon through the thick green liquid.

They finished the main course of venison and sweet potatoes. "Anna, what is wrong with you? You sit there like a lump tonight. I might as well be dining alone."

Anna looked up, her eyes watering in spite of her determination to stay calm. "You do not like me as your wife any more."

"Wife? Good God, girl. You're not my wife. I bought you as a slave, and I've let you be in the Big House and be a mistress to me. That should be enough for you. Besides, you are large with child now. It is not fitting that you come to my bed."

Anna could feel herself bristling. "The child is yours. Does that mean anything to you?"

"Anna, for God's sake." He paused and looked at Anna. His eyes softened. "Sometimes I forget that you are not much older than a child yourself. Our custom here is no different than in Africa. I have many slaves, over a hundred. They all have jobs to do. Some do the field work, some are blacksmiths, some cook. Your job is to be my mistress. Some, like Abraham, are given more responsibility as they are able. I have given you more and more responsibility, too. I honor you in that way."

Anna nodded.

"Any children you have by me, I will look out for. They will be educated, and they will not have to do the work of slaves."

"But will you love them?"

"Love? Love doesn't enter in, Anna. I will care for any children of mine. I will protect them. Isn't that enough?"

"And me? Will you care for me and protect me?"

He looked at her tenderly, and Anna read the caring in his face.

"Of course, little Anna Majigeen. I do care for you, and I admire the quick way you are learning things. I expect you to become a helpmate to me as I run the plantation, and," he hesitated, trying to find the right words. "And you will have a good life here."

"And you will protect me?"

"Of course."

"When our child is born, you will make me free?"

"Give you your freedom? Why, I never thought of that. Why? Why would you want to be free? I will always take care of you."

"Everyone wants to be free, Master." Anna struggled for the words. "For me, to keep my spirit in the cage of a slave is like...is like drowning. I gasp for air. I want to push against what is drowning me, to fight it. 'I must get air' is all I am thinking. I must be free."

Master Kingsley laughed. "Anna. Anna, you have such a strong spirit. I saw that in you at the slave market, and it was one of the reasons I chose you. We'll talk of this no more now, but someday, perhaps we'll talk again. We'll see. In the meantime, I wanted to tell you that I'll be going to Charleston tomorrow. I have some business there. Do you want me to bring you a present, a new dress perhaps?"

Anna looked down quietly, momentarily defeated. "I like presents," she said softly, as she dipped her spoon in the custard that Mariah brought. *Does he understand about my freedom? I dare not say any more. What should I do? What CAN I do?*

\* \* \*

June of 1807 blew in with a heat Anna remembered from Senegal. There was a difference, though. Here, afternoon thunderstorms built up and crashed around them, the lightning zigzagging across the skies like the swish of the tyeddo warrior's sword. Anna loved to watch the fierceness of the storms from the safety of her new home. She delighted in the sense of excitement in the air, the feeling that something amazing was going to happen soon.

Anna had the sense of that something in the air. She wandered though the downstairs rooms of the Big House, feeling restless and slightly out-of-sorts. She knew, from the older women, that it was time for her baby to come, but she hadn't yet felt the pains they told her to expect. She did have a persistent back ache that was annoying.

Anna walked to the slaves' cabins. She knew Sophie would be working in her garden at this time of day. As she lumbered awkwardly along, she rubbed her aching back. Anna was disappointed to find Abraham sitting on Sophie's cabin step with Sophie. They were so deep in conversation they did not notice Anna until she stopped in front of them.

"Anna." Sophie rose to hug her. "How are you feeling?"

"I don't feel well today."

"Here, sit down." Abraham looked at Anna blandly.

"So where is your Master these days?" Anna asked Abraham, irritation seeping into her voice.

"You know as good as me, girl, that he gots all dose ot'er plantations to see 'bout, and he gots dose boats to sail and make trades."

"I know, but when is he coming back?"

"I 'spect him today. He could ride up any minute now."

Sophie patted Anna's arm. "Has he been teaching you a lot?"

"When he's here." Anna wanted to tell Sophie more, but not with Abraham sitting there.

Abraham stood and looked down the road. "That may be de Massa now. I see de dust stirrin' on de road, so someone's acomin'. I best go see." He ambled away without any farewell.

"What's troubling you, chile?" asked Sophie.

"Oh, Sophie, I'm worried. I think things are changing, and maybe he's forgotten about me. Maybe he'll forget this is his child and won't give me my freedom."

Sophie nodded her head in understanding.

"He hasn't bedded me since before that night he was with Munsilna."

"Of course not. You are too large with child."

"But I thought...."

Sophie laughed gently. "You think too much, Anta Majigeen."

"But...," Anna started again.

"But what? You thought you would be the only one? It is the same in Africa. Why did you expect a man to be different here? Your father had more than one wife, didn't he?"

"Yes."

"So, Massa will have several slaves as his mistresses. That

is just the way it is."

Anna rested her head down on her knees. "I know."

Sophie looked at her with concern. "Why don't you go up the Big House and get out of the sun? It's awful hot out here." Sophie patted Anna's arm gently. "Anyway, I've got to get to work in my garden."

Anna rose awkwardly and said her farewell. *Doesn't anyone care about me? I bet she just wants to get back with Abraham.* Anna wandered back up the path to the library and tried, unsuccessfully, to find a book to interest her. She felt a pull of pain across her abdomen. Perhaps, this was the beginning of the labor they had told her about.

Anna made her way through the kitchen, stopping when she saw Celia. "Celia, I'm having this feeling, this aching across here." She rubbed her huge abdomen. "Do you think it's time for the baby to come?"

Celia put down the wooden spoon and came over to Anna. She placed her hands on Anna's abdomen. "Lordy, Lordy. You tight as a drum. You get on into yo' bed and I call the midwife. Hurry, now."

The feeling of lightning Anna had anticipated all day was crackling around her. She felt her breath quicken as she undressed down to the plain shift she wore under her clothes. She sat on her bed as a sharp pain gripped her. *Oh, Mama, I wish you were here.* Anna remembered when babies were born back at Yang Yang. Those occasions were always times of celebration and joy. Then she remembered the births that occurred during the Middle Passage, the screams of anguish, the grief. She looked at the Jesus on the cross.

"Papa God, I'm excited and I'm scared. Father Mendez says You walk beside us even though we can't see You. Will you please...Ohhh." Another pain tore through her. Excitement that she would soon hold her baby in her arms was replaced with fear. She gripped the edge of her bed.

Celia bustled in with the midwife. "Now, Anna, everything gonna be all right.  You see." She eased Anna back onto the narrow cot and pulled up the stool she brought in with her. "I'se gonna stay right here wid you, girl. Dere's nothing to be scarit of.  Lots of babies been borned on dis plantation, and Sissy, here, done brought dem all into de world. But dis be a special birthin'.  Dis be the first baby borned here in de Big House. You jus' relax and do what Sissy tell you do."

This was a different Celia, a new Celia that wasn't scolding Anna. *Does having a baby change everything?*

Many hours later, Anna felt she could not bear another pain. She lay on her rumbled sheets, sweat pouring off her brow, as Celia gently wiped her face  with a damp cloth.

"I can't...," she began through clenched teeth.  "I can't."

"Ah, little one, you can, and you will," Sissy said in her strong, soothing voice. "Be not long now."

Anna gripped Celia's hand. She wanted to think about this change in Celia, this kindness for the first time, but she couldn't make herself focus. Celia had always been so cross with her, yet now she was where Anna wished her mother could be.

The last few pains made Anna feel that she was being torn apart. "Mama!" she screamed. "Mama!"

Anna felt the push of something greater than she could imagine, and the midwife laughed aloud. "It be a boy. Massa have a son."

Anna gasped. "I have a son." Her eyes shone brightly with the news. "I have a son, and my son and I will be free." She felt herself relax, exhausted, into the pillow, smiling.

Celia took the baby, wiped him clean, and brought him to the new mother.  She laid him gently in Anna's arms. "Here be de Massa's son," she said with a cackle in her voice. "De firs' chile borned in de Big House, and it be under my charge. I mighty proud."

Anna looked down at the tiny face and marveled at the chocolate color of his skin, at his tiny fuzz of black hair. *He looks like a little old man.* She laughed with joy.

"I gots to tell de others." Celia scurried out through the kitchen.

Anna heard her announce, "Massa have a healthy son," and she heard the shout of glee rise from those gathered by the kitchen steps. She looked into the puckered face of the new baby.

"See, you are very special," she told him. "They say you are the first baby born in the Big House." She smiled at the boy. "And you and I...we're going to be free. Yes, free."

# Chapter Fourteen

*Laurel Grove*
*June – September 1807*

Anna was relieved to hear Celia tell Charles he could go report to the master that a son was born. *He got home just in time.* She waited with a tingling sense of expectation. Minutes later, the women scooted out as Master Kingsley entered Anna's small room. He sat beside her on the bed and looked down into the baby's sleeping face.

"You did a good job. You gave me a son."

Anna looked into her master's eyes. "He is beautiful, isn't he?" she asked. "What will his name be?"

"I've always liked the name George. I think George would be a good name."

"George Kingsley. Yes, that is a good name."

"I have a gift for you, Anna, to mark this special day."

Anna's eyes sparkled as she smiled. "Oh, you remembered."

"Remembered? Remembered what?"

"Why, my freedom papers. You know, we talked about it."

Master Kingsley sat up straighter and the smile left his face. "We talked about it and I said that someday I'd think about it, but ...I hadn't...it isn't time yet. That's not the present."

Anna felt the tears come to her tired eyes, and she

lowered her gaze and bit her lip to keep the tears back.

"Come, come, little Anna. This is no time to be sad. Look at what I did bring you." He pulled the gift box from his jacket pocket and handed it to Anna.

With one arm around the baby, Anna was unable to open the box. He took it from her, opened the box, and removed the ring. He took her free hand and slipped the ring on her finger.

"Anna, my dear, with this ring I am showing the world that you are special to me, that I truly...care about you." He gently kissed her forehead.

Anna looked into the face of this man who had such control over her. There was tenderness in his eyes, a gentle smile on his mouth. She was too tired to fight for more. "Thank you. It is a beautiful present. I thank you... Zephaniah."

He smiled at her for using his first name. "As soon as you are strong again, I want you to move your things into the room adjoining mine. I want...I want us to be closer. You will be as a wife to me. You have been becoming that by helping me with the running of the Big House. We will have the nursery for George set up next to your room. Would that please you?"

Anna looked at Zephaniah a long time before she answered. *You know what would please me, and yet you do not give me my freedom. I am still a slave...your slave.*

"Yes. That would please me. There is something else. I would like Sophie to come help me with the baby."

"Sophie? But she is a field slave."

"Yes, but she speaks the Wolof language and she is a friend."

Zephaniah sighed as if conceding something. "Very well. Sophie may come help with little George until it is time for harvest, but only till then. She will stay in her own cabin, though. I can't have field slaves staying in the Big House."

*A small victory, but it is something, at least.*

"I'll let you rest now." He paused at the door and looked back. "You did well."

After he left, Anna stoked the baby's face. "You will be my bridge, baby George. Because of you I am starting my way to freedom, and someday...someday, I promise you...I will get there. Someday, you and I will be free."

\* \* \*

Celia finally let Anna up after two weeks. Sophie came to the Big House to help Anna move her things to the bedroom next to Master Kingsley's.

"What you doin' here? You a field slave. G'wan about you business," Celia stormed at Sophie when she appeared at the doorway.

"Celia, I asked her to come," Anna's voice came firmly from the doorway of her room.

Celia gave Anna a slow, deliberate look. She turned and went off muttering, "Girl so uppity. Let some field slave in de house. We see about dis."

Anna and Sophie's glance met and their faces broke out in matching grins.

"That Celia," said Anna, shaking her head. The two young women gathered up Anna's things. Anna led the way through the house, noting Sophie's amazement at all the luxury.

The room given to Anna was not as luxurious as Master Kingsley's, but Anna marveled at how beautiful it was. A single walnut sleigh bed covered with a crocheted white spread was centered against a wall. Next to the bed, a small pine table had an oil lamp on it, and a pine dresser along the other wall held a large white washbowl and pitcher. Against the third wall was a walnut armoire. Sophie walked to it and hung Anna's three dresses.

"I can hardly believe this," Anna confessed. "When I first arrived a few months ago, I had only my brush and comb set, my blue scarf, and the dress I was wearing. Now it takes two of us to carry all my things."

Sophie laughed. "It is more than amazing. You are fourteen years old, and you are living like the mistress of this plantation."

Anna walked to the window, pushed aside the white eyelet curtains, and gazed out.

Sophie put her hands on Anna's shoulders. "You should be very proud, Anna." When Anna still said nothing, Sophie turned her around gently. She wiped the tears from Anna's face with her fingers. "Anna, I know. But he may still give you your freedom. Do not despair."

Anna leaned against Sophie's strength. "I will not give up. I will never give up."

\* \* \*

"Anna...Anna, wake up. You're having a bad dream." Zephaniah's voice cut in to the smoky haze of Yang Yang through which she struggled.

She sat up in bed and put her face in her hands. *Mama. Papa.*

Zephaniah sat close to her and put his arms around her. She leaned into the strength and found comfort there.

"What is it, little one? What were you dreaming?"

"It was that terrible night....The night that started everything." She shivered slightly.

"Tell me about it."

She looked into his face and saw only tender concern. For the first time, she began to tell the story. "We were all sleeping. My father rushed in and yelled, 'It's the tyeddo warriors. You must run.'.... I didn't know what to do....There was fire...and smoke ...and dust. I could hardly breathe....I was so scared.....The warriors were like masked monsters....They were on horseback....I ran....I ran as hard as I could. I tried to get to the baobab tree to hide...." Anna's breath was coming faster and faster. She could see it all.

Zephaniah held her close as she poured out the horrors: her parents killed,...the walk to the coast,...the dungeon at Gorée Island,...the Middle Passage,.... Madu's death. Once she started the telling, she couldn't stop. It spewed out as she trembled in Zephaniah's arms. When she got to the part when he bought her, she stopped and leaned against him in exhausted silence.

"Anna, my little Anna." He kissed her gently on her forehead. His tender stroking brought warmth back to her body and stilled the trembling.

"You will never have to be afraid again, my little one. I will always take care of you."

He made love to her tenderly. For the first time, Anna felt that it was not as a master taking his slave, but as a man making love to a woman. She slept that night as though a burden had been lifted from her heart.

\* \* \*

Anna stood at the window, nuzzling George's soft skin. She loved watching the change of light as the late summer sun moved over the orange grove. A carriage rolled up to the wide front porch, and a couple got out. The man was a tall, aristocratic-looking man, his features finely chiseled, his nose long and slender. As he removed his hat, Anna noted his sandy brown hair. The woman was dressed well, her forest green parasol matched the quality gown she was wearing. As she lowered the parasol, Anna gasped. The color of her skin was almost as dark as Anna's. The woman took the white gentleman's arm as they ascended the steps. Anna could hear Zephaniah greeting them warmly.

"Anna," he soon called. "Anna, come down here please."

Anna handed George to Mariah, who had become his main nursemaid with Sophie helping with harvest. She quickly brushed her hands over her hair.

"Ah, there you are," Zephaniah said as Anna entered the parlor. "This is Anna," he said to his guests. "Anna, this is Mr. and Mrs. Fraser. Their plantation, Greenfield, is south of here. Remember? I told you that they would visit one afternoon."

Anna greeted them with as much poise as she could muster, trying to remember the things Zephaniah had taught her. "Would you like some tea?" she offered.

"Mr. Fraser and I have business to discuss in my study," Zephaniah commented. "But why don't you order some refreshment for you two ladies. Please excuse us." He turned and gestured to the other gentleman to precede him down the hall.

Anna used the few moments of ringing for Celia and asking for tea things to compose herself. She did remember that Zephaniah told her the Frasers might visit soon, but she was expecting a white couple like the Matthews. She felt slightly off balance at meeting a mixed-race couple. It made her feel happy and hopeful.

As they settled down with their cups of tea and the thin slices of pound cake that Portia had brought, Anna could not hold back her curiosity. "Where are you from, Mrs. Fraser?" she asked.

"I am from the Rio Pongo River area in Guinea. John, my husband, owns a port there where the slave trade is processed."

"You mean your husband is involved in the slave trade, and yet he married you?" Anna asked with surprise.

Mrs. Fraser laughed. "Oh, yes. I am a free woman."

"And you are accepted as his wife?"

Mrs. Fraser paused slightly and seemed to choose her

words carefully. "I am acknowledged as his legal wife. I have not been treated disrespectfully, yet we do not participate fully in the social life of our area. I would not say I have close friends among many of the planters' wives. However, there are several couples like us here in Spanish Florida. The Erwins have a rice plantation on the St. Mary's River. George Clarke is an official with the Spanish government, and he has two black wives."

"There are several?" Anna asked, amazed by this information.

"That's right. Most here seem to have the attitude that there are the two classes, slave and free, but just because a person has black skin does not mean he or she has to be a slave. There are a number of freedmen here."

"How did they get to be free?" Anna asked, almost holding her breath to absorb all this new information.

"I would guess that most were able to buy their freedom or earn it in some way. Some women have had children and have been granted freedom."

"How did you get to be free?"

"I have always been free. Mr. Fraser was a ship captain and was involved with the slave trade. We lived in Bangalan on the Rio Pongo, and my father worked for Mr. Fraser to select the slaves to be transported to the Americas . It was a few years later that we married, perhaps to have someone to go on with the business after my father died. We continued to live there for several years."

Anna remembered the *signare* who stood regally looking down on her as she arrived on Gorée Island. *Would Mrs. Fraser have been like that? I can't believe she would have been so uncaring.*

"My husband then decided to move to Charleston and establish a business. He bought plantations and used many of the slaves he brought here. We have a cotton plantation along the St. John's River and also a rice plantation along the St. Mary's."

"Do you have children? Are they free also?"

Mrs. Fraser smiled at Anna's earnestness. "We have a son and two daughters. Yes, they are all free and have always been so."

"We have a son, George. I had hoped when he was born....I thought I would be made free, but...."

Mrs. Fraser gently rested her hand on Anna's arm. "Don't be discouraged. It can still happen. Perhaps when you have another child, Mr. Kingsley will give you the manumission papers."

"Manumission papers? What are they?"

"Those are the legal papers that state you are free. Once you have them, no one can put you back in slavery."

Anna sat back. "I will get those papers. Someday, I am going to have them, and so is our son, George."

"You will be interested to know what my husband came here to discuss."

Anna looked at her with curiosity. "What?"

"There was an article in the paper. In the United States, their Congress passed a law that prohibits the importation of slaves from Africa. Anyone who knowingly buys an illegally imported slave is fined $800. If someone equips a ship for slave trade, he will be fined $20,000. All that will go into effect on the first of January, 1808."

Anna sat back in surprised silence. *That will affect Zephaniah's trade business. He will have to be very careful,* she realized. "But, that is for the United States. We are under Spain's rule here in East Florida."

Phenda Fraser nodded. "True. But, John thinks it will not be long before the United States takes over much of Florida. Someday, we may find ourselves part of that country."

"What will that mean? What will be different?"

"A lot, I'm afraid. Spain allows persons of color to be free. We can hold property, testify in court, all kinds of things. It is very different in the United States. For one thing, they do not allow marriage between blacks and whites. Our children would not be allowed to inherit anything."

A stab of fear made Anna's stomach tighten. So, now even if she and George got their freedom, there would be another danger to worry about.

"One reason our husbands support manumission is so that the free blacks will keep the slaves from rebellion and from causing even more problems, perhaps even joining those who would be against us."

"I did not realize there is so much danger." Lines of worry creased Anna's brow.

Mrs. Fraser smiled at Anna. "But let's talk about more pleasant things. I noticed your beautiful roses as I came in. Do you like to garden?"

"I don't know anything about gardening," Anna confessed. "I would like to learn, though. I love the things that bloom and look so pretty."

"Well, I would be glad to teach you. Gardening is a passion of mine."

Conversation of the men as they entered the room interrupted the talk of gardens. "Come, my dear. We must be leaving."

The four walked together to the front of the house. Before getting in the carriage, Phenda Fraser turned to Anna. "I hope we will become friends. Please call me Phenda. I will come visit you soon and we will do some gardening."

"I would like that very much."

After the Fraser's buggy started down the long drive, Anna and Zephaniah turned back to the house.

"I liked her," Anna said. "I was surprised to meet a black person married to a white man."

"Umm." His silence told Anna that he was obviously absorbed in thought.

*He is worried by what Mr. Fraser told him. I wonder what this means for us.*

# Chapter Fifteen

*Laurel Grove*
*Fall 1807*

The months flew by after George's birth. Anna's days were
full of a million details to see to. Phenda Fraser visited several
times, and Anna discovered a love of gardening. She also
spent many hours with Harriet, who was fitting her for the
new clothes Zephaniah had insisted she needed. Not only did
Anna have new dresses, but there were also cotton petticoats,
chemises and drawers, underdresses, and even worsted stock-
ings. Zephaniah brought her two shawls from Charleston, a
heavy wool plaid for warmth and a shimmering tapestry for
special occasions. Anna felt more like a princess than she ever
did before...most of the time. *Something always comes along to*
*slap my status as a slave in my face.*

Anna watched her new friend closely whenever she
visited. Phenda seemed so at ease with herself, so knowledge-
able about the many aspects of running a plantation, and
Anna wanted to be like her.

Zephaniah was often gone from the plantation and, more
and more, he left things in Anna's hands. She consulted daily
with Celia and Charles about the running of the house, and
by late fall, Zephaniah had her working with Abraham in the
running of the plantation.

"Massa Kingsley set up de 'task system,'" Abraham explained to her. "I finds out what gots to be done dat day, and

I gives de orders to de drivers."

"Who are the drivers?" Anna asked.

"Dey be de most trusted slaves. Dey gots to earn dat. Drivers be in charge of a group of de field slaves, and dey gots to see dat de work is done. Everyone wants to get de work done because den dey be free for de rest of de day."

"So, once they do their tasks, they can go fishing or work in their own gardens?"

"Dat's right. So, we don't gots to beat anyone to do de work. Massa Kingsley he don't want no slaves beaten."

Anna sat back, mulling over the information. "It makes a lot of sense. A lot of sense."

One morning as the two sat together in Master Kingsley's study planning the tasks of the day, Anna asked, "Have you been with Master Kingsley long?"

Abraham chuckled. "Mos' of his life and all a mine, I 'spose."

"That long?"

"Oh, yes. I was borned and raised at Master Kingsley's papa's place. In Charleston, it be. My daddy was de white overseer and my mama was a slave dere. Yes, we gots a long history."

Anna sensed that Abraham no longer judged her harshly since they had begun working closely together. Because she relied on him to guide the work, he had relaxed with her. Now she dared to ask something she had wondered about.

"Tell me, Abraham, are you liking Sophie? I see you with her a lot in the afternoons. I know she likes you."

Abraham's chuckle came from deep within. "Well, Anna, you needs to get yo'self down to Sophie's to hear de latest. I been after dat gal, and she finally say yes to me. We goin' to jump de broom on Saturday. Massa done give his permission." Anna sat back with surprise. "I didn't know."

"Cuz you hain't come down for awhile. You too busy wid little George. Dat Sophie, she takes a long time to makes up her mind."

"And Master Kingsley knows?"

" 'Course. He like for de slaves to be married and live in famblies. He don't never sell off famblies from each other like so many do."

"Oh," Anna said in surprise. *I guess I still have a lot to learn about Zephaniah.*

"Dat's right. And he say dat we is Africans and we should do like we done in Africa, jump the broom and all."

"This 'jumping the broom,' what does it mean? I've heard talk of it for getting married, but why?"

"I don' know if it come from Africa, or if de white massas done thought it up, but dey say that when a mans and his woman jump de broom, dat makes 'em married. It mus' hol' some kinda magic, I figure." He shrugged his broad shoulders.

"Well."

"But, I was goin' to ax you to tell Father Mendez next time he come 'round. We still want him to bless us like he do."

"Abraham, I just don't know what to say," said Anna, smiling at the overseer.

"Don't need to say nothin'. Jus' give me de jobs for de day, so we can all gets to work."

* * *

Anna, carrying baby George, arrived at the slaves' quarters on Saturday for the celebration of Sophie and Abraham's marriage. She almost felt like she was back in Africa. She heard many languages spoken, including the Wolof . The familiar sounds warmed her. Many of the slaves dressed in their native style for this special occasion. Anna wished she had a colorful, loose-fitting cotton dress to wear instead of the simple rose muslin dress Master Kingsley had bought her. She had wound the powder-blue scarf around her head turban-style and that simple connection to the style of her people helped to make her feel at home.

Anna made her way through the milling crowd to Sophie and Abraham and squeezed their hands with her free one.

"I am happy for you," Anna told her friend sincerely.

Sophie's eyes sparkled with joy. "Abraham is a good man. He will look out for me."

"Yes, he is a good man." She kissed Sophie's cheek and moved away to give someone else a chance to congratulate the newlyweds.

Anna moved slowly through the gathering, suddenly feeling shy. *I really don't know any of these field slaves except Sophie and Abraham.* Several stopped her and patted George, clucking at him and trying to win a smile.

"Come, put your baby on dis quilt with mine," one young mother offered. "Den you has your hands free to gets some food."

Anna didn't want to leave this warm feeling of Africa she had found. "Thank you." She settled the baby next to the other little one.

"Dey is food set up on dose trestles over dere. You go hep yourself and I watch de babe."

"Thank you," Anna repeated, and she eased her way over to the make-shift tables. Looking at the array of food, she was sure Celia had seen to setting up the feast. There were platters of ham and turkey, bowls of sweet potatoes, collard greens, biscuits and corn bread, and several kinds of pie. Anna heaped her plate and went back to sit with the young mother.

"I be Mattie," said the girl, who looked almost as young as Anna. She was of medium height, much lighter in skin tone than Anna. Her black hair was held back in a simple, brown head rag, and her dress was of the same brown color. Her face was round, her dark eyes deep set, her nose broad, and her mouth drawn up in a friendly smile.

"I'm Anna."

Mattie laughed, showing her large white teeth. "Everybody know you, girl, and everybody know dis baby be Massa's."

Anna felt nonplussed and could not think what to say. Just then George started cooing and turned both mothers' attention to the babies. For at least an hour Anna forgot she was a slave in a strange country as she and Mattie shared the conversation of mothers everywhere.

As Anna lay in her bed later, she felt a sense of contentment. The afternoon had been full of good things: joy over Sophie's marriage, hearing her native language, meeting another young mother, showing off her precious son. Maybe this was the beginning of change for her, change from fear and sadness to a time of happiness. She sensed possibilities for herself and her son.

The next day she was checking the silver in the butler's pantry to see what needed polishing. She heard a commotion coming from the kitchen, set down the pieces of silver, and went into the kitchen. Sophie was at the door in an agitated conversation with Celia.

"What is going on?" she asked, her irritation showing. Celia and Sophie both turned to Anna, and their matching expressions of despair made Anna's heart skip a beat.

"What is it?"

Sophie walked to Anna and putting her hand on Anna's arm. "Mattie's baby. During the evening, he started burning up with fever and broke out in a rash. He's worse today, near death. Sissy says it's the scarlet fever. She asked Mattie who'd been near the baby that might be infected." Sophie paused and looked at Anna with eyes filled with pain. "Mattie told her that just you...and baby George."

Anna felt her legs start to go limp, but she had to get to George. She turned and fled up the stairs, her heart racing with fear and sobs tearing through her throat.

Anna took the stairs two at a time and raced down the hall to the nursery. Bursting through the door, she ran to the rocker where Mariah was rocking George and grabbed him from the slave's arms.

"Has he seemed sick?" she asked, her breath ragged, her hands trembling.

Mariah was perplexed by Anna's behavior. "No. He be fine."

"Yesterday." Anna began, still trying to catch her breath. "He was with Mattie's baby. Her baby has scarlet fever. He may die!" She cuddled George tightly to her.

"Oh, no!"

Anna unbound the baby from his blanket and sacque and checked him carefully for signs of a rash or fever. His body was clear and cool, and he smiled up at his mother.

Sophie and Celia appeared at the doorway.

Turning to them, Anna said, "There is no sign of the illness."

Celia walked to Anna and quickly looked George over. "We gots to keep watchin him. Dis sickness, it can lie in wait, den pounce."

Anna gasped. "How long? How long before we know he's safe?"

Celia shrugged. "I dunno. We best ax Sissy."

"I'll go ask her," said Sophie.

Anna nodded, afraid to take her eyes off George.

The hours of the day were long for Anna. Sissy had told them it might be as much as a week before George showed signs of the dreaded fever. *Why did Zephaniah choose now to visit his other plantations? If he were here, I wouldn't feel so frightened. He'd know what to do.*

Anna spent much of the afternoon and evening pacing, holding George to her as if her nearness would protect him. Mariah stayed patiently in the shadows of the room as night fell around them. That night, and the next, and the next after that, Anna pulled the cradle close beside her bed. Every time George stirred, Anna bolted upright and watched her son. *I have to keep you safe, little one. I have to protect you so you can grow strong and free someday.*

The third day Sophie came to Anna in the nursery. Her expression told Anna what she feared hearing.

"Mattie's baby died last night."

# Chapter Sixteen

*Laurel Grove*
*Fall 1807 – Fall 1809*

A sob choked in Anna's throat. "Oh, Sophie, I'm so scared."
Sophie nodded. "I know."

"I wish Master Kingsley would get home."

"Abraham said that Massa should be back soon. But look
at you. You've hardly slept in days. You haven't left George
for a minute. You've got to take care of yourself, too, Anta
Majigeen. What if you get sick?"

Anna jumped up from the rocker. "I can't get sick. I have
to be ready to take care of George if he gets that scarlet fever."

"Yes. So let Mariah do her job for a while and you get
some rest."

"I want to rest, but I can't. I'm so afraid."

"Anna, there will always be danger possible for our
children, for us. We can't let it win over us. You've been so
strong in all you've been through. Be strong now. Don't let
fear be your master."

Anna sat in the rocker and placed George gently in the
cradle. She put her face in her hands and felt despair wash
over her.

Sophie put her hand on Anna's shoulder. "Be strong,
Anta. I will be strong with you. I am carrying a baby
inside me now. I might have been alone with this babe, but
Abraham wanted us to be a family. See, good things can

happen. You're afraid to believe that, but it's true."

"A baby? You, too?"

Sophie smiled and nodded.

Anna took Sophie's hand and held it to her cheek. She took a deep breath. "I will try to be strong, Sophie.... I will try."

Anna asked Mariah to sleep next to George that night so she could rest. She was surprised when the morning light slipped through the window to waken her. She had thought she would not sleep. She slipped quickly into the nursery and smiled at the sight of George sleeping peacefully, his fist curled by his mouth. She gently touched his chubby cheek and his black hair. Another day without the dreaded fever.

Zephaniah returned to Laurel Grove a week later. Anna was proud that she could report to him in a calm voice the scare of disease to their son. By now, she felt confident that George had not been infected. *I feel like I have been victorious in some way.* Deep inside, she knew they had been lucky. This time.

The seasons spun their web around life at Laurel Grove. Fall gave way to the busy holiday season, bringing visits from Zephaniah's two sisters and their husbands. Anna hoped they would greet her warmly as the mother of Zephaniah's son, but that was not to be.

When Zephaniah introduced them, Anna smiled and gave a curtsy as she had been instructed. Both sisters looked down their noses at Anna and didn't say a word. Their husbands acted as if Anna and George did not exist. Anna, taking baby George from Mariah's arms, felt herself flushing at the insult. Zephaniah didn't appear to notice as he ushered everyone into the parlor.

"I must go put George to bed," Anna whispered to Zephaniah. She turned and fled the room. No one seemed to care.

Anna was furious. "Who do they think they are?" she

fumed aloud as she settled George in the baby bed. "You're their nephew, George, and they look at us as if we aren't even there." She gazed down at her son. "Yes, I know we really are slaves, aren't we, my son?" She stroked his hair. "But, I promise you, we will not always be slaves. I promise you."

After the celebrations for Christmas and the New Year, there was a quietness about the plantation that Anna enjoyed. She and Zephaniah spent hours in his study planning what to plant in which field, which should lie fallow for the year, and which fields should have the timber harvested.

Spring burst, with much rain encouraging new growth. There was a satisfaction as the crops erupted in the fields to grow in abundance. Families were growing, too, and Anna delighted in the birth of Flora, Sophie and Abraham's first child.

Anna most enjoyed supervising the planting of the vegetable crops. Corn, beans, and potatoes were the staples, but Anna added lettuce in the early spring, and later squash and pumpkins.

The fanfare of flowers, especially with the addition of cuttings from Phenda Fraser, made spring Anna's favorite season. Oleanders and lantanas waved their colorful blooms, and roses added their deep reds. The best, though, were the snowy white blossoms of the Mandarin orange trees. Their fragrance carried up to the Big House in March and April. From Phenda Fraser, Anna learned of other plants and trees. She added narcissus for their bright yellow-white blooms, and fig and banana trees for extra treats for their meals.

Summer was a busy time, with the big fields of corn and cotton coming to fruition. Anna walked or rode beside Abraham, secure in his intuitions about the plantation. Zephaniah often used the summer months to sail on one of his several ships. He traded cargo from the colonies, loaded slaves for the next port, and then traded for other cargo for the return trip. Anna worried about his continued involve-

ment in the slave trade, but Zephaniah thrived on the danger.
When he wasn't sailing, he made short trips to his other
plantations, always leaving Anna in charge.

"Are you lonely when I am gone?" Zephaniah asked. It
was December, and he had been gone for several weeks.

"A little," Anna answered matter-of-factly. "But you know
I enjoy the challenge of running Laurel Grove. And George
keeps me busy."

Zephaniah laughed.

Anna looked at the man she considered her husband. *I
might as well tell him now.*

"Zephaniah, things will get even busier. I am again with
child."

"Splendid. I hope this next one is just like George."

"And I hope with this next one you'll give me my
freedom," Anna said forcefully.

Zephaniah slapped down his wine glass. The wine sloshed
slightly as the click of the crystal against the table indicated
his irritation.

"Why do you persist in this? You have everything a
woman could want. I acknowledge you as my wife. You have
every comfort. You do not need to be free."

"You are wrong. Freedom is my deepest need." Anna's
hands gripped the edge of the table as she fought to keep the
anger from her voice.

His fist slammed against the table. "Enough. I am glad
you will have another babe. This child will be cared for and
protected as well as George. We will discuss this no more
tonight."

Anna clasped her hands together in her lap and took
several deep breaths. She knew Zephaniah well enough to
know she must drop the subject. *I will go see Sophie tomorrow.
Sophie will understand.*

\* \* \*

Anna held tightly to two-year-old George's hand as they went down the path to Sophie and Abraham's cabin. George, distracted by every bug and stick, had to be pulled along. Anna was anxious to talk to her friend. She smiled as they hurried, thinking how much harder it was to have a conversation with George and Sophie's toddler, Flora, with them now. There was always a tear to kiss away, something to admire, or, simply something to chuckle over. Whatever the visits brought, it was always a joy to slip back into the Wolof language with Sophie.

They had not been visiting long before Sophie said, "I can see you're upset, Anna. Tell me."

"Oh, Sophie, I get so angry. I finally told Master Kingsley that I was going to have our second child. He still won't promise me my freedom."

"But, Anna, you live as the mistress of Laurel Grove. All the slaves do your bidding. Isn't that enough?"

"No, it's not enough." Anna's eyes flashed anger. "I thought you would understand. You are my only real friend. I need you to understand." She leaned back in her chair. "I can't talk to anyone else. Since I had George, Celia and the other house slaves have not been as cruel to me, but we cannot really be friends. I worry that on one of Master's trips he might find a white woman to be his wife. What will happen to me then?"

"I understand. You have always been independent. You have fought against being a slave. But, Anna, until he frees you, you are a slave. It would be easier for you if you just accept that."

"I can't accept it. I told you about Bella and the things she taught me. She made me see the strong spirit inside me. Using that strength is how I survived all the horror. That spirit is a part of me. I will not be complete until I am free."

"You also told me how Bella urged you to look at the good things. Massa introduces you as his wife. He has taught you to speak and read and write as if you were born here.

133

He has promised to educate your children. Those are good things that matter."

Anna sighed, then smiled at her friend. "Sophie, you are a good friend. Of course, those are good things and I need to be grateful for what I have. I am almost seventeen years old; I have a beautiful son; and I live on a profitable plantation with a good man acting as my husband. From Father Mendez, I am learning about a loving God. And I have you for my friend. I promise, I will be thankful for those blessings."

"Good." Sophie patted her friend's arm.

"But, can't I still get mad when I think about it?" Anna's eyes twinkled with humor.

Sophie's hearty chuckle brought her toddler, Flora, into her arms. George crawled up in his mother's arms, and the two mothers sat in the fading December sunlight, rocking their children and thinking separate thoughts.

\* \* \*

Anna had forgotten what the pains of childbirth felt like. On this bright July morning in 1809, as the tightening around her middle got stronger and stronger, she remembered.

"Mariah, take George away for the day....maybe take him to Sophie's. And tell Sissy that it is time." She issued the orders with a breathlessness, anticipation, fear, and hope all mixing together.

The afternoon sun slanted through the eyelet curtains. Anna did not notice the sunshine or anything else in the room. She was glad for Celia's hand to squeeze as the pains became more intense and for the leather strap that Sissy had put between her teeth. Three years had taught Anna that Celia considered anything that happened in the Big House to be her business. The birth of this second baby was to be under her watchful eye.

*I don't care why she's here. I'm glad to have her hand to hold.*

Through the haze of pain and exhaustion, Anna heard Sissy say, "It be a girl dis time."

*Will Zephaniah be disappointed? Will that keep him from granting us freedom?*

"A baby girl," crowed Celia. "She be a pretty little thing."

Anna took the new infant in her arms. "Oh, she is pretty." She gazed at the dark eyes, button nose, and tiny rosebud mouth of her daughter. *This baby is the color of the coffee mixed with milk that Zephaniah sometimes fixes for me in the mornings.* She kissed the soft cheek as she felt the first stirrings of love for this precious bundle.

Zephaniah got back to Laurel Grove the next week and came to Anna's room at once.

"Did you see her yet?" Anna asked.

"Not yet. I came to see you first. So, it's a girl. Well, that's fine, Anna. I hope she will be as bright and capable as you."

Anna waited. *Will he give me the gift of freedom this time?*

Zephaniah sat in silence for a moment, his mind obviously somewhere else. "Oh, I almost forget," he said, reaching into his pocket. "I have a gift for you." He handed a small wrapped package to Anna.

Anna's heart sank. *Freedom papers would not be in this tiny package.* She unwrapped the paper around the gift and almost laughed at the two tiny chocolates.

"I remembered how you like chocolates. Well, I'll go look at the babe."

"What will we name her?"

He stroked his chin. "Hmm. Let's name her Martha, after my sister."

*I wonder what high and mighty sister Martha will think about having a mulatto child with her name.* "Yes, Martha is a good name."

"I must get back to my responsibilities. Good bye, Anna dear." He reached down and patted her cheek.

"Good-bye....And thank you for the chocolates." As Zephaniah started away, Anna called, "Zephaniah, please... can I talk to you for a few minutes?"

He turned and came to her bedside, pulling the chair closer. "Of course. What is it?"

"You seem...you act...troubled? Are you disappointed that we have a daughter?"

"No, no, Anna, not at all. Any child is a delight. I will educate your daughter as I will your son."

*He always says MY son or daughter, never OURS. But at least he's not disappointed with a daughter.*

"What is it then? What's troubling you?"

Zephaniah sighed. "I am concerned. On my way back, I stopped in Georgia. There is a strong movement to take over Florida for the United States. That will change a lot of what I can do with my ships and my trade business. In some ways I agree with those plantation owners who are starting to be called "Patriots." There would be some benefits in being governed by the United States, but on the other hand...."

"On the other hand," Anna continued for him, "it is good to have Spain in control because they are so busy elsewhere, they do not bother you. You are free to do as you please."

Zephaniah chortled. "Anna, you are always quick to understand. Now, do not worry about this situation. Nothing will happen anytime soon." He stood again. "You must rest now."

\* \* \*

Anna sat at her writing desk in the July afternoon sunlight. She paused and looked over at the cradle where Martha was sleeping. Sighing, she picked up the note she had been writing and reread it.

Dear Phenda,

It was so nice to be able to have another visit with you a few short weeks ago. You were kind to come visit me during my confinement. Since that visit, I have given birth to a beautiful little girl named Martha. As you know, I had hoped that Mr. Kingsley would give me my manumission papers after this second child was born, but it was not to be. My heart longs for the day when I will be free, and I still have hope that it will happen. Mr. Kingsley does not understand why I should so desire it since he now acknowledges me as his wife, and, sadly, I cannot find the words to make him see. Perhaps, if there is another child....

Anna put down the paper and gazed out the window. *It appears that I have everything I could want, and yet there is this one need that burns within me.*

# Chapter Seventeen

*Laurel Grove*
*Fall 1810 – Fall 1812*


Anna's third pregnancy in 1811 was the easiest yet. She had never felt better, and almost until the day the third child was born, Anna continued walking the plantation with Abraham, overseeing all that was going on. She and Abraham worked well together. He was aware of how much she valued his knowledge and wisdom. She decided to confide in him. "I know I shouldn't have any expectation of the manumission papers when this child is born, but I can't help myself. How can Master Kingsley not give us our freedom? He knows I want it, and this is our third child." Frustration made her voice sound strident.

Abraham shook his head. "He know I wants my freedom, too. I growed up a slave to his daddy, and I done proved my worth. Dats why he brought me here as manager. I been his manager for dese seven years now, and still I be a slave."

Anna stopped walking. "Abraham, I'm sorry. I never thought...I didn't realize. Of course, you would want freedom, too. But, what would you do if you became a freedman? Where would you go?"

"Oh, I wouldn't go nowhere. Sophie and me, we be stayin' right here. Dis our home. But den I would be my own man, dat's all. Dat's the only thing be different."

Anna understood.

* * *

Early in February 1811, Celia laid Mary, a new daughter, in Anna's arms for the first time. Anna waited expectantly for Zephaniah.

He entered, beaming. "Another daughter, is it, Anna? Well, that's all right. If she's like her mother, she can run a plantation as well as any man."

Anna closed her eyes and shook her head after he left. She didn't really mind that this time there was no ring, no gift, not even chocolates. She did mind that there were no manumission papers. What would it take to make him understand?

Anna watched gentle March arrive out of the nursery window. The fire in the grate had warmed any chilly corners of the room. She smiled at her children playing on the rag rug. George was almost four years old, Martha almost two. The children were her constant joy, and when he was at Laurel Grove, Zephaniah seemed to enjoy them, too.

Anna loved the afternoons when she gathered George and Martha on her bed and told them stories of Yang Yang. She took them to visit Sophie and her three children, hoping that the Wolof language would become as familiar to them as English.

Anna picked up one-month-old Mary from the mahogany cradle, carried her to the rocker by the window, and began rocking and humming. In these quiet moments, she let herself be carried back to Yang Yang, singing the songs her mother sang.

"*Kuy laal Mademba sagger gatha Naayandey?*
*Kuy laal?*
*Kuy laal sama doome djey?*
*ayo beyyo beyyo.*" George looked up and smiled.

Mariah came in to help with the children. "What dat you singin'?"

"It's a Wolof song. I'll always love those songs. I can hear my mother's voice in my head as I sing."

"Don't dat make you sad?"

"Sometimes. And then sometimes I feel a comfort, as if Mama were here with me. I think what my life would have been back in Yang Yang at eighteen. Instead, here I am living as the wife of a wealthy planter-trader, with three beautiful children, and I really run the plantation of Laurel Grove in Master Kingsley's absence." She didn't voice her next thought. *The hardest part for me to believe is that I am still a slave.*

Mariah put her hand to her mouth. "I almost forgots. I 'spose to tell you de Massa want to see you. He in his study."

Anna handed the baby to Mariah's welcoming arms and smoothed the pale yellow sateen dress as she headed downstairs. She knocked at the study door and opened it.

"Ah, come in, Anna."

Anna pulled the extra chair close to his desk as usual He had been gone for several days, so she assumed he wanted to go over details of the plantation work with her.

Zephaniah leaned back in his chair and smiled.

"Yes?" Anna asked.

"Anna, you know I care deeply for you and your children." He paused, as if waiting for Anna to comment.

"Yes."

"Anna, I consider you to be like a wife. As such, you and the children are to participate in what I have, but..."

Anna felt a twinge of concern.

"But, I am concerned that if something should happen to me on one of my journeys, you and the children would simply be considered slaves and would be sold off, heaven knows where."

The words sent a chill down Anna's spine. She knew the truth of it.

"And so, my dear, I have drawn up this paper." He picked up one of the many documents covering his desk. "It is written in Spanish, of course, the legal language of Florida, but I will read it to you in English."

Anna sat still, almost afraid to breathe.

Zephaniah read. "*1 March 1811. St. Augustine, Florida. In the name of Almighty God, Amen: Let it be known that I, Zephaniah Kingsley, resident and citizen of the St. John's River region of this province hereby state: That I have as my slave a black woman named Anna, about eighteen years old, who is the same native woman that I purchased in Havana...I recognize her children as my own; this circumstance, and as well considering the good qualities of the already referred black woman, and the truth and fidelity with which she has served me, impels me to give her freedom graciously and without other interest, the same accorded to the aforementioned three mulatto children whose names and ages are for the record: George, three years and nine months old; Martha, twenty months old; and Mary, a month old...I remove my rights of property, possession, utility, dominion, and all other royal and personal deeds which I have possessed over these four slaves. And I cede, renounce and transfer (my rights) to each of them so that from today forward, they can negotiate, sign contracts, buy, sell, appear legally in court, give depositions, testimonials, powers of attorney, codicils, and do any and all things which they can do as free people who are of free will without any burden....*"

Anna was stunned. "...free people who are of free will without any burden..." The words shouted themselves over and over in her mind. "...free people who are of free will without any burden...." Was she really, finally, hearing those words she had longed for, dreamed of, begged for? She could not take it in. Tears coursed down her cheeks, her hand to her mouth.

Zephaniah sat back and dropped the paper on his desk. He smiled at her. "Well, Anna, are you pleased?"

Anna, unable to speak, rose from the chair and went to his side. She knelt beside him, and gently took his hand. She opened it tenderly, kissed his palm, and held his hand to her damp cheek. "You have given me the gift above all others. The most precious gift. I thank you from the deepest part of me." She sensed that the depth of her emotion embarrassed Zephaniah.

"Come, come. You have earned the right to be free. You are so bright and capable. The next thing for us is to work toward getting some land of your own. You have shown how well you can manage."

Anna took Zephaniah's face in her hands and kissed him on his forehead. "Would you read it to me again?"

Zephaniah's deep, rolling laugh burst out. "Of course."

This time, she took every word into her memory and her heart. She would never forget the words. Never.

\* \* \*

Anna visited Sophie several days later anxious to tell her the news. She took George and Martha with her as she hurried down the path to the slaves' quarters. She heard Sophie singing. The sound of song in the Wolof language warmed Anna, quickening her steps.

"Sophie," she called. "Sophie. It has finally happened."

Sophie turned to Anna with a wide grin. "Ah, yes. Finally. It is so wonderful."

Anna wondered how Sophie could know her good news already. "So, you know?" she asked.

"Yes." A joyful laugh rolling out with the words. "Massa came yesterday and told us. 'Abraham,' he said, 'You been a loyal and faithful worker all this time. I'm making you free.' We all just knelt down on the floor and praised the Lord."

Anna looked at her in amazement. "Abraham is free?"

"Yes, praise God. He is a freedman. Now he can be working to get enough money to buy my freedom and our children's."

"Sophie, I didn't know. I came to tell you that he gave me

my freedom. He didn't tell me that Abraham was free, too."

Anna and Sophie fell into each others arms, laughing and crying at the same time. Their children looked up at them with such puzzled expressions that the two laughed more.

The two friends sat on Sophie's doorstep, basking in the springtime sun and in their good fortune.

Sophie looked out over the fields where slaves worked. Slipping back into their Wolof language, she asked, "What will really change with this freedom, Anna? How will our lives be any different? Abraham and I will still live here, still work for Massa. He will be free, but I will still be a slave. Our children will still be slaves."

"But it will be different," Anna insisted. "Abraham will earn wages. You could build yourself a bigger house if you wanted. He can save more money toward buying your freedom. For me, things may not seem different on the outside, but I will be different. I am no longer a slave, no longer someone's property. That is the difference, and that is the most important difference. Besides, Zephaniah is going to help me get some land of my own to manage."

"Land of your own? And just what would you do with land of your own?"

"Why, I'd make it work for me, of course. I would grow things on it. With land, you can earn money and power. I learned that from Zephaniah. I have learned a lot from him, things I can use for myself and my children."

\* \* \*

Anna glanced at the fall sky as she walked the plantation. Heavy gray rain clouds formed in the south. She hurried her steps to be sure the slaves had finished the second picking of cotton before the rains came. Zephaniah was busy in his study, and Anna knew he was relying on her for observations.

As they finished their noon meal and sharing of information, Charles returned to the dining room from the front hall.

"Mr. and Mrs. Fraser are here. They be waitin' in the parlor for you and Ma'am Anna."

Anna and Zephaniah rose and hurried to see their friends. Anna was disturbed to note their tense expressions.

"Is something wrong?" asked Zephaniah.

"Not yet, but we wanted to warn you," replied John Fraser. "It's this continuing trouble with Americans wanting to take over Florida. Those rebels calling themselves "patriots" are continuing to stir up trouble, and the skirmishes are becoming more frequent."

"I know they have been harassing the planters to force Spain to give East Florida to the United States," Zephaniah said. "They have been here at Laurel Grove to talk once, but that is all."

Anna remembered when two scruffy looking white men had come to talk to Zephaniah. She had wondered what they wanted, but Zephaniah didn't mention it, and she forgot about their visit.

Phenda Fraser turned to Anna. "I don't know how much you have learned of the politics of our area. It may not seem important to you whether Florida is part of Spain or of the United States, but I tell you, for you and me the situation is critical. If we become part of Georgia, or even a separate part of the United States, we and our children could be taken into slavery and sold."

Anna drew a hand to her mouth. "We would lose our freedom?"

"Yes."

Anna looked at Zephaniah with frightened eyes. "Is that true? Could they make us slaves again?"

"It is a possibility. But as long as we are under Spanish rule, you are safe."

The crack of thunder boomed through the air, as if an ominous warning.

Mr. Fraser rose from his chair. "We must get home before the storm. We just wanted to warn you to beware."

Anna and Zephaniah stood on the porch and watched them leave. Anna felt drained by the news, and she held tightly to Zephaniah's arm. He patted her hand. "Don't worry. I will do all I can to keep you free. This threat, though, is all the more reason why you need to be established as a landowner. We will work for that immediately."

Anna felt a rush of emotions. She was thrilled with the idea of having land, but the Fraser's warning left a sense of foreboding. The world around her mirrored that feeling. As they turned to go inside, a streak of lightning sliced from the dark gray heavens to the fields, shimmering its frightening power, and heavy sheets of rain wept from the sky.

# Chapter Eighteen

*Anna's Place*
*1812 – 1813*

Zephaniah found a five-acre plot of land across the river from Laurel Grove and arranged for the Spanish government to grant it to Anna.

"The land is not much, Anna, but it will be a useful tool for us. I am expanding my retail business to that side of the river, and with your property there, I will not have to build another store. We can send things across the river in smaller boats to sell and receive goods that way. I will put Abraham in charge of that."

"But it will be my land. Isn't that right? I will own the land."

"Yes, of course. You will own it. But I still want you at Laurel Grove. I need you to run things for me."

Each winter month found Anna spending more and more time on her own land. She confessed to Sophie, "I feel such a pull to be across the river. I haven't shirked any on the responsibilities Master Kingsley has given me here, but I am so much happier working on my own land."

"Of course. That is your very own. It is natural that you would feel that way."

"I have started a flock of ducks and chickens. When they see me coming, they rush to me, squawking for food. They know I am the one looking out for them."

Sophie chucked.

"Sophie, I wish...."

"You are always wishing for something you don't have. Then when you get it, you wish for more. Can't you be content?"

Anna paused before answering. "Not yet. I just cannot be content yet. There is more I need."

* * *

Anna entered Zephaniah's study, where he sat working on accounts. She sat quietly as he worked, watching him dip his quill in the crystal ink well that stood on his desk.

He looked up and smiled. "I see you are admiring my inkwell," he said. "This inkwell is very special to me. It belonged to my grandfather and then to my father. When I came here from Charleston to start my own plantations, my father passed it on to me."

"It's beautiful."

"Yes, isn't it?" He bent his head back to his work.

"Zephaniah." He looked up, at the serious tone of her voice.

"I need to have a house built on my land. I need to be on my own land and live there."

Zephaniah frowned. "Why? You have everything you could want here. You have a comfortable home, slaves to do your bidding, help with the children. I give you a free hand concerning the plantation." He sounded more exasperated with each word. "You are free." He slapped his quill down angrily, splashing ink across the wooden surface. "What more could you possibly want?"

Anna chose her words carefully. "All that is true, and you are good to me. Things will not change for you if I have a house on my own land. I will still manage Laurel Grove as you want me to, and I will stay with you here when you want me to. But....but you told me it is the land that gives you power, Zephaniah. I do not feel the power of my freedom here. I want to be on my own land. It is a deep need within me."

Zephaniah shook his head, the anger gone from his face. "Anna, Anna. It should not surprise me. Your fierce, independent, and strong spirit that first attracted me holds me to you still. I do understand your need." He sighed deeply. "Very well. I will send carpenters over to build you a house. What's more, I will send Joseph and Moses and their wives and children as your slaves and Mariah to help you with the children. You will be your own person with home, land and slaves of your own."

* * *

Anna could not keep from frequently crossing the river as the dream of her home became a reality. If no one was available to row her across, she took the small canoe and paddled her way the two-mile stretch of river. The land had been cleared for crops the previous year. Now, a block house with stone walls on the first floor and chinked logs for the second took shape.

"I will build this for you," Zephaniah told her firmly as they worked on the plans. "But, remember, this is to be for my trading on the east side of the river. The first floor must be for storing tools, grain, and whatever I want Abraham to sell. The second floor will be for you and the children."

"I understand."

"Where would you like the slaves' cabins to be?" he asked.

She pointed. "I think, here. They will not be too close to the house, and they will not take up land I may want to cultivate in the future."

Zephaniah looked at her with admiration. "A good choice." His look turned serious, and his tone changed.

"Anna, I want you to be very careful in your coming and going. The United States is at war with England now, but there are still those who are interested in taking over Florida."

"But they would not bother with my small acreage, would they?"

"No, I think not. But I want you to be careful as you come and go from Laurel Grove. I understand that forces have taken over Fernandina. It is only a matter of time until they try for St. Augustine. I only want you to be aware. Be careful."

Anna looked into his troubled eyes and a shiver of fear ran through her.

* * *

Anna was delighted with her new house's charm and comfort. The first story was solid stone and was divided into two main rooms, one for storage and the other for a kitchen. The large stone fireplace on the north end was very similar to the one at Laurel Grove. A wooden staircase went to the second level. The house was furnished with left-overs from the Big House at Laurel Grove, but it was Anna's. The main living room contained a sofa and two chairs, a walnut desk and chair against a wall, and a scratched mahogany table with six chairs for dining. Large windows opened to a view of the river. On the east side of the living area was a doorway to Anna's room, with her sleigh bed, pine dresser and armoire. On the other side of the house were two rooms with small beds for the children and a single bed for Mariah. Harriet had helped Anna make bright blue cotton curtains for the windows.

Early summer sun poured on Anna as she fed her ducks and hens in the yard. She looked and waved a greeting as she saw Zephaniah coming up from the dock. "Come and see everything," she called. Zephaniah was impeccably dressed, as usual, with a brown broadcloth double-breasted tail coat in cutaway style. A deep green cravat was tied around his high collar. Zephaniah took off his wide-brimmed hat and brushed dust off his buckskin breeches and black boots.

His serious expression as he joined Anna made her uneasy.

"Is something wrong?" she asked.

"Nothing we can't handle. Just some news. I'll tell you later, but first, show me around your home."

Anna paused, wanting to know the problem.

"Later, Anna. It can keep."

They walked to the vegetable garden where Anna had neat rows marked for lettuce, peas, beans, onions, and black-eyed peas.

"Things are coming along well." Zephaniah smiled. He shielded his eyes from the sun as he watched Joseph and Moses working the mule and plow in the corn field. He nodded with approval.

"Come see how I have organized all the tools and produce in the lower level. Abraham said he will take some of the things next week to sell to the farmers and the Seminoles on this side of the river."

Zephaniah inspected everything. "All is in good order, Anna. You are doing a wonderful job here."

"I love working here. I love seeing things planted and starting to come up. I love planning what work should be done each day and seeing that it is done in the best way possible. I love...."

Zephaniah's deep laugh interrupted her. "I know, Anna. Believe me, I know. You are finally your own person again." He put an arm around her shoulder.

She looked at him fondly. *He does understand me.*

George escaped from Mariah's supervision and ran to his father.

"Come see my room, Father," he urged, pulling on Zephaniah's hand.

"Of course."

They mounted the stairs and entered the living area of the house.

"You have made this a warm and welcoming room, Anna," Zephaniah said.

George kept tugging at his father's hand. "Come on, Father. This way."

Zephaniah followed the boy into the room where he and his sisters slept. He looked around and nodded. "Very nice, son."

He turned to Anna. "Are you happy with the slaves I have given you?"

"Oh, yes. They are all good workers, and I enjoy having their children around to play with our children. I will have Marva fix us some tea, and you can tell me your news. Let's sit on the bench under the trees. It is pleasant there with the river breeze."

George appeared determined to stay with them, and Zephaniah did not seem inclined to send him away. Anna was touched at the way Zephaniah tousled George's hair. Marva brought them cups of tea on a tray, and they sat in the shade of a live oak dripping with Spanish moss.

"I do have some news, and it is not good. It is about the Patriot Rebellion."

George settled himself at his father's feet.

"I feared that. What has happened?"

"The rebels still have control of Fernandina, and they are moving southward, trying to control the river and St. Augustine."

"I've heard from Abraham that there have been many little battles. Do you know how the Frasers are faring?"

"They have not had any trouble since they are farther south. But, what I must tell you is...yesterday, after I got home from my trip, they took me captive. I wanted to come tell you myself before you heard it from someone else."

Anna gasped at the news. "Took you captive? When?

What happened?"

Five-year-old George stood and leaned close to his father, his small face etched with concern. Zephaniah drew his son closer to comfort him.

"Oh, I was safe enough from harm, but I knew I would not be freed until I pledged them my support."

"But you didn't, did you?"

"I had no choice. It does not mean anything. Of course, I do not really support them, but I worry that they will be using Laurel Grove as a base for some of their activities."

"Taking you captive....How did they get to you?"

Zephaniah laughed a bitter laugh. "It wasn't hard. I was out riding by myself, farther from the house than I should have been. You know that dense copse past where we plant the cotton?"

Anna nodded.

"Well, there was a small band of them, real ruffians they were. They jumped out, spooked my horse, and I fell. Then they grabbed me and tied me up."

George grabbed his father's arm. "Father!" he exclaimed in alarm.

Anna put her hand to her mouth. "Oh, Zephaniah."

Zephaniah patted George's hand. "Don't worry, George. You can see I'm fine."

"How awful. Were you hurt?" Anna asked.

"My pride was hurt more than anything," he admitted. "They made me sit until their leader arrived. He was a sallow-looking fellow with a mean countenance and a bullying nature."

"Did he hurt you?" George asked, his eyes still wide with fright.

"Oh, no. He didn't touch me. Sit down, son. I'm fine." He turned to Anna. "The leader said that the 'patriots' were taking over some of the plantations to use for their bases, and they wanted access to Laurel Grove. He said we would all be

better off if we were under the flag of the United States and
that it was in my best interest to cooperate. He said that John
McIntosh, who has the plantation on Ft. George's Island,
is their leader. I wasn't surprised. I'd heard rumors to that
effect."

"How long did they hold you captive?"

"Not long. A few hours. I told them I would cooperate
but that I expected they would let me go on with my business
of running the plantation, and they agreed."

"Was that all?"

"Not quite. They also wanted to know how many free
blacks were at Laurel Grove."

"Why did they want to know that?"

"The Spanish are using the free blacks and the Seminoles
to fight against these rebels that have come down from
Georgia."

"But you didn't tell them about Abraham?"

"No, of course not. It's not only Abraham. Don't forget
that many others, carpenters and the blacksmith, are all
freemen, too. No, I told them there were no free blacks at
Laurel Grove. Also, I am having a fortification wall built
around the big house, and I have purchased two cannons
from the Spanish. They will be mounted this week at the top
of the house, aiming through the attic windows. I hope those
measures will discourage anyone from actually attacking us"

Anna was disturbed by the news. The danger was so
much closer now. "But, Zephaniah....if they win...."

"They will probably not win. Although I have learned
that they are secretly supported by President Madison of the
United States. That means, I suppose, that their financial
backing is coming from wealthy sources there."

Anna felt a rising sense of terror. "If they win, the children and I will be slaves again."

"Oh, I do not think so. After all, you are a free person
and a property owner. I do not think you have anything to

worry about. If East Florida does become part of the United States, I will see to it that you remain free,"

Anna wrapped her arms around herself. Zephaniah rose and stood behind her, putting his arms around her as if to warm her. "Don't worry. It will be all right. Now, I must be off. I just wanted to warn you to beware. And I think it best if you do not come to Laurel Grove for awhile. I will come to see you here, and I will let you know when you can safely return."

"Not come to Laurel Grove? But...."

"Just for now. I know you will miss your visits with Sophie, so I will arrange to have her come with Abraham when he brings goods over to this side. Also, you will see some Spanish gunboats patrolling the river occasionally from now on. I asked the commander to stop by and meet you, so you'll know who to turn to for help. His name is Moreno."

"Gunboats, Father?" interrupted George.

"Son, go back to Mariah now. I am talking to your mother."

George lowered his head, stuck out his lower lip, and kicked up the dust with the toes of his boots as he walked away.

"Oh, Zephaniah," she turned and leaned into his strength. "I thought once I was free I would be safe."

"You are safe, little Anna. I will always look out for you, remember?"

Anna nodded as they separated. She walked with him to the dock and stood back as he climbed into a little skiff. Before he pushed off, he looked at her. His eyes seemed to promise her something...safety?...love?

Anna stared after him as he rowed away.

George came back and pulled at her skirts.

"Are we going to have to fight the Patriots, Mama?"

"Surely not, son," Anna replied. "Why would they come here with all these big plantations around?"

Rosalie Turner

"They'd better not try to bother us."
"No, they'd better not."

# Chapter Nineteen

*Anna's Place*
*1813*

Anna felt the late summer sun beating down on her bare arms as she hoed the weeds between the potato plants. Mariah sat with the children in the shade. The air hung heavy with August heat as flies buzzed around the leafy plants. Distant sounds of Joseph and Moses calling to each other in the cornfield was soothing to Anna. Moses' wife, Jane, and Marva folded clothes that had been drying over bushes in the summer sun.

Anna paused in her work as she saw the Spanish priest trudging up the lane from the dock toward her house. She pulled off her large straw hat and wiped perspiration from her brow with her arm. "Hello, Father Mendez, and welcome."

"Anna, I always find you working hard."

Anna laughed. "And what else would I be doing? Come, let us go inside and have something to drink." She beckoned to Joseph's wife as they approached the house, "Marva, bring us some lemonade, please."

Anna and Father Mendez settled themselves in the comfortable chairs that Zephaniah had provided.

"How have you and your family been since my last visit, Anna?"

"We have been well, but concerned. Do you think the so-called "patriots" and their rebellion will bother us and my small acreage."

"They have certainly been a problem. You should be safe, but do not be complacent." Father Mendez nodded toward the river. "Your location on the river is a good one, and they may want it for themselves. Most of the patriots have gone. The ones remaining are just bandits. Who knows what they will do?" He turned to face her. "But let's talk of you. Have you read the book I left with you?"

"Yes, I have." She answered his questioning look. "I understand why you want me to have the children baptized in the faith. I know now that it is not enough simply to have me become a Catholic."

"I knew you would understand. And are you ready for me to perform that sacrament?"

"Almost ready. I want to think a little more about choosing their godparents."

"Is that such a hard decision?"

She looked deeply into his kind, brown eyes. "Yes, it is. Our freedom is a fragile thing, and I want to select godparents who will always be in a position to protect my children, to ensure that freedom. Can you understand that?"

The priest regarded Anna closely. "You are wise beyond your years, my child."

"I have to be."

* * *

A few days later Anna saw another visitor approaching from the river. He climbed out of a small boat that two sailors had rowed to shore. By his uniform Anna knew that this must be Commander Moreno. The commander, probably a little younger than Zephaniah, was a slightly built man, but his military bearing and his large uniform hat made him look taller. His swarthy complexion, black hair, and dark eyes made him look stern and imposing.

Plumed hat in hand, he bowed slightly. "Mrs. Kingsley?"

"I am Anna Kingsley."

"I am Commander Moreno. Mr. Kingsley suggested that I stop by and introduce myself. You have, no doubt, noticed our gunboats on the river. We are here to protect you. If you should need our protection, we should establish a signal of some kind."

"Yes, of course. What do you suggest?"

"Could you have one of your slaves make a flare? If they could wave it from the dock, we would see it if we were any-where near."

"Yes, Joseph or Moses could do that."

"Very well." He bowed again, turned smartly and headed back to the dock. A few yards away, he stopped and turned back to Anna. "I should warn you that the rebel leader, Colonel Alexander from Georgia, has occasionally been seen on this side of the river."

Anna's heart skipped a beat. "Near me?"

Commander Moreno shook his head. "No. Quite a bit to the north. I simply wanted to alert you." He nodded his farewell.

*He is not very friendly. I hope I never need his help.* As she turned back to her work, she wished for peaceful days back at Laurel Grove.

\* \* \*

Anna surveyed the work going on in the yard around her two-story house. Marva and Jane were making soap in a heavy black caldron over an open fire in the yard. The soap would soon be ready for shaping. Joseph sharpened the tools that would be stored for the winter, and Moses burned the dry corn stalks in the field. The fall air was comfortable on Anna's skin, with the gentle breeze from the river. Anna saw a skiff quickly approaching the dock. A sense of alarm traveled through everyone as they looked up from their work.

Anna soon recognized Abraham as the visitor. She sensed tension in the way he held his tall, sturdy body as he walked toward her.

"What is it? What's wrong?"

"It was Indians, Seminoles." Abraham caught his breath. "Dey attacked Laurel Grove two day ago, trying to get dem 'patriots.' De Indians figgered it be a base since dose rebels done be comin' and goin' all de time. Dey didn't care we was dere, too. It be terrible shooting. We had to escape. They kilt some of the field slaves, took some captive. They kilt Big John."

"But Master Kingsley...was he hurt?" Anna interrupted fearfully.

"He be all right. We got away, and now we at his other place, at White Oak Plantation. De rest of de field hands, dey be hiding in the woods, and dey spose to be comin' north to White Oak. De drivers be bringin' dem in. But, Anna, Laurel Grove, it be ruin't."

Anna put both hands over her mouth. "Oh, Abraham. And Sophie, is she with you?"

"Massa Kingsley sent her and de babes to White Oak awhile ago. I sure thank God for dat."

"How could they get Laurel Grove with all those fortifications around it? That fence, those cannons....How could they get it?"

Abraham shook his head. "Dose cannons, dey pointed at de river. De attack come from de woods. Dey kilt slaves in the fields before we even gots to our guns. We couldn't do nothin' but run."

"Did Master Kingsley send me any message?" Anna asked.

"Jus' want you to know what happen and dat all de bad stuff is goin' on our side of de river so you be safe here at yo' place. Want you to know he hidin' out at White Oak. He say dem rebels have Laurel Grove now, and don't you go dere no mo'." His next words sent chills of fear through Anna. "He say dat if you and de chill'un get captured, dem rebels, dey gonna take you to Georgia and make you slaves again."

Anna muffled the moan in her throat. "We can't let that happen, Abraham."

"No's, we can't. I scarit Sophie and de chill'un gonna be sold away from me before I can buy dey's freedom. Massa say don't worry, but I is plenty worried."

"But Master Kingsley wouldn't do that."

"I know he wouldn't, but if dey get captured, I jus don't want to think about it."

"Well, we must stay on our guard, that's all. Tell him I'm glad he's safe and that we will stay safe, too."

"I tell him." Abraham turned back toward the river.

"And Abraham, tell Sophie I miss her."

Abraham nodded and hurried on. As he rowed away, Anna's slaves gathered around her.

"What do dis mean, Ma'am Anna? What goin' to happen to us?" Fear showed on Joseph's face.

Anna drew herself up tall and straight. "Now, don't get all worried. This has nothing to do with us. The fight is between the Spanish and those patriots coming down from Georgia and the Carolinas. They attack only the big planta-tions because they want them for themselves. They're not going to bother us. Besides," she added, "we've got those Spanish gunboats that patrol the river. They'll protect us if we need them."

"Like dey did for Laurel Grove," Moses muttered under his breath as he turned away.

Anna walked quickly toward the house. She would not, could not, let them see the fear that filled her. She had survived capture, lived through the Middle Passage, become a free person of property. She was Anna Kingsley, a free African princess. She would not let them take her freedom, nor her children's freedom.

\* \* \*

By November, Anna could no longer stand the suspense. "Joseph, you or Moses take the canoe and slip over in the dark tonight to Laurel Grove to see what the damage is."

"Ma'am Anna,... don'... make me... do dat," stuttered Moses. "I confess it, I'se too scarit.... Besides, I gots me a fambly to think of. What would happen to dem if'in I was captured?... Don't make me or Joseph go."

She understood, but she wanted to know what had happened. The plantation was directly across the river, but the river was at least two miles wide. Finally, she went herself. The moon was only a sliver, sending little light on the softly lapping river as Anna crossed. She pulled the canoe under the willows slightly north of Laurel Grove. She waited several minutes, her ears acutely tuned to the night sounds around her. Her heart was pounding so hard she feared it could be heard. An afternoon shower helped mute the sound of her footsteps on the leaves and pine needles as she crept closer to the Big House. A hoot owl startled her. She forced herself to breathe slowly to calm her nerves.

At the edge of the cedars that lined the yard of the plantation house, Anna sat back on her haunches to watch and listen. She was horrified by the scene before her. The barn, the kitchen house, and most of the slave cabins lay in splintered ruin. The noise coming from the Big House was loud and raucous. She had no doubt that the rebels there were numerous and drunk. She tried to estimate their number as she watched them come and go. Anna guessed there were at least fifty.

Her glance went to the top of the house, where two brass cannons facing the river were silhouetted against the night sky. *It would be important for any Spanish gunboat to take those cannons into consideration.*

After watching for about an hour, Anna slipped away as

quietly as she had come.

As she pulled the canoe up to her dock, Mariah was waiting.

"I'm glad you back safe, Anna. I don't like dat you went over dere."

"Are the children all right?"

"Dey fine. Dey sound asleep. I worried 'bout you, dat's all."

"I needed to check on Laurel Grove. I have a plan."

"What your plan?"

Anna wondered about confiding in Mariah, but the young woman had become more than the slave caretaker of the children. "The next time I see the Spanish soldiers on the river, I'll give them a report about the activities at Laurel Grove. In return, I'll ask them to provide my family and slaves protection. I'm sure the soldiers will help us. Commander Moreno came ashore yesterday to check on us. He was warning me that a rebel bandit had been tracked closer to my property." Anna put her hand on Mariah's shoulder. "We may have to act soon. I want you to pack enough for us to have several changes of clothes. Tomorrow, you and Moses, Jane, Joseph, and Marva pack our valuables and hide them in the woods. We must be ready to leave at a moment's notice."

Fear showed on Mariah's face.

Anna took Mariah's arm. "I told you because I thought I could trust you to be brave."

"I try," whispered the slave.

"I have been through worse, Mariah. If we remain calm and brave, we will get through this, too."

"What you want I should pack?"

"Pack the silver, and...let me think. Pack the linens and enough of the things we use every day, like pots and pans, so that we'll have something to start with again when we come back. Just look around, Mariah, and think what is important to us. That's what you should pack."

Anna woke at dawn to a gray sky and a fine mist. The slave families stayed in their cabins, and Anna, Mariah, and the children confined themselves to the second floor living space. Anna walked slowly through each room, evaluating every possession. *What do I need to hide? What should I take with us?*

She took a tapestry satchel and packed some books for her and the children. She ran her fingers across the silver brush and comb set, Zephaniah's first gift to her. From the small top drawer of her pine dresser, she pulled out a rolled paper tied with a blue ribbon. She untied the ribbon and straightened the paper, again reading the precious words."... impels me to give her freedom.... Free people who are of free will without any burden...." She took the powder-blue scarf Zephaniah brought her from Charleston, and wrapped the retied paper in it, and placed it in the satchel.

# Chapter Twenty

*Anna's Place*
*Laurel Grove*
*November 1813*

After breakfast, George leaned against Anna's lap. "Tell us about Yang Yang."

Anna smiled and put her hand against his soft cheek. "All right," she agreed. Martha joined them and climbed up in Anna's lap. Mariah sat in the other chair rocking Mary.

Anna heard the gentle rain on the roof as she began. "In Yang Yang, where I grew up, we all lived in mud huts with thatched roofs...."

As usual, George interrupted. "I forget. What are those?"

"If we took palm branches and wove them together and put them over a small, round, mud hut, that would make a thatched roof." Anna went on with her story. "The huts would keep out the cold winds and the hot air. My father, your grandfather, lived in the center hut. My mother, your grandmother, lived in another hut with me and my two sisters. We were very happy. There was always good food to eat and someone to play with...."Anna allowed her imagination to go back and see the place of her birth and her family. When she would tell the children about her beginnings she always felt torn. She found such comfort in remembering, but also pain. The memories made her realize how far from those roots she had come. Even so, she knew she would continue to tell the stories and sing the songs because she wanted to connect the children with that place and the family they would never know.

The afternoon cleared, and everyone wanted to be outside in the gentle fall air. Anna spent the afternoon walking over all her land. *I wish I could hold it close to me. I must prepare myself for what is to come.* She saw to it that the slaves had packed most of the household things, silver, china, cook ware, linens, tools, and small decorative items. Then she instructed them to pack their own belongings.

Anna was awakened at daybreak by the sounds of cannons and gunfire. She ran to the window, heart pounding. Moses, Joseph, and their families scurried toward her house, and Mariah and the children burst in her room.

Memories of the tyeddo raid flooded her. She shook her head to clear her thoughts. She saw the Spanish gun boats, the *Inmutable* and the *Havanera*, anchored not far off the dock of Laurel Grove. The thunder of the cannons was soon silenced, but the sound of gunfire from the gunboats continued. Anna gathered the frightened slaves and children around her.

"It is time for us to go. Everyone, quickly get dressed. Mariah, Marva, and Jane, take all the children to the woods along the river bank where I showed you yesterday. Keep hidden and wait there until I come for you."

She pointed to the men, saying, "Joseph and Moses, you will go with me in the canoe to the gunboat. Let's go."

Jane clung to her husband. "No, Ma'am Anna. Let Moses stay with us. Who will protect us if they come? Please, Ma'am Anna."

"Stop that." Anna said. "I know you're frightened, but you must be strong for the children. You will be safe if you do exactly as I say. Those rebels are not on this side of the river now. The gunboats must have made the rebels flee into the woods around Laurel Grove. Now, hush. Go on."

The two men paddled the canoe toward the gunboat. Joseph turned to Anna, his voice shaky. "What if dey think we be rebels? What if dey shoot at us?"

"They know me. Keep paddling," Anna ordered.

As they pulled alongside the gunboat, Anna took the hand offered to her and pulled herself up into the gunboat.

"Commander Moreno, I have come to ask asylum for my three children and my slaves and their children. In return, I can give you some information."

"Of course you may have asylum. What information could you have that we do not?"

"I could have told you that there are two cannons pointed at the river, but you have discovered that on your own already. I have watched the rebels at Laurel Grove, and I believe there are between fifty and seventy-five holding it."

"That is not much information, but it does not matter. Go and get your dependents, and we will keep them safe." He turned away.

Anna put her hand on his arm. "Wait. In return for our safety, I will lead your soldiers to Laurel Grove and show them how to get rid of the cannons."

"You? You, a black woman, barely more than a girl?"

Anna bristled. "I may be only twenty years old, but I am the wife of Zephaniah Kingsley and the mother of his three children. I have survived more than you can imagine, certainly more than you have in all your years." Her heart was racing at her boldness, and she was frightened that she had ruined her chance for her children's safety.

Commander Moreno eyed her coldly. "Very well. Get your children and your slaves, and then we will see."

Anna and the two slaves pulled the canoe onto the bank of the sheltered area where Anna had instructed the others to wait. The women seemed calmer, perhaps for the sake of the children.

"We will go in shifts," Anna said. "Moses, you take my children and Mariah in the canoe. As soon as you let them off, come back for the rest." She bent to her children. "Sit quietly. We do not want the canoe to tip." She stood and looked at Joseph. "Go back to the dock, get the flatboat, and bring it over here. You will take your family to the gunboat. We will all be safe. Don't worry. Go quickly."

The children and slaves were soon huddled against the cabin of the gunboat. All gunfire had ceased, and the river was calm The sun marked the middle of the day as Anna climbed into the canoe again.

"You do not have to be involved with this," the commander said as he watched her settle herself in the canoe. "I will keep your people safe regardless."

Anna looked up at him. "I know. But this is something I must do...for myself...and for Mr. Kingsley. I know the layout of the house. I can show your soldiers the easiest way to get to the cannons."

"We can do that without you. Our gunfire has chased the rebels away from the house for now."

"Perhaps. But they will be back. I can get your soldiers in and out quickly."

"You convince me you need to do this, so I will allow it. Go quickly. I will send two boats of my men behind you, and I will be watching everything." He lifted his spyglass. "Be careful."

His caution chilled Anna, but she shrugged it off. *I have to do something, take some action. When the tyeddo warriors came, I was defenseless. I am not defenseless now.* She signaled Joseph and Moses to begin paddling.

She watched the faces of her children and her slaves as they diminished in the distance. Anna led two small boats of ten soldiers toward Laurel Grove. Commander Moreno swept the area around Laurel Grove with his spyglass.

Anna was almost to the dock of Laurel Grove, and she

had seen no activity. The soldiers were a slight distance behind her when they heard a shout from the deck of the *Inmutable*.

"We must turn back," came the command from the boat behind her. "Commander Moreno has ordered us back. Quickly."

Aboard the gunboat, Commander Moreno stormed up to her. "You were leading us into an ambush. Did you think you could deceive us?"

Anna was stunned. "An ambush? But I saw nothing."

"The insurgents were creeping back to the house. I could see a stirring of branches in the woods. All my men could have been killed."

"What of me? Do you think I want to be killed? I assure you, Sir, I was not leading you into an ambush. I had no idea the rebels were headed back."

Commander Moreno turned and walked away. The afternoon was punctuated with intermittent gunfire as Anna tried talking to the commander again and again.

"Why would I lead you into an ambush? I value my life more than that. Look at my children. Do you think I would desert them?"

The commander sighed. "Very well. I believe you. Now, please, let us not discuss it any more."

Anna tried to think of a way to show him her loyalty. She knew that she had a lot more to fear than simply being shot at by the rebels. If she and the children were captured, her life of freedom would be over, probably forever. With the rebels at Laurel Grove, the possibility of her capture and that of her children was greater. Slaves could buy or earn their freedom in Spanish Florida, but there was no chance of that in the United States. She could not let that happen.

Anna stood at the railing of the gunboat, staring at what was left of Laurel Grove. She thought of Zephaniah and what he would want. She knew he would give up Laurel Grove before he would let an enemy take it and use it. She knew what she had to do.

"Commander, this is what I will do. Let me go in my canoe with my two slaves. I will sneak into the plantation house at dusk, and I will burn it to the ground, along with the cannons."

He stared at her in amazement. "I cannot let you do that."

"But you must," Anna insisted. "If you send your soldiers, they will be seen and shot at. If no one goes, the rebels will just come back and retake control of the house and cannons. You must let me go."

"How can I let you do something so dangerous?"

"How can you not? Until Laurel Grove and those cannons are destroyed, you and your men will never be safe on the river, and if the rebels are in control, all of us remain in danger."

Commander Moreno was silent for a moment. "Very well. You may go, and I pray God will go with you." He paused as he looked toward Laurel Grove. "We will send a fusillade of gunfire toward the outskirts of the house to scare off any of the patriots who have tried to return. You will go in daylight so that we can see and fire on the returning rebels."

Anna motioned Joseph and Moses to get into the canoe as she slipped over the side of the gunboat. Her heart was racing and her lips were dry, but she was determined to appear calm.

The humid late afternoon air clung to her as they pushed off. Moses and Joseph trembled with fear. They paddled the canoe to a sheltered spot. Anna gestured for them to wait as she stole off through the underbrush. The distance from the river to the house had never seemed so far. Anna stayed off the path and in the shadow. She tried to be silent, but her breaths were coming in gasps, and her heart was hammering. Every few yards she paused and listened. There was no sound of rebels returning to the house.

She crept to the kitchen door and listened, scanning the outer reaches of the yard. She opened the door and stopped, horrified.

# Chapter Twenty-One

*Laurel Grove*
*November 1813*

Ashes from the huge fireplace were scattered in the middle of the floor; pots and kettles were overturned; the smell of rancid food permeated the air; broken plates lay in piles. Anna grabbed a smaller pot and scooped still hot coals into it with a soup ladle. She hurried through the butler's pantry and the dining room. The massive mahogany table was scarred and covered with dirty dishes. The lump in Anna's throat grew bigger, and tears slid down her cheeks. *I must keep going.*

She stopped again at the hall threshold. Silence. She paused again on the stairs, set down the pot, and ran back to Zephaniah's study. The condition of that room made her gasp. All Zephaniah's papers were strewn about the room. Someone had taken his ink and thrown it over everything. The beautiful damask draperies were torn down and splattered with black. His chair was thrown aside. Anna ran to the desk. Under a haphazard pile of Zephaniah's records, Anna found the crystal ink well. It was not broken. Anna grabbed the heirloom and shoved it deep into her pocket.

She picked up the coals and continued to the third floor. Anna gathered the thin curtains in the slave bedrooms into a pile and tipped a few coals to smolder. She put another pile near the stairs that led to the attic and the cannons.

She retraced her steps to the second floor and to the

storage room. She wanted to use bolts of cloth for another fire, but she found the room locked. Frantically, she looked around. She had no choice. She ran into Zephaniah's room, pulled the drapes down, and made a pile near the wall. She left more coals in the center of the pile. She tried not to look at the bed where Zephaniah held her and made her feel safe. *I must do this.* She swept the heavy spread to the floor, leaving more coals on top of it.

Anna let the sobs come as she ran from room to room, setting more fires. She remembered how awed she had been the first time she saw all the beautiful things in this house she had come to love. *What will Zephaniah think when he learns this is all gone?*

Anna ran down the last flight of stairs to the hall. She ran to the kitchen and gathered more coals. In the parlor she pulled the drapes into more piles, leaving coals on each pile. She caught sight of herself in the big mirror, a dark shadow of a young woman with hair flying wildly about her face, her body glistening with sweat. She put her hand to her mouth, grieving for the girl that had once studied her reflection there, the young girl who had acted as mistress of this beautiful home, the one who had found freedom and strength here.

She smelled smoke and heard the crackling sound of fire. The smell and sound took her back to her last night in Yang Yang as she ran down the path to the river.

It was dusk when Anna and the two slaves returned to the gunboat. The evening sky over the river had softened with the setting sun. The river lapped gently against the boat.

Commander Moreno helped to pull Anna aboard. "Well," he said, his voice sounding more sad than angry. "You said you would burn it to the ground, and I do not see any flames."

Anna looked at him, her own eyes like burning coals, the emotion behind them almost overwhelming her, her body glistening with perspiration. "Wait," she said. "Wait and watch."

She turned to face what was left of her first home with Zephaniah, the birthplace of her children, the place where she first tasted freedom again after the tyeddo raid took it away. Anna stood as if carved in stone. Her hands gripped the gunboat railing. The sun was setting behind the ruined outbuildings of Laurel Grove, painting the sky in a rosy hue, lining the clouds with gold. With the peaceful river running in front of the plantation and the pastel sky behind, the tragedy of loss seemed even more bizarre, and Anna felt the grief like a physical blow.

"There! I see it!" Commander Moreno's voice brought her back to the present.

Anna saw her success, too, the first wisps of smoke, curling almost lazily into the sky. Soon, more strands of smoke came together, filling out, until the sky above the plantation house roiled with dark smoke, and flames danced out of the windows and roof to join with it in a crackling, ominous specter. The smell of fire and smoke carried out to the gunboat. She could almost see the silhouette of the baobab tree with the smoke from the village behind it. A sense of panic rose up within her, and she forced herself to breath more slowly. *I am safe on this gunboat, and my children are safe.*

All the soldiers watched now with Anna's family and her slaves. With two loud crashes, a cheer went up from the soldiers aboard the gunboat. The dreaded cannons had been silenced.

The commander faced Anna. "You did it, young woman. I don't know how, but you accomplished that destruction by yourself."

Anna allowed a small smile to form on her lips. "I dragged curtains and drapes in piles and lit them, knowing that it would take awhile for the fire to spread. That gave me time to get away. I could not let them catch me."

"I will send a report on this to the authorities in Spain.

You can be sure you will be rewarded for what you have done here tonight, Mrs. Kingsley."

"My reward, and Mr. Kingsley's, will be that the rebels can no longer use Laurel Grove for a sanctuary. It is important that we do not let anyone use against us what we have built. That would be more painful than seeing it destroyed by ourselves."

"I assure you, madam, your reward will be a lot more generous than that."

"There is still something I need to do. Please take me across the river to my place."

Commander Moreno hesitated, taking the full measure of the young woman before him. "Of course."

As soon as the gunboat anchored near Anna's dock, she lowered herself into her canoe.

"Let me send soldiers with you," Commander Moreno said.

Anna looked at him, her eyes clear, her face set with determination. "No, this is something I must do myself." She eased the paddle into the water and headed for her dock.

Anna pulled her canoe alongside the dock and tied it. Every fiber of her body was taut with tension. She scanned her property - the slaves' cabins, the poultry yard, the small barn, and, finally, the sturdy two-story house. The first home of her own. The mules, ducks, and hens had been herded into the woods the day before, and the emptiness of the place tore at Anna's heart. Tears slid down her cheeks.

The sky darkened as the afterglow faded and a tiny quarter moon appeared. The wind was gentle, and Anna heard it rustling as the breeze traveled through the nearby trees along the river. The water lapped softly against the shoreline. Was it her imagination or did the smell of smoke from Laurel Grove began to slip across the river, burning her eyes and tearing at her heart?

She entered her house and picked up two large torches

Moses kept made up for checking the animals at night. The coals in the fireplace were still glowing from the last meal Marva had cooked there. Anna thrust the torches in the coals. Anna mounted the stairs with one flaming torch in each hand.

With a last glance at the beauty of the home she loved, she thrust a torch against the curtains she and Harriet had made, and then she threw it on the bed she had left only that morning. A lifetime ago. With the other torch, she ran to the slaves' cabins and torched each one. Heart breaking, with one last thrust, she tossed the torch into the barn and stood back.

Standing in the center of her property, Anna's face and body shimmered from the heat that vibrated around her. Her breathing was labored from the effort and from the grief. She wanted to drop to her knees and wail but feared she would not be able to rise again.

"My home," she whispered. Tears streaked her soot-stained face. She raised her arms, stretched them wide as if to embrace what had been hers. She dropped her arms to her sides, empty. Her throat ached from harsh sobs at the agony of what she had done. Just as she had done as a captive on that terrible trek from Yang Yang to Rufisque, she put one foot in front of the other and moved on.

At the dock, she looked one last time.

As Anna returned from her final foray, she felt as though she had absorbed the smoke into the deepest part of her. She wondered if she would ever rid herself of the acrid smell. She felt a tiredness that was more than physical and longed to curl up somewhere and sleep. Strong hands were waiting to help her up from her canoe. The commander handed her a canteen of water. She drank eagerly as the commander spoke. "There is little moonlight," Commander Moreno told her, "but we will set out immediately. I want to get you and your family to safety at San Nicolas. There you will find sanctuary and you may stay as long as you need to. We have given your people and your children some biscuits, dried beef, and water. Please take some for yourself."

"Thank you."

Commander Moreno looked as if he wanted to say more, but Anna turned away to go to her children and slaves. In spite of the late hour, two-year-old Mary was the only one asleep, cuddled in Mariah's arms. Anna slid down on the deck and pulled George and Martha into her lap, nuzzling the sweet smell of them. She wanted to explain to them, to tell them why she had done what she did. She wanted to let them know that while the land is so important, it is more important not to let others take it from you for their own destructive use. She wanted to say so many things, and maybe someday she could. But for tonight, there were no words. She hugged the children to her and closed her eyes.

# Chapter Twenty-Two

*Fort San Nicolas*
*November – December 1813*

The gunboat bumped against the landing dock of Fort San Nicolas, jolting Anna awake. She stiffly got to her feet. The children and slaves began to stir.

Commander Moreno stood talking with another officer on the dock. The officer was the same height as the commander but more stocky. His uniform matched the commander's except the new officer's was more rumpled. There was a lot of gesturing and nodding toward Anna before they approached her.

"Mrs. Kingsley, this is Capitan Gonzales. I have told him of your heroic acts, and he will see that you, your family, and your slaves are comfortable here at San Nicolas. You may go with him now. You have nothing to fear."

"Thank you." Anna turned to follow Capitan Gonzales. *Safe. I remember when Zephaniah first taught me that word. He said I would be safe now, that he would protect me. Where are you, Zephaniah? I miss you and I need you.*

In the deep hours of the night, shoulders sagging, spirits low, Anna, with her group, walked up the dock to a large blockhouse. The square stone building loomed like a dark fortress. Anna was too tired to take in any of the details. She carried the dozing Mary, and Mariah gently pulled George and Martha along. Moses, Joseph, and their families followed, carrying the few supplies they had packed.

"Here are three rooms you may use for now." Capitan Gonzales held the lantern high. "In the morning, we can see if you need other arrangements. Right now, I would imagine you just need a place to rest."

Anna nodded and entered the first of the rooms with the children and Mariah. Capitan Gonzales used the flame from his lantern to light another candle in the room.

There were two beds, but a pile of extra bedding on one would do for a pallet on the floor. A small washstand in one corner had a pitcher full of water, a washbowl, soap, and a stack of clean towels. Anna and Mariah settled the two older children on one bed, and they fell asleep immediately. Mary never woke as Mariah laid her on the pallet. Mariah washed and then settled herself beside Mary on the pallet, leaving the remaining bed for Anna.

Anna went to the washstand and poured some water in the bowl. She wet her hands and face, and lathered with the soap. She dipped her hands in the water and splashed the water on her face to rinse away the soot, relishing the coolness against her still too-warm skin. Patting her face dry with a towel, she glanced at her reflection in the mirror above the washstand.

Except for the fly-away strands of hair, the young woman Anna stared at no longer looked that different from the one she had glanced at in the mirrors of the Big House in calmer days, or in her own home. Anna smiled grimly. *You were right, Bella. Nothing anyone does to me - no matter what terrible things happen to me - nothing can touch my soul, my strength. I am still standing strong.* She disrobed to her cotton underdress and lay down, knowing that she would sleep that night and go on with life the next day.

\* \* \*

Anna awoke to the sound of a bugle blowing and men's voices outside. For a split second, she wondered where she was. As the memory of the previous day washed over her, she wanted to lie back down.

George sat up in bed. "Mama." Anna knew she had to be strong.

They changed into clean clothes and went down into the main area of the fort. Anna was surprised to see that several other families were already housed there. The main floor was one large room with a stone fireplace at one end for cooking. Breakfast awaited along a wall. Soldiers and the families were eating at a grouping of large trestle tables. Slaves ate in another area. Anna felt the eyes of the white families looking her over, judging her. They took in her fine clothes and her mulatto children. Anna bristled. *You don't know me. You don't know anything about me.*

Capitan Gonzales walked over. "Good morning, Mrs. Kingsley. Did you sleep well?"

"Yes. We were all very tired." She looked at him more clearly this morning. There was warmth in his dark eyes. His thin mustache matched his black hair. Anna looked around. "So, we are not the only ones seeking safety?"

"We have a number of forts in this area, and all of them are providing sanctuary for residents. After you and your family have something to eat, I would be glad to show you around."

"That would be nice," she said, ushering the children toward the food.

Anna had not eaten since the morning before. She and Mariah filled plates for the children and themselves with bacon, biscuits, and fruit. There was hot tea, Spanish coffee, and, Anna's favorite, thick hot cocoa. The rich chocolate flavor of the drink revived her spirit.

"Fort San Nicolas has been built and rebuilt several times," Capitan Gonzales explained as they later walked the perimeter of the blockhouse. "It was first built because we expected an attack by the British. After Spain reoccupied East Florida in 1784, it was rebuilt, and the moat was added. However," he chuckled, "the officers' quarters and the soldiers' barracks are located outside the safety of the moat in that long building there." He pointed to another stone building on the other side of the wide, water-filled ditch.

"Why was it rebuilt so many times?" asked Anna.

"You, better than anyone, know of the destruction that has come our way from Georgia. Rebels attacked here in 1796. The windows were all shot out, and they fired cannons at the blockhouse, taking out large chunks of the wall. That made the whole structure unsafe. We rebuilt later, and then, during this so-called "Patriot War," they came and destroyed it again. We retook it not long ago and have made it secure once more."

"Is it really secure?"

"Oh, yes. We have many troops in the area now. You will be safe here for as long as you need to stay."

"I confess, I do not know how long that will be. I guess I will have to wait until I hear from Mr. Kingsley." Anna sighed as she realized the void her life had become. *I may not be a slave, but Zephaniah still controls my life. Even if I were completely free, though, where would I go? What would I do?*

\* \* \*

Two weeks seemed to go by in slow motion to Anna. She was not used to so much idle time. At first, she welcomed the relaxation. What she had to do to Laurel Grove and her own place had exhausted her in body, mind, and spirit. The first quiet days at the fort gave her time to rest.

The families usually spent their time walking the perimeter of the fort or visiting together in the main room. The first morning after showing her around, the captain introduced

Anna to the other plantation owners. They acknowledged her presence with a brief nod, occasionally a few words of conversation.

Before long, the children began playing together, white and black, making up the usual games of childhood. The slaves stayed apart, tending to laundry, cooking meals in the huge fireplace, and looking after the children.

Captain Gonzales had let her know that she was the only free person of color there, and she felt that she didn't belong with either the blacks or the whites. She sat by herself much of the time, wishing for Sophie.

That afternoon, Anna walked around the outside of the building and settled on a bench looking at the river. The December day was cool, but she was comfortable with her warm shawl wrapped around her. She watched two Spanish gunboats passing each other, a barge moving slowly. Gulls squawked as they darted about looking for food. The river was so much narrower here than it was between Laurel Grove and Anna's property, but sitting and watching the river made her think of the days at home. *I never thought I would find myself torn away from my home again. Will I ever really be safe?*

"May I join you?" a soft voice by her shoulder startled her from her reverie. Anna looked into the kind blue eyes of an older woman she had noticed that morning. The woman was not tall, but rather heavy-set. Her face was round, her cheeks full and dimpled, emphasized by her smile. Her light brown hair escaped from her gray bonnet in little tendrils around her face.

"I would be pleased. Have you just arrived?"

"Yes. My husband and I managed to get through in our buggy last night. Our plantation is on the Nassau River north of here."

"Oh, Mr. Kingsley is north of here also. He is at his plantation on St. Mary's River. Do you think the rebels are heading that way?"

"Zephaniah Kingsley?" Her voice reflected her surprise.

"Yes. He has several plantations here. We lost one, Laurel Grove, and he escaped to another, White Oak. I haven't heard from him since."

"I know of White Oak, of course, and we know Mr. Kingsley slightly. I do not know what has happened there, though. We heard only that the rebels were coming, and so we left before we had a confrontation."

"When is this fighting going to end?"

The other woman shook her head sadly. "I'm sorry. I haven't introduced myself. My name is Rebecca Cowles. My husband is Phillip Cowles."

"I am Anna Kingsley."

"I saw you this morning with several children."

"Yes. We have three. Do you have children?"

"No. We were never blessed with any."

"I'm sorry." Sympathy showed in Anna's eyes

"And you have three. You must have married very young."

"We....we have been together for seven years." Anna felt herself drawn into the quagmire that Zephaniah had put her in. He called her his wife, he introduced her as his wife, and she had begun to think of herself as his wife, yet there had never been a marriage. She grew quiet.

"Well, I must go rejoin my husband." Mrs. Cowles rose and smiled a farewell.

"Good-bye." It had been pleasant for a few moments of simple, social conversation with another woman. *I don't wish the Frasers bad luck, but if they have to flee, I hope they come here. I am lonely.*

Anna filled much of the time reading to the children and telling them stories. Many other hours stayed empty. The nights were especially hard. Those thinking times gave her time to brood about Zephaniah and all he had given her, and what he had come to mean to her. There has been no word from him since the day that Abraham had come to her place. *Was he still safe?*

Anna worried about a Christmas celebration. Now that George was six and a half, Martha was four and a half, and Mary was two, they were old enough to look forward to the holiday. She had nothing but the few clothes they had brought with them. She knew that Zephaniah would make Christmas happy for them if he could, but where was he?

*I must get out of this fort and to a store. If I could just get some corn husks or fabric, I could make dolls for the girls, and I'll think of something for George.* Anna took some money from a small coin purse she kept in the tapestry bag.

Finding Mariah outside with the children, Anna whispered, "I am going outside the fort. I want to get something for the children's Christmas."

Mariah looked at her with fright. "Oh, Anna, please don't. It mayn't be safe out dere."

"I think it's safe enough with all these Spanish soldiers about. I won't be long." She slipped away from the children and wandered about the perimeter as she often did. When she thought no one was looking, she slipped out a side door of the fortification and made her way over the narrow bridge that spanned the moat.

Anna wrapped her woolen plaid shawl tightly around her and tried to appear as unobtrusive as possible. A few short blocks from the blockhouse were some buildings. There was a saloon, of course, but Anna thought one of the buildings might be a mercantile store. Anna walked along quickly. The area bustled with the pre-Christmas business. The women were well dressed in English fashion Phenda Fraser had told her about. The skirts were wide and bell-shaped and the hems decorated with flounces and bows. The men all wore frock coats and sported tall beaver hats. Many of both sexes had billowing capes against the cool sea air. Anna was aware of the drabness of her blue muslin dress, but the powder-blue scarf she wore as a turban made her feel more regal.

Anna found a mercantile store and hurried inside. It felt good to be free of the restrictions of the garrison. She browsed through the merchandise, wondering what might make a good gift for George. Coming upon a basket of tin whistles, Anna decided one of them would be just the thing for George. Among all the bolts of fabric, she found several small pieces that she could use to make dolls for the girls. She was glad she had thought to pack needles and thread in her tapestry bag. Waiting to pay at the main counter, she selected a stick of horehound hard candy for Mariah.

"Are you shopping for your mistress?" the proprietor, a large, pudgy man with a balding head, asked as he made the change. His eyes were small and mean-looking under bushy gray eyebrows. His hairy arms protruded from rolled up sleeves, reminding Anna of large ham hocks.

Anna was unsure how to answer. She didn't want to arouse any attention to herself, but she didn't see any need to lie.

"No," she responded. "I am shopping for myself, to have things for my children's Christmas."

"Are you new here?"

"I....I am here just temporarily."

"Who do you belong to?" he continued to question her, holding her change in his hand so she wasn't free to leave.

"I am a free person." Anna held out her hand for the money. Several people were waiting behind her to make their purchases, and Anna was becoming uneasy.

"We don't take to freein' our nigras around here." Spittle sprayed from his lips.

"May I have my change please?" Anna was firm, but her heart was beating fast and she felt her body trembling. *Why did I come out of the fort? No one but Mariah even knows where I am.*

"Give her the money, Sam. We've got things to do, and

we're tired of waitin'," called a male voice from behind Anna.

The proprietor glared at Anna and spilled her coins on the counter. "Next," he said loudly.

Anna snatched up her parcel and change and left the store. She hurried along the plank sidewalk by the buildings, not looking left or right. In the second block, she heard heavy boots behind her.

The echo of the footsteps increased as she walked faster.

She entered the third block and was almost to the fort. The sound of the boots came closer and closer. Anna felt a rising sense of terror. Should she run? The boots were almost upon her. Anna's breath came in gasps. Someone grabbed her arm.

"Stop." a male voice hissed in her ear.

# Chapter Twenty-Three

*Fort San Nicolas*
*December 1813*

Anna felt she would faint from fright and stumbled. The firm hold on her arm held her up. Only determination to get back to her children kept her from collapsing. The grip was like a vise. Anna dreaded turning to look at her captor. She had seen the rebels around Laurel Grove from a distance, and she didn't want a closer look. Their oily-looking, scraggly hair, unkempt beards, and scruffy clothing made their appearance intimidating.

"You are from the garrison. I have seen you there. You should not be out here alone." The words were English, but with a strong accent.

Anna turned. The voice belonged to a Spanish soldier. His uniform was immaculate, and his serious face had a frown. "I will see that you get back safely."

Relief washed over her. She took his offered arm to steady herself. "Thank you. Thank you so much." They turned to walk the short distance to the garrison.

"You should not do this again," the young man mildly reproached her.

Anna was able to laugh softly. "Don't worry. I never will."

\* \* \*

Anna felt a continuing restlessness. She spent much of the afternoon walking back and forth to the dock. She stared out at the river, willing Zephaniah to come, but there were only the usual gunboats. *Like the sand washing out with the tide, everything goes. I have my manumission papers, but I am not free. I must stay here in this jail-like place, waiting. Zephaniah, where are you?* She watched the sunlight skim over the water, sparkles catching the high places. The sight reminded her of the horrific Middle Passage. She remembered Bella's words, and straightened her shoulders. *I have survived much. I can survive this. Zephaniah and I will build again. I am a free person.* Daily, it seemed, Anna went through this swing of emotions, from discouragement and despair to determination, and back again. She walked to the tall cedar where Mariah entertained the children and settled herself at the base of the tree.

"Shall I tell you a story?" she asked, smiling at their bright faces.

"Yes...Yes. Mama."

"Tell us about Yang Yang," George made his usual request. It pleased Anna that he was interested in those roots, a place that he would probably never see. She tried to make the connection real for him with her stories.

"Well," she began, "if it were a day like this, a day in December in the village of Yang Yang...."

A commotion at the front gate of the fort caught their attention. The gate opened, and a group of people hurried through, accompanied by a number of Spanish soldiers. Anna searched for Zephaniah in the group.

A man looked like Zephaniah, but were her eyes playing tricks on her? No. It was Zephaniah. Anna jumped up and ran toward the group, the children behind her. As she approached them, she slowed. She wanted to run to Zephaniah, to feel his comforting arms around her, but suddenly she felt shy. Would he want her to make such a public display? How would he react when he learned she had burned Laurel

Grove? She drew closer, joy and relief overcoming her hesitancy and pushing her on.

Zephaniah looked her way, and his face broke out in pleasure. Anna saw the caring in his smile and in the sparkle in his eyes. She knew then that he was glad to see her, too. Anna walked toward him, slowly at first, then running the last few steps. Zephaniah opened his arms to her, and Anna found the comfort she had been longing for. Her face buried against his chest as her arms locked around him. She felt his strength as he held her close.

George and Martha circled their pudgy arms around each of his legs and looked up at him with bright smiles. Zephaniah knelt and put his arms around the children.

"Father, Mama started a fire! She burned the house down," George announced.

"And we went on a big boat and watched the fire," added Martha.

He looked at them and smiled. "Yes, I know all about it. You can tell me more later."

Mary toddled up holding Mariah's hand. The child lifted her arms to be picked up by her father. Zephaniah was pleased. He lifted her to him and kissed her soft cheek.

Setting Mary back down, he looked at Anna. "The Spanish captain who escorted us in to the fort told me you were safe, but I did not dare believe it until I could see you with my own eyes."

He took Anna's hands in his. "Are you well?"

"As well as can be expected. And you?"

"I am better now that I know you and the children are safe." He stooped to scoop up Martha with his right arm and circled George's shoulders with his left. Mary had toddled away with Mariah.

"We have a lot to catch up on. Let us go to your room so we can talk."

As they sat on the rope bed in the spartan room that

Anna and the children shared, the two children sitting close by on the floor, Anna's eyes took in Zephaniah. His hair was still brown, his countenance strong, and yet she noticed a subtle change in him. The escape from Laurel Grove and this latest escape from White Oak Plantation had aged him. Anna knew that Zephaniah had passed his fiftieth birthday, but he always seemed so strong and vital to her that she could not imagine that he was aging. The thought made her sad.

"I have heard about what you did at Laurel Grove and at your own place. That was so brave of you, and I am so proud. I always said you had spirit, but you were wonderful."

Anna flushed at his praise. "I dreaded having to tell you. I was sure you would understand, that it was what you would have wanted, but, even so, I was afraid. All those beautiful things...gone. It broke my heart to do it."

He took her hands for a moment. "I know. When I heard about it, I grieved for you. You had already lost everything once. But it was the right thing to do. We will build again."

Anna felt the warmth and strength in his hands. Her heart was filled with gratitude to this man who had given her so much, and who continued to give her what she needed. "Tell me what has happened to you since you left Laurel Grove."

Zephaniah's shoulders slumped almost imperceptibly. "Oh, Anna, it has not been easy. We lost many slaves during the attack at Laurel Grove. Now, the whole plantation is gone. We suffered loss at White Oak Plantation, too. Of course, there are still the rice plantation and the Drayton Island plantation, and there are still a good number of slaves left to carry on our work."

"I have been so worried about you, Sophie and Abraham, Charles, Celia, the other house slaves, and the field slaves."

"Other than the ones we lost in that first attack on Laurel Grove, everyone is safe at the other plantations. Abraham and his family led the remaining slaves to Drayton Island.

They will be safe there."

"I wish they could be here. I miss Sophie, especially. It would help to have her to talk to." Anna paused. "It has been hard thinking of all we have lost."

Zephaniah took her hand in his again. "We have both lost our land, but there is still much land available. We can rebuild. We can start again in a new place. I will find a place that is safe for us, and we will create a new plantation. We can work it out together."

Anna looked into his brown eyes and saw the hope and determination that would carry them through. "Yes, we can work it out together."

Zephaniah stood abruptly. "Let us rest here for a few weeks while I gather information and see about materials. By spring, we can have a new start." He looked down at the children, with their eyes still watching him.

"The quarters are crowded here. I will arrange for my own room, and you can join me there. Mariah will stay here with the children."

"Before you go, I have something for you." She went to the tapestry bag. "I saved this from Laurel Grove for you. I knew it was important." She handed him the crystal ink well.

"I don't know what to say."

"You do not need to say anything. I wanted to save something for you. This seemed like the right thing."

"It was exactly the right thing."

He took both her hands in his and kissed her on the cheek. "We make a good team, Anna. We will be fine."

She smiled and nodded her head. Anna watched him until he was out of sight. For the first time in weeks, she no longer felt as though she were in limbo, floating along without direction. *Zephaniah. My anchor.*

"We'll be all right now. Your father's here."

* * *

The next weeks were pleasant ones. The weather was calm and cool. Anna worked with the children and walked around the fort with Zephaniah. In his bed again, she felt alive and safe. *What is it about him? When I am with him, I feel that anything is possible. He makes me feel whole, complete. Do I dare trust him enough to believe in those things?*

Anna loved to listen to his strong, enthusiastic voice as he reeled off plans he had for the future. He was rebounding from the discouragement that he had shown when he first arrived. Now, he reminded her of a horse, chafing at the bit, yearning to run free again. He stirred the same feelings in her. Anna was used to working toward something, her freedom, her own property, always more than she had at that moment.

"Anna." Zephaniah sat at one of the tables set up under the live oaks. "Come here a moment. I want to show you something."

Anna looked over his shoulder as he spread a large map on the table.

"This area," he pointed to Ft. George Island. "This is where we should settle and build a plantation. I have been looking into all the possibilities, talking to people to see what might be available. I like this the best. It belongs to John McIntosh. Remember, I told you about him once? He was a patriot sympathizer." Zephaniah rushed on without waiting for an answer. "It is a beautiful piece of land. It is at the mouth of the St. John's River, accessible from the ocean yet protected by this extension of Florida on the south and by Talbot Island on the north. It will be the perfect setting for my trade business. We can plant orange trees again."

"What I want us to do," he continued, "is rest here another week or so, then go to Fernandina. There is a large Spanish garrison there that can protect us until the area is safe. Then we will go to Ft. George's Island and begin our new life."

"But will we really be safe?" Anna asked.

Zephaniah settled himself on the table. "As far as the marauders are concerned, we will be safe. They are being chased out of Spanish Florida. The real Patriots had already gone, and those doing all this devilment were just thugs. But..."

"But, what?" His tone made her uneasy.

"I am afraid that eventually Spanish East Florida will belong to the United States, and that will not bode well for you and the children. The laws in the states are harsh for Negroes. Their thinking is that all people of black skin should be slaves."

Anna shuddered. "Zephaniah, I was born free. After I was captured and made a slave, you saw fit to free me and give me land of my own. Then, I lost that. I cannot lose my freedom again. We cannot let our children lose it."

Zephaniah's eyes reflected Anna's despair. "I know. And I promise you that I will work hard to keep you free."

"I know you will, but I also know that things happen beyond our control." Memories of the tyeddo raid and the fires at Laurel Grove and her own place swirled in her mind like billowing smoke clouds.

# Chapter Twenty-Four

*Fernandina, Florida*
*December 1813 – 1814*

Anna followed Zephaniah up the gangplank to the *Esther* and
nodded a greeting to Captain Wright. *How strange to board this*
*ship as free woman rather than slave.*

She stood at the railing with George, Martha, and Mary
as the crew untied the moorings, and the boat creaked away
from the safety of San Nicolas and made its way northward on
the St. John's River toward Fernandina on the Atlantic. The
slaves gathered in small groups around the deck. Zephaniah
joined the family at the railing. He appeared to have regained
his enthusiasm and zest for life.

George was beside himself with excitement. Anna knew
the boy had felt so restrained at the fort and that he longed
for space to run and explore again. Martha, as always, exuded
her calm nature. "Mama, are you going to burn the fort before
we go?"

Anna laughed at her daughter's assumption that a river
trip was always preceded by a fire. "No, Martha. There's no
need for that here."

Mary, barely two-years-old, smiled as she felt the sea
breeze on her face.

"How long do you think we will be at Fernandina?" Anna
asked.

"Not long. I want to gather what materials I can salvage

from the other plantations, and I want to complete the purchase arrangements with McIntosh for the Ft. George Island plantation. That shouldn't take much time because he is anxious to sell."

"Is he afraid of more uprisings?"

Zephaniah laughed. "Not at all. He was a leader of the Patriot Rebellion, and he has fled to Georgia to avoid reprisals. Remember? I told you there were rumors to that effect. When they captured me that day, they said McIntosh was their leader."

"Well, good riddance then."

The family watched together in the cool December morning as they passed the plantations along the river. Anna winced every time she saw the destruction left by the rebels.

"Look, Anna, children." Zephaniah pointed to the white plantation home barely visible on the tip of an island. "That will soon be our home. That is Fort George's Island. See what a marvelous location, here at the mouth of the river and the ocean on the other side?"

Anna stood on tiptoe to see. There was obviously destruction to the plantation buildings, but the Big House appeared to be in good shape. A surge of excitement went through Anna. A *new beginning*.

\* \* \*

The garrison at Fernandina was much larger than at San Nicolas. Huge earthen-work construction and ten cannons surrounded the ramparts.

Anna gazed at the garrison walls as they walked in. The fort formed an outer square with many rooms along each side. In the center was a large grassy area where groups of soldiers and civilians lounged.

"That is the commandant's home." The soldier who was escorting them to their rooms pointed to an impressive

looking building. Spanish soldiers were in evidence everywhere.

Anna, Zephaniah, the children, Mariah, and several other
house slaves were soon settled. The field slaves were housed
on Zephaniah's schooner, which remained at the dock.
Life at the fort eased into a routine. Zephaniah went often to
his other plantations, gathering remaining supplies, and Anna
again had too much time on her hands. White women often
came together to visit, but they seldom included Anna. She
could tell by the clothing of the others that she was the only
free black woman there. No one snubbed her since she was
there as Zephaniah's wife, but no one tried to be friendly,
either.

* * *

Anna walked toward the ocean, her warm shawl protecting
her from February winds. Her path angled through a grove of
tall palms and brought her to the sandy shoreline. She gazed
at the vast ocean before her and remembered the days of
nothing but ocean and sky on her long voyage to Cuba. She
almost could see Madu, cruelly chained, see him dragged to
the edge of the ship.... She forced herself to think of something else.

"Hello." A cheerful voice behind her startled Anna. The
young woman standing before her appeared to be in her late
teens although already as tall as Anna. Her blonde hair was
drawn back in a chignon of curls, and her blue eyes sparkled.
Her dark blue silk gown with lace at the collar and cuffs was
expensive and well made. The plaid shawl around her trim
shoulders was a heavy wool of good quality.

"Hello," Anna acknowledged her.

"I've seen you at the garrison, but we haven't met. My
name is Susan....Susan Fatio."

"I am Anna Kingsley."

"Oh, I know who you are. Everyone knows you are a heroine who helped the Spanish. Weren't you scared to go alone to set fire to your home?"

Anna was taken aback to think she was considered a heroine. "I....I wasn't....I just did what needed to be done."

"Please, don't be modest. I'd love to hear all about it. Would you tell me?"

Anna smiled. "There is nothing to tell. I knew where the heavy drapes were. I snuck in and lit them, then got away before the fire was too great."

"I heard my parents talking, and they said that Zephaniah Kingsley bought you as a new slave from Africa. You looked so sad, looking out at the ocean just now. Were you thinking of your family back in Africa?"

Anna was surprised at both Susan's perceptiveness and her bluntness. As they headed back toward the garrison, she found herself sharing her experiences with this young girl. Each day after that they found some time to walk and talk together. Anna finally had a friend in this place.

* * *

March brought spring gently to Fernandina.

"When are we going home?" George and Martha often asked.

"We'll go to a new home when your father has everything ready," Anna answered. She understood their impatience.

Zephaniah was preparing to leave on another trip. "This will be my last trip. I plan to bring Abraham and his family back with me. Then we'll be ready to go to Ft. George Island."

"I will be so glad to see Sophie. How soon will you be back? When will we leave for our new home?"

Zephaniah laughed. "Anna, Anna, you are as impatient as George or Martha. I'm glad there is still Mary, who does not always ask 'When?'"

Each day, Anna watched from the ramparts of the fort for Zephaniah's return by boat. Finally, she saw his small schooner and two barges full of supplies and furniture enter the port. She rushed to the entrance of the garrison, where she waited impatiently for Zephaniah and Sophie. The sight of her short, stocky friend coming along behind Zephaniah filled Anna with a sense of comfort. She smiled and waved.

Anna's eyes twinkled with excitement as she welcomed Zephaniah. "And now, are we ready to go?"

He laughed as he took her hands. "Very soon, my dear. Very, very soon."

Anna squeezed his hands and moved on to hug Sophie.

"I am so glad to see you. I was so worried, not knowing what had happened to you."

"And I was worried about you, Anta. But here we are, safe."

Midmorning of the next day, the family and slaves loaded onto the schooner. It had already picked up all that could be salvaged from Laurel Grove, all the valuables Anna's slaves had hidden, along with many of the field slaves from the other plantations. Zephaniah had spent weeks gathering all he anticipated they would need to restore the plantation at Ft. George's Island. The schooner was followed by several rafts with furniture and supplies.

Anna watched the land that they passed with great interest. They sailed south from Fernandina, past Amelia and Talbot Islands. Martha and Mary were content to stay in the cabin with Mariah, but George scooted from one vantage point to another, the wind ruffling his curly black hair.

"How could they do so much damage?" Anna questioned Zephaniah as they stood together at the railing, viewing destruction. "Why couldn't they be stopped?"

"That is one problem about being ruled by Spain. They have so many other problems, they cannot give us the protection we need. That lack of protection was one reason I thought to support the patriots at first. The United States could look out for us better, but that is a bitter double-edged sword for us. The price we would pay for that is the danger of returning you and the children to slavery." He shook his head sadly. "A bitter double-edged sword."

Anna leaned forward against the railing and turned her face up to feel the sunshine warm it. She would not let herself be saddened by thoughts of what might be. She was going to a new beginning. She had learned to live in the moment. If it were a bad moment, it would pass. Good moments, like today, were savored.

# Chapter Twenty-Five

*Kingsley Plantation, Fort George Island*
*December 1813 – 1819*

The schooner bumped against the battered-looking dock at
what Zephaniah told her would be called Kingsley Plantation.
Anna took George and Martha's hands and started toward
the main house. Mariah followed with little Mary. All the
slaves began looking around the grounds, inspecting the
ruined slaves' quarters. The land was flat and low, the fields
spreading out from the back of the house. Cedar trees lined
one edge of the yard of the Big House, their branches spout-
ing the tender green of new leaves. Palms were abundant as
well as magnolia, live oak, and hickory trees.

From the shore, things did not look too bad, but as they
got closer to the house, Anna could see that there was much
work ahead of them. Zephaniah went to inspect the outbuildings and the slave quarters. Anna left the children in the yard
with Mariah, walked up to the wide porch which ran across
the north side of the house, and went inside.

The main door hung at an angle, shutters on the front
of the house were awry. The main house looked bruised and
violated. Anna found herself in a large room with fireplaces
on each end. An overturned table with two broken legs lay
defeated on one side of the room. Sunlight spilled through
dirty windows and filled the room, spotlighting the destruction.

Anna tried to picture the room cleaned and full of Zephaniah's new mahogany furniture, the windows draped with a deep green fabric, the pine floor smoothed and polished. A lizard scuttled across the floor, bringing her back to the present. She sighed and went on to examine the bedrooms, one on each corner of the first floor. Outside, a staircase led to more bedrooms. Another staircase led up to an observation deck.

Anna made her way to this highest part of the house. From there she saw the children playing tag below. Farther away, Zephaniah and Abraham peered into what was left of the barn. Anna surveyed the entire plantation from the lofty deck and made a quick assessment. The slaves' cabins had been burned down and could not be used. Most of the outbuildings were damaged, but many were restorable. Anna dusted off her hands. There was work to be done.

She climbed down and made her way back to the porch. Zephaniah was headed her way from the barn. The path he was walking on was made of sand and crushed shells. *What a clever use of a material that was on hand.*

"Well, what do you think?" Zephaniah mounted the porch steps to join her.

Anna smiled. "We have a lot to do. I'll get the house slaves busy cleaning out the rooms of the Big House before we move in any furniture."

"And I'll get the field slaves started on building some temporary cabins for them. The old slave cabins are beyond repair."

"I noticed that. I have a suggestion. To get the slaves in something more quickly, why don't you let me show them how to weave together palm branches to make thatched roofs like we had in Senegal? We have an abundance of palms here. The women could be doing that while the men put up the basic cabins. Sophie will know how to do it, too, and she can supervise that activity."

Zephaniah looked at Anna with admiration. "An excellent idea. I would not have thought of it."

Zephaniah and Anna walked the vast plantation the next week. Slaves were busy working at every corner of the island. The house slaves scoured the walls, floors, and windows of the Big House. Field slaves rebuilt the barn and other outbuildings while others worked on the slaves' quarters. A few were already at work in the fields, clearing the land for a spring planting.

New livestock had been purchased and brought in. Anna's ducks and poultry seemed none the worse from their experience. Meats from Drayton Island Plantation filled the smokehouse, and there were vegetables in the root cellar. Anna had insisted that the furniture not be brought in until the house was ready, so Zephaniah had it covered with sailcloth and palm branches.

"I want this to be like Laurel Grove," he told her. "We will have fields of our Sea Island cotton and sugarcane. They do so well here. And I want to grow the foods we need to feed everyone, corn, potatoes, and beans."

The two meandered southward following a sandy path, exploring all the land. Anna was delighted with all the sea birds she noticed, not only the gulls and terns, but the shearwaters and even a few pelicans.

"Look there, Zephaniah." She pointed toward some old ruins. "What was here before, I wonder?"

"McIntosh told me about that. It was an old mission village. There were Indians here, and a Catholic mission was established. Both were long gone before the plantation was built."

Anna tried to imagine an Indian village there with Catholic priests wandering through like the missionaries had when they came to Yang Yang.

Almost to the end of the island, Anna again stopped him. "Those shells in such huge piles....How did they get like that?"

"It had something to do with the Indians, I think."

"But so many in one place. The mounds of shells are taller than a house."

"Yes, those piles must be thirty or forty feet high."

Anna walked nearer to the heaped oyster shells, glimmering in the sun. "I wonder." She scooped up a handful and let the pieces fall through her fingers. "Zephaniah, look at this. There was something they did in Senegal....I remember my father bringing the idea from a trip to the coast, and I saw it on Gorée Island, but I didn't realize it at the time.... You can make bricks out of this. You add sand and water...and something else....I don't know..."

Zephaniah went to her side by the huge mound of shells. "Yes, you're right. I've seen it done, but I had forgotten. It's called 'tabby.' We can mix this with sand and water and lime until it becomes thick. It can be poured into molds for walls or made into bricks. Anna, you've done it again. We can use this to build the slaves permanent cabins."

"And at least for a base of the other outbuildings."

"You are a marvel. What would I do without you?"

Anna slipped her hands around his arm and leaned against him.

* * *

Anna loved the way the morning light played over the furnishings of the great room. Everything had been restored to order, and the mahogany furniture was in place. The windows sparkled, and the pine floors shone like burnished bronze. Zephaniah was finishing his breakfast in the dining room as he read the mail. She hoped for a letter from Susan Fatio.

"Anna, I have a letter from my sister Isabella. She, George, and the boys are coming to Florida for a visit. Will you see that rooms are ready for them?"

Anna's spirits sank a little. Her memories of visits from

Zephaniah's sisters were not pleasant, but she knew she could never say anything to Zephaniah about the way his sister snubbed her. "Of course. When do you expect them?"

"They should arrive next week. Their sons will be with them."

Anna had not seen Isabella and George Gibbs and their children since before the trouble with the rebels. Zephaniah's relatives had not been rude to her, but they treated her as if she weren't there. It made Anna feel as if she were still a slave. Zephaniah seemed oblivious to their treatment of her.

Two weeks later Anna greeted the Gibbs as they left their skiff. Zephaniah had ridden to the outskirts of the plantation.

"Welcome." Anna put on her friendliest, most confident smile. "Charles will show you to your rooms and have your luggage taken up. When you are rested, please come down to the great room for some refreshment. Zephaniah should be joining us by then."

Isabella looked her slowly up and down as if to say, "Are you still here?" Instead she said only, "Thank you."

She had not changed much since her last visit a few years before, Anna noted. She was a short, thin woman with sharp features. Her brown hair made a tight cap around her head, parted in the middle, with large coiled curls pulled to the back. Her brown eyes were small and deep set, and her mouth seemed always pursed in displeasure. Her husband was a contrast, tall and lanky with the beginnings of a pot belly.

Without saying a word, Isabella made Anna feel young and defensive. It infuriated Anna that anyone could make her feel that way. She drew herself up straight and tall and re-minded herself of her own royal blood and, most importantly, that she was a free person.

George nodded slightly at Anna as he turned and helped his wife up the stairs. The two boys, Kingsley and Zephaniah, stared at Anna. The last time she had seen them, they were small boys. At ten and twelve, they were growing tall and thin like their father.

As they sat at the massive dining table that evening, Anna looked at every detail and was pleased. The crystal chandelier cast a muted light over them, reflected in the gleaming dark wood of the table. Celia and Charles had set the table with Wedgwood china from Europe and new crystal goblets. Zephaniah had brought rich Madeira wine on his last voyage. Anna had arranged the menu. Celia's special turtle soup, followed by roast pork, clam fritters, new potatoes, early peas, biscuits, and a dessert of rich trifle. After dinner, they moved to the great room, excusing the boys to play outside. Mariah brought the three Kingsley children in to say good night.

"Zephaniah, we're thinking of moving to Florida," his sister told him after the children had left. "Do you think the troubles with the rebels are finally over?"

Zephaniah puffed on his clay pipe a moment before answering. "Yes, I really believe we are safe from them now. The last of these rebels have been chased from the area."

"I've been inquiring about the matter," George said. "Their original purpose was to agitate the plantation owners so they would want to become part of the United States. That will evidently happen soon anyway, so why would the rebels need to continue?"

"Exactly," replied Zephaniah.

The tension rose in Anna at those words. "So, we really will become part of the United States?" She tried to keep the emotion from her voice, but by the way everyone looked at her, she knew she hadn't disguised her true feelings.

"But that would be a good thing." Isabella looked at her harshly.

Anna's retort was brusque. "Not for me and our children."

"Now, Anna, don't upset yourself. We've talked about this. It won't happen for awhile, and even if it does, you will be safe from those laws that would threaten you and the children." Zephaniah shot her a warning look that let her know she should drop the subject.

The rest of the evening dragged for Anna. The idea of returning to slavery chilled her soul. A huge wave seemed to race towards her, and she could do nothing to save herself and the children from being caught in its fury. She had seen debris tossed about in the violent waves during a storm over the ocean. She did not want that to happen to her.

# Chapter Twenty-Six

*Kingsley Plantation*
*1820 – 1823*

The ripples had barely settled from the Gibbs' skiff leaving Kingsley Plantation when Anna flounced to Sophie's cabin.

Sophie clicked her tongue. "Well, I see you're mad about something. You might as well go on and tell me what's wrong, chile."

"It's that sister of his. She makes me so angry. She looks down that nose of hers and acts like I'm...I'm...dirt under her feet."

"Umhmm."

"The only time she speaks to me, it's to tell me to get something for her."

"Um hmm."

"And her husband. He never says a word."

"Maybe that's a good thing." Sophie smiled, but Anna rushed on.

"You would think Zephaniah would say something to her about it. But he just ignores the way she treats me."

"He probably isn't even aware of her behavior."

"That's what makes me so mad. I heard her talking about me. She said, "That black servant of yours, that negress from Africa.... she acts like I don't even have a name."

"Anta Majigeen, are you finished spewing?"

Anna sat back. "I guess so."

""Cuz, my dear Anna, that's all you can do about it. The Massa will never notice, nor pay any mind. And that sister of his, she'll never change. In her eyes, you'll always be the young slave that her brother bedded, nothing more."

"But...but I am of royal lineage and now I am a free woman...and...and"

"That doesn't matter to them, and it never will."

Anna's anger evaporated, and the hurt Isabelle's snubbing caused took its place. "That's not fair, Sophie."

Sophie smiled her calm smile and patted Anna's arm. "Now where did you ever hear about 'fair' for us? It will never happen."

"But...." Anna's shoulders slumped. "I know you're right. Isn't there something I can do?"

"Why, of course. You can come visit me and pour your anger out right here on my floor."

Anna smiled. "That's just what I'll do then."

The two friends laughed together, and Anna felt all her bad feelings slip away...and slide from Sophie's floor right out the door.

* * *

Anna and Zephaniah sat in compatible silence on the front porch of the main house watching the July evening steal its way around them. The sky softened from the strong blue of summer to a rosy, hazy covering. The water of the river darkened slightly, and the ripples from fish jumping could be seen as they tried to catch a low-flying bug for supper. The terns and egrets made their evening appearance. The children's voices could be heard as they played with some of the slave children, dashing about the yard catching fireflies. George, at fourteen, was almost too old for such activity, Anna thought. Martha and Mary, at twelve and ten, were children one day and trying to be young ladies the next.

Anna turned in her chair. "I have something to ask you."

"What is it, Anna?"

"We have accomplished a lot since we arrived here, haven't we?"

"Yes. We have restored this house to its original beauty, we have made great strides on the slave quarters, and I have followed your suggestion about their arrangement in a semi circle. Now the slaves are hard at work clearing more fields for planting, and we already have good crops of potatoes, corn, beans, and cotton, just like at Laurel Grove."

"We have also had a lot of visits from your family since we have made our home here. Isabella and her family were here recently, and Martha and her family not long before that."

"That is true. Has that been a problem for you?"

"No, not really a problem. But it has made me think that I should have my own place again, a place for the children and me. You have other co-wives now, Munsilna and Sarah. I don't want to be far away, or across the river as before. I was thinking of a house to the rear of this one. We could use the lower level for a kitchen, cook there, and bring the food to the main house. It is so crowded and difficult to cook below stairs here and bring the meals up to the dining room."

Zephaniah looked at Anna tenderly. "Is it so difficult for you to be here when I take someone else to my bed?"

Anna smiled at him. "No, Zephaniah. I grew up in a culture where a man had several wives. I have gotten over my youthful jealousy that I should be your only wife. I just think it would be better if we lived as people did back in Yang Yang. My father had a separate hut, and each wife and her children lived in a different hut around his."

"You always surprise me. I never know what you're thinking. I do want you to stay close because you are the one who oversees everything. I need you here to run the house and see to the food, but you also have such good ideas about the work of the plantation."

"Thank you. Then you'll agree? You'll build me a house?"

"Of course. How could I refuse you?"

Anna smiled in the darkness. Tomorrow she would show him house plans.

* * *

Within the year, the house was finished. Life on Kingsley Plantation continued with a rhythm of seasons, planting and harvesting, life going on, year after year. The only real cloud on the horizon which weighed on Anna's heart had been the threat of the United States taking over Spanish East Florida, and now that threat was a reality.

Anna made her way up the stairs to the observation deck on top of the main house. This secluded post had become her special place when she needed to get away and think about things. The past seven years had been wonderful ones for Anna, the most serene of her entire life. She had loved every day here on Ft. George's Island. Anna had known this day would come. Zephaniah had arrived home the night before with the news. He did not seem unduly alarmed. Whether or not that was to keep her from being frightened, Anna was not sure.

He had brought her the newspaper. The article told about Andrew Jackson coming into Pensacola. Anna could just see him. She pictured him sitting arrogantly on a big white horse. He was now governor of Florida, his appointment coming from President Monroe. The article told that five million dollars was paid to Spain, and Anna pictured it in bags of gold half-eagle coins, which was based on the Spanish model. How ironic that would be, she thought. The paper said that all Floridians could renounce their allegiance to Spain.

*I might have to renounce it publicly, but in my heart I will always feel a connection to Spain. It was a Spanish grant that gave me the first property that was really mine. Spain saved us when the rebels were about to attack my home place, and it was Spain that gave us sanctuary at San Nicolas. Spain gave a land grant on the east side of the St. John's River of 350 acres as a reward for my actions against the patriots. And now they expect me to pledge loyalty to the patriots?* Anna remembered from her days of capture that people could make you do things outwardly, but they could not control your heart, your soul.

Anna stood at the railing of the observation deck, the hot July sun radiating off her soft, yellow muslin dress. She looked over the plantation she had helped Zephaniah build. The sunlight shimmered on the lush tropical beauty of Florida. Her own house, referred to as "Ma'am Anna's house" now, stood off to the side, its tabby brick first floor and the wood frame second floor a visible statement of the security it provided. Anna surveyed the plantation from a 360-degree angle, took it all in and held it close to her heart.

She could see her hand in so much there. The palms she had urged Zephaniah to plant lined the long drive winding from the main house back to the fields and on to the ancient Indian village. They were growing fast, making a stately entrance. To the east, outside of the picket fence that boarded the three open sides of the main living quarters, stood a sturdy row of cedars. The barn stood just south of the cedars. Farther in that direction began the row of slave quarters with their gardens. Between those cabins and the Big House were the large vegetable gardens they relied on for their food. In the distance, Anna saw the fields of sugarcane, corn, and Sea Island cotton, just as they had grown at Laurel Grove. To the east were the beautiful orange groves, and beyond them the marsh with its grass dancing in the breeze. She turned all the way around and viewed the river and the dock, where there always seemed to be some kind of activity.

As she looked at all the bounty before her, tears came to Anna's eyes. *I cannot lose this. I cannot lose the land again.*

Through her tears, Anna saw Susan's small flat-bottomed boat being rowed toward their dock by two slaves. Susan nestled under a parasol. Over the years, their friendship had grown. Her arrival lifted Anna's spirits. She wiped her eyes and hurried down, anxious for any comfort her friend's visit might be able to give.

* * *

In the three years since the United States had obtained Florida, Anna's hopes had risen, only to be dashed like a strong ocean surf. In 1823, President Monroe surprised her by appointing Zephaniah to the Territorial Council, East Florida's legislative body. She had been sure that he could influence the law-making body to protect free blacks' freedom.

"This is very good for us," he had told her before he set off for the first session. "I know I can make them understand that just because a person's skin is black, he or she doesn't have to be in slavery. After all, it is in the interest of all of us to have some free blacks on our side. That can help in preventing the racial riots we fear."

"Racial riots? There is no talk here of racial riots."

"Perhaps not at Kingsley Plantation because we are very lenient with our slaves. But throughout the white population of Florida, there is a strong sense of fear. If the slaves decided to band together to overtake the whites, like what happened in Haiti years ago,..." Zephaniah shook his head.

"If the plantation owners would all treat their slaves well, there wouldn't be anything to be afraid of," Anna said firmly.

"That is true, but the whites, out of their fear, will probably make laws to keep the blacks from being able to form a revolt."

"Harsher laws do the opposite of what they should do."

Zephaniah smiled at her. "You are right, of course. I intend to use my position on the Territorial Council to make them understand." He turned to pack some papers from his desk. Anna walked out on the porch. Watching the moonlight on the river had the calming effect on her it always did. *I will have to trust Zephaniah to work this out.*

\* \* \*

With Zephaniah on the council, Anna felt that her freedom would not be in jeopardy. That sense of security lasted only until Zephaniah returned.

"It was worse than I ever imagined. No longer can free blacks come into Florida. They cannot gather together in large groups, nor carry guns. What will I do about Abraham? When I am not here, he is in charge of the slaves and the security of the plantation. He needs a gun."

Anna saw the anger in his eyes. Her emotion was not anger, but fear.

"I think things will get worse before they get better."

"Will I lose my freedom?" she asked.

"No, I do not think they can do that because you were free before the land was ceded."

"And the children? What about our children?"

"I believe the children will be safe, too."

Anna turned from Zephaniah and shivered. Would she ever be safe?

Zephaniah put his arms around her. "Do not be frightened. I told you I would keep you free, and I will. Each time I travel north I try to learn more about what we can do. I will keep you safe."

Anna felt his strength. Zephaniah had always been shelter for her. Perhaps she could trust him in this matter. Perhaps....

"Anna, stay with me tonight. I will make you feel safe. I will comfort you.

# Chapter Twenty-Seven

*Kingsley Plantation*
*1820 – 1829*

When Zephaniah returned from the next session of the Territorial Council, Anna waited until he was alone in his study before she knocked at the door and entered.

"Anna, come in." He looked up from his work with a smile.

"We must talk."

Zephaniah placed his pen down on the papers before him, and sat back. "What is it?"

"I am with child again."

"Anna, that's wonderful. It will be good to have a baby about again after so long a time."

"But, Zephaniah, think." She almost spat out the words. "This child will be born without the freedom that surrounds the other children. Can they say this child will be a slave?"

Zephaniah sat quietly. She knew the truth of what she said shocked him.

"Well, can they?" Her voice sounded bitter and angry.

"Anna." He chose his words carefully. "I must admit that it is possible. I will try to do more through the council. If I am not successful there, I will move you all to safety. It is something I have been thinking about."

"Move us? Leave here?" Now Anna was shocked. "Where would we go?"

Zephaniah looked at her with despair. "I do not know yet, but if the time comes, I promise you, I will have a place to take you."

Anna crossed her arms over her chest, as if in holding herself she could find comfort. *What I long for most is freedom and safety. Why must those things always be out of my reach?*

\* \* \*

Anna sat with Sophie on the steps of the house Abraham had built for his family. The early fall sunshine still carried the summer's warmth. Anna smiled as she felt the new life moving inside her.

"This is an active baby." She put her hand to her large abdomen to feel the fluttering kick. "Perhaps this will be a boy again."

"That would please Massa, wouldn't it?" commented Sophie.

"Yes, I think so. He has enjoyed teaching George about the plantation. With George turning eighteen next year, he could be able to take over the plantation if necessary."

Sophie sat for a few moments. "Anna, do you think we are safe? With the new laws, will Abraham and you and your children lose your freedom?"

"There is that chance, and it terrifies me. I counsel my girls to marry wealthy white men. With their education, their lighter skin, and Zephaniah's entrée into white society, those marriages are possible for them." She sighed. "But I have to put the fear of losing our freedom out of my thoughts. If it happens, I do believe that Zephaniah will get us all to safety somewhere."

"But where? Where could we find sanctuary?"

"I don't know. Every time he goes north now, he tries to learn more from the abolitionists."

"I have heard that word, but who are these abolitionists?"

"Zephaniah says it is a movement to end slavery that grew out of a religious...I think he called it a religious revival. It's been going on for awhile, but now the movement is getting bigger. The states in the north have been saying that slavery is illegal, that it's not right for someone to own another person. They're starting to write more about it and to gather together so their message will have more strength. Massachusetts was the first state to ban slavery, back even before I was born, so that's where a lot of people are who believe in freedom. When Zephaniah goes to Boston, Massachusetts, on business, he has met with some of those people, the abolitionists."

"But, he is a slave trader himself."

"No longer. He stopped when more and more places outlawed slavery."

"He keeps slaves for his plantations, though."

"Yes, because they are necessary for the economy of the plantation. But he is fair to his slaves. He allows them to buy their freedom at half their appraised value, and he frees those who have earned it. He freed Abraham. He freed me."

Sophie sighed. "I don't understand how he can have things both ways, have slaves and believe in abolition of slavery."

"I have slaves, too, don't forget. We, Zephaniah and I, don't believe that just because a person has black skin, he must be a slave. We believe slavery is necessary for some cultures, but only if we are fair to our slaves. It was the same in Africa, remember?"

Sophie shook her head. "I can't really understand it. I don't want Abraham to lose his freedom."

"Zephaniah will look out for us."

"If we have to flee from here, it will be hard."

Anna looked out at the beauty she had helped create stretching before them. "Harder than you know, my friend. I love this place with my whole heart. These years have been the best of my life. The children have been so happy. Except for the threat that hangs over our heads, I feel so much peace here. I can't let the worry take away from the joy, so I must not think about the possibility of losing it all."

The afternoon sun slipped from the sky as Anna made her way back to her house. The slight breeze whispered through the cedars and laurel oaks as she walked, and she stopped to listen and savor the moment.

\* \* \*

Anna had spent the morning planning the upcoming Thanksgiving meals for the extended family that seemed to surround Zephaniah. His three nephews had moved onto Kingsley Plantation, learning to run a plantation from their uncle in preparation for the day they, too, would be property owners. Zephaniah's sisters and their husbands were frequent visitors.

Anna was glad she had insisted on her own place, even if it was only sixty feet from the main house. "Ma'am Anna's House" suited her perfectly. Zephaniah took her to his bed less often. He had, in fact, taken up with Flora, the daughter of Abraham and Sophie. Flora already had one child by Zephaniah, and he had moved her and the baby to a plantation on Goodby's Creek.

Although it had been thirteen years since her last pregnancy, Anna recognized that the backache she had been bothered with all morning was moving into the pains of labor. Sophie and the midwife arrived quickly. The pains came faster and harder, and Anna no longer found herself thinking endearing thoughts about Zephaniah. In between the moans that wrenched from her body, she managed to tell Sophie, "I promise you. This is the last baby I will ever have."

Sophie patted her old friend. "You got your freedom from that last baby, Anta Majigeen, I don't know why you bothered with one more. I'm still hoping that he will give our Flora her freedom some day now. Maybe, he even will get around to me."

Anna always felt comfort when Sophie called her by her birth name. It brought Yang Yang a little closer. With the pains pulling her into a different reality, she could almost feel that she was back in her mother's round mud hut in Senegal, with her mother's gentle hands helping her instead of Sophie's and the midwife's. She could almost pretend that terrifying night of the tyeddo raid never happened, that none of it had ever happened, and that she was the wife of a tribal prince, and that....

"Push, Anna. Push now." ordered the midwife, bringing Anna back to the reality of Ft. George's Island.

Anna grasped Sophie's hand and squeezed as she pushed her hardest. She was exhausted from this labor, and she moaned as she felt herself torn apart. The sound of a lusty cry filled the ear, and Anna sank back in the bed, grateful her hardest work was done.

"It be a boy. He look fine," the midwife told her, as she placed the baby in Sophie's outstretched hands.

Anna leaned back against the pillow, exhausted. "Well, that will please Master Kingsley. Will you go tell him?"

"So, it's another boy." Zephaniah arrived a few hours later, settling himself by Anna's bedside.

"I thought you would be pleased. Have you thought about a name for him? Should we name this one Zephaniah?"

Zephaniah chuckled. "Oh, no, my dear. With my nephew here and myself, there are too many Zephaniahs as it is. No, I had thought we would name him John Maxwell Kingsley. What do you think?"

"That is a very impressive name. It will do well." She looked into the face of the sleeping child. He had the same creamy-coffee coloring as the other children, with the dark, curly hair that George had. He was the biggest of her babies, and Anna thought he would grow to be taller than his father and older brother.

"Things are going well in Florida now. I am thinking that this is the time to buy more plantations. What do you think?"

Anna handed the new baby to Mariah and thought a moment. "The situation is better as far as any trouble from rebels, and there is a lot of land available, but what about the race problem? You told me yourself when you came home from the last territorial council meeting that racial problems are getting worse."

"Yes, they are getting worse. I cannot seem to convince the council of the practicality of more lenient racial laws." He slammed his fist into his hand. "Don't they realize they are setting up a situation that will eventually lead to radical measures?"

"If you buy more plantations, you will need a lot more slaves to work them. Where will you get them? If you bring in a lot more slaves, our neighbors will worry about the possibility of an uprising, and then the council will make harsher and harsher laws against the blacks. John Maxwell will be in danger, if not all of us."

Zephaniah nodded his head slowly, measuring her words. "What you say is true. But, whether or not I buy more plantations, the laws will continue to go against you. Those plantations will be insurance for you and the children for the future. They will be your inheritance. When I go north the next time, I will inquire about a sanctuary for you, for all of you."

"The day will come. We have got to have a plan."

"We will. In due time, we will."

The next few years did not increase the urgency for action to protect themselves from racial discrimination. Anna rarely left Kingsley Plantation, and when she did, she went with Zephaniah, never alone. The three older children were almost adults now. George was nineteen, Martha seventeen, and Mary fifteen. Because of their light skin color and good education, they were accepted more readily. They were able to be part of the social scene among the plantation owners, and Anna was glad of that. George was starting to see a lot of Anatoile Vantrauvers, the beautiful daughter of a wealthy neighboring family. John Maxwell, at four years old, was content to play with the slave children at Kingsley Plantation. Life went on, and Anna waited, trying not to worry.

# Chapter Twenty-Eight

*Kingsley Plantation*
*1828*

Anna heard the news from one of the kitchen slaves. A few years before she would have heard the news from Sophie, but their paths did not cross as often. Sophie was uncomfortable around her since Zephaniah gave Flora a farm and three children. Anna didn't mind, however, about Zephaniah and Flora. Their relationship did not take away from what she and Zephaniah had.

"It be true, Ma'am Anna," Estelle, the slave, said. "Massa freed Sophie jus' three day ago, and today he done freed Flora."

"Well, it's about time."

"Yes, ma'am. Dat girl ain't old enough to be his granddaughter, and here dey jus' had a third baby."

"Now, Estelle, don't you go talking about Master Kingsley behind his back. What he does is no business of yours."

"Yes, ma'am." Estelle looked chagrined.

Charles appeared from the main house. "Anna, Miz Fatio be here, and Master Kingsley say fo' you to come fo' lunch now."

"Thank you, Charles. Please tell them I'll be right there." As Anna entered the formal dining room, Zephaniah and his guest rose to greet her. "Susan, I am so glad to see you. I wondered if we would have many visits now that you are married to Captain L'Engle."

"Oh, Anna, you know that wouldn't stop me from visiting my old friend."

Taking Anna's hands in hers, she kissed Anna on both cheeks. "I'll be the proper visitor by having lunch with Zephaniah too; then you and I can go off by ourselves and have a good visit."

Susan's laughter was like the tinkling of fine crystal to Anna. "I'm glad you're here." Anna took a seat at the mahogany table. She smiled at her friend, glad that they had remained close since the days at Fernandina and thinking what a lovely young woman Susan had become.

As they were finishing their meal of ham and peas, Anna picked up her fork and pointed at Zephaniah. "I understand that you have finally given Sophie her manumission paper." She daintily put the forkful in her mouth.

"Yes. You have been urging me to do that for years. I thought it was time."

"Time? Hmm. Let's see, this is 1828, and Sophie and I came to you in 1806, and you freed Abraham and me in 1811....Yes, I'd say it was time."

Anna was amused to see Zephaniah squirm. "Well, the important thing is I listened to you and granted her freedom."

"Oh, it was because you listened to me? I thought perhaps the fact that Flora had your third child might have something to do with it."

Zephaniah scowled, as Susan laughed her gentle laugh. "Now, Anna, don't tease Zephaniah. After all, he's an old man."

Zephaniah shook his head. "It is futile for me to take on both of you, so I will excuse myself. You ladies enjoy your afternoon visit." He stood and made a slight bow at each of them, and left the room.

Susan patted Anna's hand. "That was naughty of you to make him so uncomfortable." Her smile lighted up her face and brought creases to the corners of her sparkling blue eyes.

"I couldn't help myself. Sometimes, I just have to make him realize that I'm still here and know everything that goes on."

"Come. Let's go for a walk by the orange trees. It's a beautiful day."

The two friends walked arm in arm by the groves, then down to the river. The slaves at Kingsley Plantation had long since stopped being startled by a white woman and a black woman walking along in obvious friendship.

"Susan, I'm glad you came today. I was feeling lonely."

"Lonely? With all these people around you?"

"You know what I mean. We are seldom invited anywhere, and Zephaniah is gone much of the time. The children are full of their own activities and lives. Even Sophie and I rarely visit anymore."

"I know it is lonely for you, Anna. You can't be close to the slaves because you are acting as mistress of the plantation. Because you are black, you don't have friends among the whites."

Anna sighed and looked toward the river. "I sometimes feel that I don't belong anywhere. If it weren't for you, I wouldn't have anyone to talk to."

Susan took Anna's arm, and they resumed their stroll. "Don't be so gloomy. Tell me some more about Yang Yang." Anna put away her sad thoughts and let her mind go back to those long ago days in Senegal that seemed to fascinate Susan.

* * *

The demon which tormented Anna, the threat to her freedom and that of her children, was kept at bay for another year. Anna's life was full with the activities of the plantation and the lives of her children.

Anna looked over the scene at the family dining table. When they didn't have company, the table was set for only the family, and Anna liked it that way. George and John Maxwell sat at her left, Mary and Martha on her right, and, as usual, they were spending the meal whispering and giggling. George seemed unusually silent.

When she and Susan visited last week, Susan mentioned that the girls would soon be of a marriageable age. The thought saddened Anna. She knew John Sammis was interested in Mary, and Oran Baxter had begun seeing Martha. It was such a milestone. Her children might soon be away from her. She liked the young men, however, and knew they had no plans to leave the area. Oran's shipbuilding business was just getting started, and his acreage was near theirs. John Sammis had a store in town and a sawmill, in addition to his plantation.

"Anna," Zephaniah interrupted her thoughts. "You seem miles away. What were you thinking about?"

"Just that the children are almost grown-ups. It doesn't seem possible."

George cleared his throat nervously. "Speaking of that, I do have something to tell you."

They all looked at George.

"I...You know I have been seeing Anatoile Vantrauvers."

Anna nodded. George had their undivided attention.

"Well, I have asked her to be my wife...and she has accepted."

Zephaniah beamed. "Very good, son. She is an attractive girl."

Mary and Martha bounced out of their chairs and ran to their brother, hugging him from different sides. John Maxwell grinned and went back to eating.

Anna smiled her approval. "You have chosen a lovely young woman." She allowed a little chuckle to escape her lips. *And I thought he was taking ill. A wedding. How wonderful. I must write a note to Susan and tell her to come for a visit so I can share with her.*

Two weeks later, Anna greeted Susan warmly. "I've been so anxious for you to come. George and Anatoile are going to get married."

"I suspected as much from your note. Do you know when?"

"The first part of May. They will marry at St. John's Bluff."

"He will be a good husband. He has grown into such a fine young man, and has learned from his father – and from you – about running a plantation. You should feel very proud."

"I do feel good about him. About Martha and Mary, too. I ....I feel a little...uncomfortable, though."

"What is it, Anna?"

"You know I have never felt accepted by white society. What if they snub me at the wedding? I don't want to put George in a difficult position. Should I not attend? But I couldn't bear that."

"Listen to me. You are accepted as Zephaniah's wife. You are George's mother. Of course, you must go to the wedding. No one will snub you. If someone does, just remember you are an African princess and snub right back."

Anna laughed. "You always make me feel that life is simpler than I make it. Thank you."

"You have been through so much in your life. You won't have any trouble handling George's wedding."

* * *

Anna knocked on the door of Zephaniah's study. "You are working late tonight. I brought you some hot chocolate."

Zephaniah looked up from the papers strewn about his desk, put his quill in his special crystal inkwell, and ran a hand through his graying hair.

"Thank you. I lost all sense of time."

"What are you working on?" She sat in the chair beside his desk.

"A treatise I want to publish. I am hoping that by putting my thoughts in writing, I will make them clearer, make the legislators see the sense of my proposal."

"Your proposal about...?"

"About slavery. About race. Of course, I support slavery. It is absolutely vital to the economy of our area. We could not possibly grow cotton, sugarcane, and tobacco without slave labor. But because people are colored should not mean that they must be a slave. My proposal is that we have three layers of people. There should be the ruling white class, the slave class, and, in between, a class of free blacks to act as a...as a buffer between the other two classes. That will avoid concerns about uprisings from the slaves. It is so obvious to me. Besides that, it strengthens the races when Negro strength is added to the bloodlines of a white family. I cannot understand why they reject my ideas."

Anna patted his hand. "Why don't you come and get some rest now. You can write your treatise tomorrow."

"We are running out of time. I must make them see, and soon. The latest laws say that even if black persons are freed, they have thirty days to leave Florida or be sold back into slavery. Do you realize what that means? If the laws consider John Maxwell a slave because he was born after Florida became part of the United States, and I granted him his freedom, we would have to send him away within thirty days. This is our five-year-old son we're talking about, Anna. Our son."

Anna reached for Zephaniah. "Then do what you must. Do everything you can."

# Chapter Twenty-Nine

*Kingsley Plantation*
*1832 – 1835*

Anna felt the need to get away from everyone, to lose herself
in the beauty of nature as she had done when they first began
rebuilding Kingsley Plantation. Walking past the mulberry
trees by the side of the house and through the picket fence
gate, she circled the large vegetable garden, feeling pride in its
bursting produce.

The late summer heat had made the palm-lined lane
dusty, and her feet stirred up swirls as she walked. She passed
the semi-circle of slave cabins and thought of going to the end
of the row where Sophie and Abraham had built their house
but decided she'd rather be alone.

Her mind wandered as she walked. *I want to remember
everything about this place. I want to fill my heart with the images,
remember all the scent of jasmine and honeysuckle and orange blossoms in the spring. I want to remember the sound of the river lapping
on our shore; the gulls calling raucously; the children playing around
the slaves' cabins; the honeybees swarming. I don't ever want to forget
the feel of the heat of our summers, or running through the misting
rain.*

The slaves working in the field of Sea Island cotton
looked up as she walked by, but she did not notice. She
paused at the ancient Indian village ruins. *I wonder why you
had to leave.* Her imagination spoke to the ghosts from that

place. *How did you feel about leaving this place?*

She walked past the now-diminished mounds of oyster shells, along the low sand hills that outlined the shore. She sat on a piece of abandoned driftwood and gazed toward the shimmering brightness that was the ocean. A trio of brown pelicans glided in a line inches above the water. *It's hard to imagine far across this water there is another home, my Senegal. I can barely remember it. Strange. I think of this as my home now.* A sob caught in her throat. *And I must lose it, too.*

Anna sat in silent thought a while longer, sighed, and started back to the house. She caught sight of a gray fox running through the scrub oaks. As she approached the lane, Sophie hurried toward her. She quickened her step.

"I've been looking for you."

"What is it? What's wrong?"

"It's Celia. She hasn't been doing good lately, and she's asking for you. I think she's dying."

Anna hurried to the cabin that Celia had moved into when she became too old to take care of the Big House. For the last few years, the elderly slave had lived comfortably, spending her days sitting in an old rattan chair in front of her quarters, bossing anyone who would pay attention.

Anna stopped a moment to adjust her eyes to the dimness inside the cabin. Several of the women moved away from the bed as Anna approached.

"Celia," Anna murmured to the tiny wisp of a woman lying under the quilt. "It's me, Anna."

The old woman opened her eyes. Her toothless mouth seemed to turn up in a smile. "Anna," she whispered hoarsely.

"I'm here. Are you in pain?"

Celia barely shook her head. "When you...first come.... I....I know'd I...was hard...hard on you, chile."

"It's all right, Celia."

"I....I done it...to hep you....to hep you grow up...and.... and be strong."

"I know that now, Celia. I understand."

"You...you...be strong...now, ya hear?"

"I will, Celia. I'll be strong like you taught me to be. Now you rest. Don't worry about anything."

The old woman closed her eyes, and her shallow breathing became weaker. Anna held on to her hand until its strength seemed to melt away, and the coolness of it turned colder.

"She's gone now," Sophie said.

Anna looked up at Sophie. In that moment, she again felt like that lost and lonely thirteen-year-old that Celia had badgered so long ago. She turned back to the lifeless form on the bed and remembered those final words. *I will be strong for you, Celia. I can do that. I remember.* She stood and gently pulled the quilt over Celia's head.

"We'll bury her in the plot behind my house." As Anna walked home, her mind filled with images of other losses: her parents, those who died on the trek to Rufisque, Madu. She shook her head to rid her mind of those heartbreaking times. This death was different. Celia was an old woman and she had lived a full life. Still, there was something about any loss that had a thread connecting it to all the others, and her heart filled with sadness. Every loss made her feel alone and vulnerable.

\*\*\*

Anna and John Maxwell sat on the front veranda of the Big House trying to eke out any coolness from the river breezes. "Look at that pelican, Mama. He's trying for a fish."

Anna smiled as she watched the heavy, awkward bird. She looked across the yard toward the river and saw a small sailboat approaching. "I think your father's coming."

Zephaniah tied his boat to the dock and hurried toward them. He mounted the steps quickly, slapping a newspaper against his thigh. "Anna, come to my study for a moment please." He only brushed his hand lightly over John Maxwell's head as he passed. Anna, puzzled, rose to follow him. John Maxwell started to say something, but Anna patted his shoulder signaling him to be still and to stay behind.

"Look at this." He thrust the newspaper in Anna's hands, went around to his side of the massive desk, and slumped into his chair. He ran his hand through his hair, a sign Anna recognized as agitation.

Anna sat in the chair by the desk as she began reading. The headline blared: "Slave Rebellion in Virginia! Many killed!"

"Look at that, Anna! This Nat Turner had sixty followers, and they killed fifty-eight whites. Fifty-eight! And they were mostly women and children. Think what that will do to race relations."

"Yes. Yes, I understand, Zephaniah. But, except for Nat Turner, they have captured and killed all the slaves who were involved, and, from this report, they have killed a lot more innocent ones, too."

"But that's just it, Anna. Don't you see? Now, whites everywhere are frightened. If there were an uprising here, they would randomly kill any blacks."

"But the threat is over. Why are you so upset by this?"

"Think, Anna. Nat Turner hasn't been captured yet. Everyone will imagine that he is coming to their area to lead their slaves in revolt. The extra fear is the spark needed to inflame those here who are so frightened of a slave revolt. Now, they will have reason to pass even harsher laws against blacks. This could be the last straw for us...for you and the children....for my other wives."

"So, the time is closing in on us, isn't it? We have to make definite plans to leave."

"I'm afraid so." He slumped back in his chair and closed his eyes.

*There is nothing more to say.* She laid the paper on his desk and walked out. Her heart felt a sadness that seemed to take over her whole body. She felt heavy as she walked.

At the front door, she heard voices. John Maxwell was talking with someone. "Phenda. Mr. Fraser. What a surprise. It has been such a long time since we have seen you."

"Anna." Phenda moved to Anna and embraced her. Mr. Fraser nodded in her direction. Phenda, as usual, dressed in the latest style of the day. Her dress of pale blue had ribbons of beige running through it. The sleeves fitted closely on her forearm and billowed widely at the top. The bodice seams were piped with an ecru fabric. A white linen capelet completed her outfit.

Anna admired her friend's good taste. "Come in. Zephaniah just arrived, and he will be so glad to see you again. Come to the living room and have a seat."

As they moved to the brocade sofa, Zephaniah joined them. "I thought I heard your voices. What brings you this far upriver?"

"Some serious decisions," Mr. Fraser replied.

The smile left Zephaniah's face. "Let me order some refreshment first." He rang for Charles and tea.

Phenda turned to Anna and took her hand. "It has been so long since we've had a good visit. At least our letters have kept us in touch. John Maxwell seems well. How are the others?"

Anna's spirits lifted and she smiled. "They are all well. George and Anatoile are expecting their second child soon."

Zephaniah interrupted. "Tell us of your 'serious decisions,' John."

Mr. Fraser sighed. "I have sold all my holdings in Florida. We are moving to the north. These restrictive laws are too much for us. Phenda and I are legally married, yet she is treated as a non-person here. It is obvious that we cannot change things." He paused. "Why don't you think about joining us?"

Zephaniah and Anna exchanged a glance. "It is impossible for me." Zephaniah's voice was firm. "I have too many plantations and too many responsibilities here."

"And too many wives," Phenda said under her breath. The truth brought a smile to Anna's lips.

"We are making plans, of course. I have decided to go to Haiti. If I can find suitable land, I will establish a free black colony there for Anna and the others."

"We have heard of President Boyer's offer. You know, I'm sure, that the land there has been abandoned, divided, and run down. I am not sure you will find anything to be salvaged."

"We will see."

Charles arrived with a tray of cool tea and slices of Sally Lunn cake. As Anna distributed the refreshments, conversation turned to local news and lighter topics, but Anna sensed the pall that had fallen. The visit did not last much longer. *Was Zephaniah making the best decision for us? My life, as always, is in his hands.*

\* \* \*

Anna's thoughts the rest of the week were of her daughters. *I know we will have to leave, and that means leaving Martha and Mary behind. How can I? They are married with homes of their own, but they are still my daughters. When they come for their weekly visit, I must tell them, prepare them.*

The skiffs eased up to the dock in the early afternoon. Anna stood waiting on the veranda of the Big House. She had a sitting room in her house, but preferred visiting with guests in the comfortable parlor of the Big House.

"Mama!" Mary rushed up the steps and kissed her mother's cheek. "Did you hear about Nat Turner's revolt? Isn't that the scariest thing?"

Martha kissed her mother. "Mary, you're always so excitable. Calm down and give Mama a chance to say hello."

"Come and sit, girls. Tell me how you are."

"But," Mary took her mother's arm and led her into the parlor. "What do you think about that? Do you think there will be a slave revolt here?"

The three sat on the sofas facing each other: Anna, dark and dramatically contrasted to the pale sofa, and the two girls, equally pretty with their soft *café-au-lait* coloring on the other sofa.

"No, I don't think there will be a slave revolt here. We treat our slaves well. They can earn their freedom. They live in family units. They have no reason to revolt."

"But, what if that Nat Turner comes here and tells our slaves a bunch of lies? He's a preacher, they say. He might get them all stirred up."

"Mary, for heaven's sake. That's enough." Martha shook her head.

"What scares me, though is....Would the slaves rise up against us because we own them, or...or, would the white people go around killing us because we're black, like those white folks did in Virginia?"

"My darling girl." Anna leaned forward and took Mary's hand in her own. "It is hard to live between both races as you have had to do. But these fears you have....these are things you do not need to worry about. You married a strong, influential white man when you married John Sammis. He has a lot of power in this area. No one is going to harm you, or Martha either."

Martha turned to Mary. "See, I told you."

Anna folded her hands in her lap and took a deep breath. "Your father and I have been talking. The end result of this slave rebellion probably will be harsher laws. We must think of George and your little brother. It will soon be time for us to move to a safer place."

"Move?"

Martha, with tears in her eyes, asked, "You would leave here?"

Anna nodded. The catch in her throat made speaking difficult.

"Where would you go, Mama?" Tears were already streaking down Mary's cheeks.

"Your father is going soon to investigate Haiti. We have a chance to build a free black colony there."

The girls knelt on each side of their mother, their arms around her waist. Anna held each of the girls to her and kissed them. The afternoon sunlight streamed through the windows and poured itself on them, highlighting them as a tableau, a picture of grief.

\* \* \*

"You are so quiet today, Anna," Susan L'Engle said. They were walking together on the rose-scented path. Both were dressed in cool organdy dresses, Anna's a striking white against her dark skin and Susan's a pastel green.

The two friends sat in the oak chairs on the wide veranda of the Big House, sipping their drinks and fanning themselves while they chatted. Anna held the chilled glass to her cheek. She found solace in her pink and red roses bright against the green leaves, her lantanas and daisies. *Can I leave all this?*

Look at the children down at the river." Susan nodded toward them. "It's good to hear children laughing and playing."

"Yes, and John Maxwell loves to be the leader. See how the younger ones follow him?"

"He is so much like Zephaniah, isn't he?"

"I think so. John Maxwell will accomplish whatever he sets out to do."

"I am looking forward to when John and I have a family."

"I'm sure that...."

Anna was interrupted by a piercing scream from the children at the riverside. *What is it? What's happening?* She was frantic as they raced to the river. *John Maxwell! Please don't let it be John Maxwell!*

# Chapter Thirty

*Kingsley Plantation*
*1835*

Anna pushed through the cluster of children and gasped in horror as she saw John Maxwell falling to his knees, crying in anguish and holding an arm hanging helplessly at his side.

"What happened?" Anna yelled.

The children moved away from him, their eyes wide with terror.

"What happened? Tell me!" Anna screamed at them as she knelt by her child. John Maxwell writhed in pain.

"A snake, Ma'am Anna," one whispered hoarsely. "Sally done picked up a snake, and John Maxwell grabbed it 'fore it bit her."

"A snake. What kind of a snake?" She held the sobbing John Maxwell to her as she tore his sleeve open. The wound was already swelling and turning red.

"Where is the snake?" Susan asked.

The little boy who had spoken up pointed to the river.

"Was it sort of tan and pinkish, with diamond markings?" Susan continued.

The little boy nodded.

Anna's heart was racing with fear. "It must have been a copperhead!"

"Mama! Mama!" John Maxwell screamed between sobs. "My arm! Help me!"

She reached deep within for control. "Susan, can you help me carry him to the house? Sammy, run and get Sissy. Tell her what happened and tell her to come to the Big House. Now!"

The children ran toward the slave quarters as Anna and Susan made a seat with their hands and helped John Maxwell into it, his cries of pain tearing into Anna's soul. "You'll be all right, darlin'. You'll be all right," Anna murmured over and over to him. Her heart raced with fear as they staggered to the house.

Joseph appeared from the fields and gathered the child into his strong arms. Susan grasped Anna's arm and followed.

"Put him on the sofa," Anna breathlessly ordered. Sissy was coming in through the back door as Joseph laid John Maxwell down.

"It was a snake. A copperhead, I think," Anna told Sissy. Her voice broke with anguish.

"It hurts so bad, Mama! Help me!"

Anna felt as though her heart was being wrenched from her body. The agony of seeing her child in pain was worse than any physical pain she had ever endured. Anna stroked his head as Sissy examined the wound.

"Bring me hot water and soap, quick now!" the midwife ordered Joseph. She opened her bag and brought out a shiny knife. John Maxwell's eyes grew huge with fright, and he began screaming louder, trying to pull away.

"What are you going to do?" Anna's voice was frantic. She reached to hold her son.

"I gots to make a cut and get out de poison. You wants to save your boy, don' you? Hold him still now."
Susan held his legs as Anna held his upper body close to her. "We have to do this, son. I'm sorry!" She tried to shield his eyes from the knife cutting into his tender, young skin. His screams ripped through Anna.

"Dat's all the cutting, now. It be over." Sissy bent over

the arm and began sucking at the wound. She spit away the
blood into a rag again and again.

Joseph returned with a basin of water, soap, and towels.
Sissy took them and wiped her face and rinsed her mouth.
She spat into a towel, then cleaned the wound. "Now, I makes
a poultice for him, and I gives him some special tea to ease de
pain." She worked with powders and leaves from her pack.

"Will he be all right?" Anna barely dared to ask.

"Too early to say. A copperhead bite ain't usually kill un,
but he jus' a boy. De poison may ruint his arm. We jus got to
do de bes' we can and leave it to de Lord."

Anna held John Maxwell close as his sobs began to
subside. She felt limp with fear. Word traveled fast. Mariah
and Sophie ran into the room. Mariah put her hand to her
mouth, stifling a gasp, and Sophie came to Anna and put her
hand on Anna's shoulder. Anna looked from Sophie's face
to Susan's and felt the support in their glances. She drew
strength from them.

\* \* \*

Anna awoke in the chair beside John Maxwell's bed. Susan
had left with the promise of trying to reach Zephaniah on
his trip to his other plantations. Sophie and Mariah sat with
Anna all night as John Maxwell slipped into semi-conscious-
ness.

Anna looked carefully at her son's face in the gray light
of dawn as she stretched to get the cramps out of her legs and
back. John Maxwell's eyes were closed and his forehead lined
with pain, his skin the color of cold ashes. His hands opened
and closed, and he continued his moaning. Anna gulped
back the sobs in her own throat. Her white organdy dress
was wrinkled and stained with blood and dirt. Her hands
trembled and she shivered. *If only I could take this pain from
him! I would gladly bear it myself. Father God, you're supposed to be*

*with us. Why didn't you look out for John Maxwell? Please...please help him now.*

Sophie came to the bedside and stroked John Maxwell's hair.

"Sophie, I can't bear to see him like this."

"I know, Anta Majigeen. I know." Sophie moved her hand from the boy's head to Anna's. "You're strong. You'll be all right."

"But will he?" Despair spilled over into her voice. Anna heard Zephaniah's voice calling through the house late that night. "Where is he? Where is my son?" The sound of boots running up the stairs echoed. Zephaniah hurried through the room. "Oh, my God." He put his hand on his son's cheek, and John Maxwell stirred. "He's burning up with fever. How bad is it?"

Anna shook her head. "I don't know. Sissy says he's fighting the poison. She puts a new poultice on every few hours and tries to get him to drink this concoction to ease his pain. But, he hasn't spoken since yesterday. I'm scared. I'm really scared." Without taking her eyes off John Maxwell, she reached her hand to Zephaniah. He clasped it tightly, caressing her shoulder with his other hand.

"Susan sent one of her slaves to find me. I was at Deep Creek. I sent him on with a note to the doctor in Jacksonville. He should be here soon, and then, maybe, we'll know more."

"It was a snake, Zephaniah, a copperhead."

"I know. Susan's note told me. She said he grabbed the snake to save Sally. The child didn't know the danger, but he knew. If the snake had bitten her, tiny as she is, she would have died, but John Maxwell saved her. My God."

Zephaniah gently pulled back the quilt that covered John Maxwell, revealing the wounded arm for the first time. He gasped when he saw the hugely swollen black limb.

Anna's lip trembled, but there were no more tears. She

took the quilt and covered John Maxwell again. She turned
to Zephaniah and buried her head against his chest. He
held her and bent his head against hers. She could feel his
anguish, and their pain became shared, not lessening, but
somehow becoming more bearable.

The doctor arrived in the early dawn. He looked exhausted. "A difficult delivery of a breech baby," he said.

Anna did not ask if the baby had lived. *I do not want to
hear any words of death.*

He examined the arm. "Your midwife has done all that
can be done. Most copperhead bites are not fatal. It's a sort
of warning from the snake. He doesn't want to waste all his
venom on a mere person."

Anna relaxed a little. She hadn't realized she held her
breath as she waited for the doctor's prognosis.

"If he can make it through the next twenty-four hours, I
think that he will live. But, he may lose his arm. We'll just
have to wait and see."

Anna felt herself swirling into an abyss. *Lose his arm?*

Zephaniah grabbed her shoulder, but she thought it was
more to steady himself than her. Then he seemed to gain his
composure and turned to show the doctor out.

* * *

The week dragged on like a slow nightmare to Anna. If she
ate, she did not know it. Sophie and Mariah took turns bringing food and urging her to eat. She stayed by John Maxwell's
bed as he eased back into consciousness. Zephaniah was in
and out of the room every few hours. Susan visited several
times, bringing tempting morsels to encourage Anna to
swallow something. Mornings came with a rosy glow to the
room. The days followed with sunlight flooding through
the windows, but Anna never noticed. The evenings muted
the light to a soft yellow and blue, but the nights shrouded

the room in darkness except for a single candlelight by John Maxwell's bed.

For several days, the arm did not change. No worse, but no better. Anna read book after book to John Maxwell, told him stories, sang to him, anything to take his mind off his pain.

"Tell me about Yang Yang," he begged. "Tell me some of the old stories."

"I will tell you the legend of my favorite tree, the baobab tree. When I was a child, I heard this often from the *griot*, the village's historian and the one who knew all the legends. In the beginning days of creation, the Great God created a beautiful place called Africa. Everything about it was perfect, like a carefully made garden. There were majestic mountains, tumbling rivers, flowers and trees, everything beautiful. Then God went back home and looked over it all. He was so happy with everything he saw." She paused and smiled at John Maxwell, and he managed a wan smile.

"Then God noticed he had forgotten one little area. There was a small space left undone. It was only sand. 'Oh, my,' he said. 'I must do something about that.'" Anna used a deep voice, and her son chuckled softly.

"And so, he decided to make the biggest, most beautiful trees to fill up this empty space of sand. Oh, they were marvelous. No one had ever seen such beautiful, majestic trees. Well, of course, the Devil heard about these special trees, and he decided to come steal them. Now, God was not about to let that happen. He looked around at where he could hide the trees, but there was no place to hide them. They were so big, they would stick out wherever He put them. 'What should I do?' God said to Himself. Then he had an idea. 'That's it!' he exclaimed. 'I know just what to do so that old Devil won't find my trees.' And do you know what he did?"

"Tell me."

"Well, he took those trees and turned them upside down.

He stuck the beautiful part deep in the sand so no one could see it, and only the bare roots stuck up in the air. And that's why the baobab tree looks like it does. Remember, I drew you a picture? The branches are all gnarly, and they stay leafless nine months of the year."

John Maxwell smiled at his mother. "That's a good story, Mama. That baobab is a funny-looking tree."

Anna smoothed back his hair. She remembered her running toward that lone tree at the edge of her village, hoping for sanctuary. Her mind flashed back to the last image she had of it, silhouetted in front of the haze of smoke.

"Mama, why are you looking so sad?"

Anna struggled away from the memory. *That sadness ambushes me. I can see those branches as plainly as if it were yesterday.*

# Chapter Thirty-One

*Kingsley Plantation*
*1835 – 1837*

Zephaniah spread the map on his desk. "Anna, this is all of Haiti. I will sail to this port, Puerto Plata, here." He pointed with a slender finger. "I have arranged for a horse and will travel throughout this area," he gestured again. "I will take as long as is necessary to find a good location. There must be good soils there. Look at these rivers. Consider the sugar export that used to come out of there....and timber. A lot of people don't realize the value of harvesting trees. It has brought us a lot of wealth here." He put his arm around her shoulder. "This can be an exciting new venture for us."

She smiled. In the past, it had been easy to get caught up in his enthusiasm, but they were older now. Although he hadn't seemed to age much to Anna, he had passed his seventieth birthday. "I know we must do this, but do not think it is an easy thing for me. We have lived here for over twenty years, the longest I have lived in one place. Our youngest son was born here; our children reached adulthood and married here. I will be leaving my daughters behind. I have put my hand and my heart into this soil, planted these gardens." She paused as her voice caught in her throat. "Do not think this is an easy thing."

Zephaniah took her in his arms and stroked her face gently. "I know that. But I must keep you safe, you and the children. I made that promise to you, and I will keep it. Trust me."

Anna pulled back and looked into his eyes. "I will try."

* * *

The heat of late September shimmered from the observation deck of the Big House as Anna scanned the plantation she loved. She wondered what Zephaniah was seeing in Haiti. She chided herself for her impatience to know the future. The last of the late summer roses were exclamation points against the drying wire-like grass of the yard. The river flowed gently to the ocean, and an osprey dove for its meal. The oleanders still waved their vibrant pink-flowered branches when a slight breeze went by. *It all looks so calm, so peaceful. But my life is that only on the surface. Inside, I am churning. I do not want to leave this place, my place. I am tired of a life where I have no choices.*

A small boat approached. She recognized Susan's vessel and hurried down to meet her friend.

"Have you heard from Zephaniah?" Susan asked as they settled on the porch with their tea.

"Not yet. It is a little early for a letter. He's been gone only a couple of weeks."

"And John Maxwell...is he completely recovered?"

Anna smiled. "He is out riding his horse. We are so fortunate, Susan. He has only a scar from where Sissy had to cut him. I still shudder every time I think of it."

Susan laughed. "So he has recovered, but you haven't quite?"

"That is so true."

Susan looked out at the peaceful scene. "If only this were the whole world. There is so much hatred and anger and fear out there in the world. Why can't it all be like this?"

Anna's laugh was bitter. "Those are my questions."

"You are my friend and have been for almost twenty-five

years. We have good conversation. We can share together. I am never aware that your skin is a different color. So, why does it make such a difference in the outside world?"

"Since Nat Turner's rebellion four years ago, people are even more frightened. Zephaniah says that now with the Seminoles and free blacks joining together and raiding plantations, things will get even worse."

"They are already getting worse. John brought me a newspaper yesterday. I thought you might not have heard since Zephaniah isn't here."

"Heard what?"

"The latest laws are forbidding anyone to teach blacks how to read or write."

Anna gasped with indignation. "Not teach them? They will trap them forever in slavery. How can they?...How can they keep tightening the shackles they have us in? The time has come. I must leave soon."

\* \* \*

Anna stood at the dock as the late fall sun eased across the sky. Zephaniah's letters were enthusiastic and informative, but she longed to hear his voice. Slaves secured the heavy ropes from the three-masted schooner, and Zephaniah bounded down the gangplank.

"Anna, I have much to tell you. You will be pleased."

John Maxwell ran from the house and skidded to a stop in front of his father. He had meant to give his father a hug, but now he wasn't quite sure what to do. He held out his hand to Zephaniah. His father pulled him close for a hug. "Have you saved any more little girls while I've been gone?"

"No, sir."

The dining table was full that evening with Zephaniah, Anna, John Maxwell, George, and Anatoile. John and Mary Sammis and Oren and Martha Baxter joined them to hear

Zephaniah's report on Haiti. "It's a beautiful country, full of promise. I sailed into Puerto Plata and rode horseback all over the land. Fall is the end of the rainy season, but I fared well enough."

"Do you see possibilities for us there?" George asked. He hadn't even touched his cream of leek soup.

"I do. There were huge plantations that have lain fallow since the slave rebellion. Most of the land that had been cultivated has been divided up into small family farms. The economy of the country will never recover that way."

"What do you think of President Boyer?" asked John Sammis. "Do you think he is leading the country back?"

"A good question." Zephaniah leaned back in his chair as the two kitchen slaves cleared the soup course and brought out venison, baked squash, and potatoes. "I met with him at the palace, and, believe me, I asked a lot of questions. He's established a Rural Code to try and get the big farms going again, but, frankly, I don't think the people have the enthusiasm to do more than eke out their bare living on small plots of land. That's why the opportunity is there for us. Haiti is the only Free Black Republic in this hemisphere. We can grab the land, and with a number of freed slaves from our plantations here, we can establish a productive, rich colony that will sustain you all."

Zephaniah made an expansive gesture with both hands. The glow from the crystal chandelier softened the gathering. Zephaniah's eyes sparkled with excitement. "You will be safe, my dear family. You will finally be safe." He picked up his fork and began to eat.

"Father, I heard that they have voodoo there. Did you see any witches?" Mary made the rest of the family smile. She always found the most dramatic element of any situation.

Zephaniah laughed heartily. "The religion of the country is Roman Catholic, Mary. But," he winked at her, "they tell me that many of the people also practice voodoo."

"Really?"

"Yes, but I learned that voodoo is not the black magic we think of. It's based on family spirits that the people have to feed with rites of food and drink from time to time. Those who can talk to the spirits and tell us what they want are called *houngan*, a man, or *manbo*, a woman. I never met any while I was traveling."

"How soon....," Martha began, on the verge of tears. She cleared her throat. "How soon will you be going back?" She reached for her husband's hand.

Zephaniah glanced at Anna, then at Martha. "It will take me some time to gather all the supplies we need; also, I will have to arrange to obtain title to the land. I would guess by late next summer we will be ready. I will go first with George and a number of freed slaves to do the building and clearing. Then, in a year or two, everything will be ready for the rest of the colony to come over." He glanced again at Anna. "Your mother and I have not had time to talk yet."

The meal continued with silence from the women at the table and bursts of questions from George and John Maxwell, George's questions about the land and John Maxwell's about the strange things he had heard about the island. "Do they really have giant lizards, Father?"

"Is it true that deadly cyclones wash over the island?"

"Do the people run around naked?"

After apple tart dessert, Zephaniah rose. "I am very tired from the trip. Anna, let us talk in the morning."

\* \* \*

After breakfast, Anna walked to Zephaniah's study. He had obviously been up early and was anxious to get on with his business.

"Anna, I have so much to tell you." He laid aside the papers he was working on.

"I have found a wonderful piece of property, 35,000 acres. It's called Mayorasgo de Koka. It's not far from where I landed at Puerto Plata, between there and the Yasica River. There have been successful sugar plantations in the region in the past, so I will want us to plant sugarcane and cotton. Our citrus crop will do well there also, and I know the rich coastal soil will be productive for vegetables you choose to plant. There are lush flowers growing everywhere and palms."

"It sounds like a beautiful place, but what of the politics? Do you really believe it will be a sanctuary for us?"

"I do, or I would never send you so far from Mary and Martha...and me."

Anna looked at him in surprise. They had a long history, and an intense one, but he now had three other wives and eight other children.

"That surprises you? It shouldn't. I've told you before, I have other co-wives now, but you are the only one who has always been more than simply a mistress, a co-wife. You helped me run Laurel Grove, and we built up Kingsley Plantation together. You have been a real partner to me, Anna. I've always been able to rely on your strength."

"I hadn't thought about....I mean, I thought you would be there with us," Anna faltered as the reality that Zephaniah would remain in Florida hit her.

Zephaniah looked at her tenderly. "George will be there to look out for you, and I will come to visit as often as I can, but someone must be here to take care of all the properties." He leaned back in his chair and seemed to be looking into the past. "I remember still my first look at you. Only thirteen, you stood so proud and regal, even on the slave block."

"That was so long ago." She remembered Bella's words to her, *No matter what they do to you on the outside, no one can touch your soul, your inner strength.* Anna let her thoughts dwell there. *That has been true. Inside myself is the only place I can find the security I crave.*

"Tell me about the political climate of Haiti, Zephaniah. Can we be sure things will not change?

"One can never be absolutely sure. You know that. Haiti has a history of turmoil, which, I believe, they are trying to change by making the country a free black republic."

"What about their history?"

"Their history goes back to Christopher Columbus. They say that when he landed there, he thought he had found India, and so he called the natives 'Indians.' They were really Tainos, which means "men of good" because they were a gentle, friendly people. Spain took over and raped the land of its gold and used the Tainos as slaves to mine it. The Tainos were wiped out. The Spaniards started importing blacks to be slaves. France and Spain fought back and forth for control of the island for years.

Anna listened quietly, trying to picture the history.

"Things were bad for slaves for hundreds of years. The slaves finally had enough and staged a rebellion. I think it was in 1791. They killed whites and chased off those they didn't kill. That's when Haiti became a black state and slavery was abolished. That was just about the time you were born. The leaders since then haven't helped the country economically, and it hasn't rebounded since the revolt."

"Why have conditions stayed that way?"

"A number of reasons, I think. The people seem content to plant and cultivate just their own little gardens. A bigger reason, according to President Boyer, is that his predecessor, Dessalines, agreed to pay France 150 million francs if they would recognize Haiti as a free, independent nation. That took all the country's money.

"And you think we could be prosperous there?"

"I have no doubt about that, Anna. The land I have in mind is good, and there is access to mahogany and cedar forests. The money we will make from Mayorasgo de Koka will support you, our sons, my other families, and dozens of slaves I will free to work the plantation."

"I am satisfied. John Maxwell and I will be ready to go when you tell us to."

"Anna." He got up from his chair and came around his desk. Taking Anna's arms, he lifted her from her chair to stand in front of him. He looked deep into her eyes as he pulled her to him and held her close. "Anna."

It was enough.

# Chapter Thirty-Two

*Kingsley Plantation*
*1837 – 1838*

In May, honeybees swarmed around the Mandarin orange trees as Anna walked to Sophie's house, hoping a visit with her old friend would settle her spirits. The two sat on the front steps enjoying the sunshine and the scent of jasmine. "Sophie, have you and Abraham decided for sure that you're going to Haiti?" Anna asked.

Sophie retied her red head rag a little more tightly. "I 'spect so. After all, Massa's going to move Flora and her six children there. Why would I stay here?"

"Hmm."

"Six children....Lawd, that man is something else!"

Anna smiled. "Yes, he is."

"Do you ever stop and wonder, Sophie? Do you ever think, 'How in the world did I end up here?'"

"I don't dare have thoughts like that. I just take one day at a time. No sense in looking back, and it won't do any good to look forward."

"I know that's true, but I can't help it. I don't want to forget Yang Yang, but it's such a faded memory now. Sometimes I wonder what my life would have been like if I hadn't been captured. What if I'd made it to that baobab tree, and I could have hidden myself in those gnarly branches? What if my parents hadn't been killed?"

"Honey, there's no use in 'what ifs.' You could spin your life away with 'what ifs.'"

"Sophie, I might have been pledged to a tribal prince. I might have...."

"But you weren't and that's what counts."

"Yes, but...."

"Listen to me, chile," Sophie interrupted. "You've never been satisfied with where you were, with what you had. First, you had to have your freedom, then you had to have land of your own, then you had your three children that gave you your freedom, and you had to have one more, then..."

"I can't help it. I always feel like there's something better over the next hill, something more for tomorrow."

Sophie laughed and patted her friend's hand. "And all that yearning and wanting more is what makes you the person you are. Don't fight it, just know that's the way it is. Now me, I've had a good life here with Abraham. We've got a family and we've got freedom. That's plenty for me."

Anna sighed. "I don't want to leave Mary and Martha, and I don't want to leave this beautiful place, but there's a part of me that wants to get on with life, that wants to see what Haiti is really like." Anna gazed out at the fields and shook her head. "Sometimes, I wear myself out with wanting."

\* \* \*

Anna stood in the forefront of the little group assembled to see Zephaniah, George, and the others off to Haiti. Zephaniah had planned to leave in the summer, but preparations had pushed into October.

"I wish I could have gone with them." John Maxwell stood next to his mother as the ship pushed away. "I'm almost a man."

Anna smiled at her youngest child. "Almost, but not quite. We'll be going soon enough."

"But I could have helped them clear the land and build the roads and houses. Father says I am a good worker."

"You are a good worker, John Maxwell, and your time will come. Now, let's go up to the observation deck and watch till the ship is out of sight."

Anna leaned on the railing at her favorite spot and strained to watch the white sails against the blue of the ocean and sky. She felt the breeze in this higher place and closed her eyes. She could almost imagine that she was on that ship with Zephaniah, and they were going to build their new plantation together. She understood how John Maxwell felt as he gave a small wave as the ship sailed out of sight.

Dinner that evening was a very quiet affair with only Anna and John Maxwell at the table. *Zephaniah brings such a dynamic force with him. When he leaves, there is really a void.* She tried to think of conversation to bring up with John Maxwell, but her efforts fell short.

After dinner, the two walked to the dock and along the river, watching the fish jump for low-flying insects. The ripples left behind spread on and on, catching the last of the sun's golden rays.

"Look, Mama! There's that old alligator that slips up the river."

Anna's glance followed John Maxwell's pointing finger until she saw the gnarled head skimming through the water. She shivered. "I don't like him."

"Oh, he won't bother us. He's just looking for some supper."

"I know, but he's ugly and mean-looking. He could be dangerous if we got too close."

The boy stopped and looked at his mother, laying his hand on her arm. "Mama, there are always ugly, mean, dangerous things in the world. The thing is to know they're there and keep away from them."

Anna looked at this son of hers and felt unshed tears

burn her eyes. "What a smart, young man you are."

\* \* \*

John Maxwell bounded ahead of Anna and Zephaniah when the day of departure finally arrived in 1838. At the gangplank, he turned and called to them, "Hurry! Let's get on board."

Zephaniah motioned to him to go ahead. At the foot of the dock, the couple stopped and turned, looking back on what they had built together. It had all been sold to Zephaniah's nephew.

"I know you are sad, Anna," Zephaniah said. "Perhaps, someday it will be safe to come back. Kingsley, I'm sure, will always make us welcome here."

Anna could only nod. The lump in her throat made words impossible. The month before had been a whirlwind of packing trunks, thinking what furnishings she would need for the house that was waiting for her at Mayorasgo de Koka. Then, it was done. Anna had taken the past two days to walk every acre of the plantation, holding images to her like cherished gems, whispering good-byes to special places.

She had wandered through the citrus groves, the fruit hanging heavy on the branches. She pulled a twig with deep green leaves to press between the pages of a book. She walked through the slaves' cabins, down the sandy road to the ruins of the Indian village, past what was remaining of the mounds of oyster shells. She stood a long time, looking back toward the plantation, seeing the fall sunshine highlight the palms she had planted, the roof of her own "Ma'am Anna's House."

Twenty-four years seemed like a lifetime. *But they were the best twenty-four years of my life. I watched my children grow up here. John Maxwell was born here. Zephaniah really accepted me as his partner here.* She sighed and started back down the lane. *I guess this is the nearest I've come to know love since the tyeddo raid.*

As the final evening before they were to sail wrapped itself gently around the land nestled between the river and the ocean, Anna made her way to the observation deck. The sun was going down in the west, and the sky became a spectacular setting before her, first turning the clouds a pale blue outlined with gold, then fading into a rosy-pink blush, which eased into the hazy grayness of dusk. With the sun gone from the sky, the air took on a slight chill, and Anna shivered. She wanted to weep her farewell, but there weren't any tears left. She climbed down to spend her last night in this beloved home.

Now, the final moment was here. Water lapped against the ship as it waited for them to board. Zephaniah put his hand on the small of her back, gently urging her to turn and move on. They walked down the dock and up the gangplank to the ship that would carry Anna to her new home.

*This man still controls me. I am free, but my freedom is bound up in him. Is that a good thing, or bad?*

\* \* \*

Anna leaned against the deck railing with Zephaniah, anxious for her first view of her new land. John Maxwell moved about the ship, looking for the best vantage points. The sea was gray and choppy, and the fresh breezes on her face refreshed Anna. The sun hid behind a bank of pearl-gray clouds. She hoped the lack of sunshine was not some kind of bad omen.

"See!" Zephaniah's voice boomed above the wind. "There is Haiti." Anna's glance followed his finger. In the distance, she saw the beginnings of land, a slight rise of solid ground on the horizon. A tremor of excitement coursed through her body. Slowly the rise became green mountains.

The ship finally bumped into the pier at Puerto Plata, and several burly dock men secured the ropes. The noise and hubbub of the busy port bombarded Anna's ears. Workers yelled, gulls squawked, boats scraped the pier, cargo slammed on the dock, horses neighed as they pulled buggies and wagons. After quiet days at sea, the sound jarred her. She took Zephaniah's arm to steady herself. He patted her hand.

The dock was full of people meeting friends and family, dock workers unloading other ships, and vendors hawking fruit, hot yams, and fried fish. Large wooden buildings, paint fading from salty winds, filled the block around the pier. *I didn't expect this much of a town.*

Zephaniah pointed. "There's George!" Anna searched the men milling around the pier.

"I see him!" John Maxwell waved his cap over his head.

"Where? I don't see him." Anna continued her search. Finally, the familiar face appeared below her on the pier as George stood tall and smiling as he waved to them.

As soon as the gangplank was in place, John Maxwell rushed off the ship ahead of them.

Anna hugged her older son tightly. "Two years is too long to be apart. You look wonderful. Mayorasgo de Koka must agree with you."

"It does. You will love it, Mother." His face was beaming with excitement, his eyes sparkling.

"Mother," instead of "Mama" took Anna aback. *He is thirty-one years old and running a huge plantation. I guess I can get used to being "Mother."*

"I've arranged wagons for all your luggage and supplies," George told them, "and I have the buggy to take us to the compound." His pleasure at having them there and his obvious pride in being in charge was not lost on Anna, and as she took his offered arm, she squeezed it and smiled at him.

\* \* \*

Zephaniah got the luggage organized as John Maxwell and Anna walked with George to the buggy.

"Tell me about Anatoile and the children." Anna and John Maxwell climbed into the buggy.

"They are well, thriving, in fact. Anatoile has made a few white friends – some are even French - although there aren't that many here. Much of our area will remind you of Florida and perhaps even of what you described for us of Senegal."

"I am so anxious to see everything."

"Your house at Mayorasgo de Koka is finished, and there is also a house for you on Cabaret Creek. We'll go to the plantation first. Later, I'll show you around the compound. Your old friends are happy living here. Sophie is so anxious to see you again."

Anna smiled. "I have missed her. We've never been apart a whole year before. John Maxwell and I would have come with Sophie, but your father wanted us to wait until the house was ready."

"That made good sense."

"Yes, but...I was very concerned. Free blacks in Florida over fifteen years old now have to pay a tax. They can be sold back into slavery to cancel any debts. They are trying to outlaw manumission, and free blacks can no longer enter Florida. It was getting very scary. I will be glad not to have that threat hanging over us."

"Well, you are safe now. You will be happy here."

Anna looked at her handsome son a moment before replying. "I will try."

"Mama, can I ride up with the driver so I can see everything?" John Maxwell begged as he saw his father approach.

Anna smiled. "Of course." She wished she could do the same.

The ride to the plantation was fascinating. Many of the houses they passed were whitewashed stucco, brilliant in the sunlight. Some were painted earth tones, ochre and mustard. Anna found them pleasing to her eyes. She was reminded of the market town of Rufisque and the houses on Gorée Island, but she put those memories out of her thoughts. She could see rugged mountains to the south, and they traveled through forests of pine and cedars. They followed the rich lowlands of the river valley, and Anna could see that it was a good agricultural area. As they got closer to the family compound, George pointed out things with obvious pride.

"Over there is the sawmill I had built. It does a tremendous business from all our timber."

Zephaniah added with a note of satisfaction, "George planned all these roads and the bridges we will cross, and he supervised their building. He has done an excellent job."

George smiled self-consciously, but Anna sensed a deserved smugness.

"Mama!" John Maxwell called down from his observation seat. "Look! There's a giant lizard!"

Anna watched with fascination as they passed a lizard at least two feet long. *I'm going to have to get used to those things. That may take awhile.*

"As they turned into a long drive, Anna felt a sense of anticipation. *Will this finally be my sanctuary?*

# Chapter Thirty-Three

*Mayorasgo de Koka, Haiti*
*1838 – 1843*

The buggy pulled up in front of a large white stucco house with windows across the front trimmed in forest green. The windows all had wooden shutters angled from the top to provide shade from the sun.

Zephaniah helped Anna out of the buggy, and she took his arm as they mounted the stone steps. Stepping over the threshold, Anna found herself in a large hallway with a tile floor. The white walls rose open to the second story, and small windows near the ceiling let in light and air. To the left was a parlor extending the length of the house. There were already some attractive mahogany and teak pieces of furniture in place. The pieces Anna brought from Kingsley Plantation would complement them well. Across the hall was a dining room, empty except for a buffet sideboard, waiting for Anna's furniture.

Zephaniah walked beside Anna as she inspected everything.

"My dear, I cannot stand the suspense. How do you like it?"

Anna looked around, taking in the good design and warmth the rooms exuded, the way it already seemed familiar to her. "I love it. I think it will be a wonderful home for John Maxwell and me."

"I designed it after the floor plan of the Laurel Grove house. Of course, the outside is different, but the rooms and that center staircase are similar."

"Yes, I see that." She started up the staircase, her hand delighting in the rich smoothness of the mahogany banister. The hem of her gray silk traveling dress brushed along the tips of the stairs.

Entering the master suite, Anna gasped her surprise. "Zephaniah! This is just like your room at Laurel Grove."

He chucked with delight. "I thought you might like it. We had such happy times there. I had the bed made to match it, as well as the highboy and desk."

Anna walked to the desk set in front of a large window. The window was open at the top, allowing a gentle breeze to stir through the sheer white curtains. The crystal ink well sat alone on the desk.

With trembling hands she picked it up.

"I wanted to give you something....something that would be very special for your new life here. I wanted it to be something that symbolized...oh, I don't know....that symbolized that we are bound together."

"It is a beautiful gift, Zephaniah, and a beautiful thought. I will cherish the inkwell. At the right time, I will pass it on to one of our sons." She placed her palm on his cheek. "Thank you."

\* \* \*

The clouds left during the night, and the morning sun smiled through the window, waking Anna. She stretched, climbed out of bed, and went to the window. She could see much of the plantation and the distant mountains. She smiled and dressed in a simple blue muslin dress, eager to see everything.

George had arranged for Hannah and Florence, two free young women born on Kingsley Plantation, to take care of things at his mother's house. Anna remembered them as children growing up with John Maxwell. They served a breakfast of biscuits, bacon, and fresh fruit for Anna and Zephaniah.

"Are you ready to take me exploring?" Anna asked.

"Of course. George has the buggy ready. We knew you would be anxious to get started."

As they rode down the streets George had laid out, Zephaniah glowed with pride. "There are seventeen homes built within our compound already, and several more are planned for the near future."

"How many slaves will you free all together?"

"I don't know yet. I am freeing those who earn freedom by their good service and those who buy their freedom. I would guess, within the next few years, the total will be between fifty and one hundred. Any who want to come here are welcome."

"Where are your other wives?"

"Flora, Munsilna, and Sarah each have their own little area on the ends of Mayorasgo de Koka."

They rode in silence, Anna taking in the beauty. "There is so much growth. I recognize the palms, and the ferns, and so many fruit trees. I know the orange trees, of course, but what are those?" She pointed to a tree near the road.

"Those are papayas. They are very popular here and very tasty."

*Papayas. One of the fruits they gave us to eat while we were in quarantine at Havana, Cuba. Will I never fully escape those painful memories?*

"Look at those trees over there. They have a hanging moss like our Spanish moss in Florida, but this kind is green. What is it?"

"Hanging Club Moss. You'll find a lot of plants that are similar to those in Florida."

"Good. The similarities will make it easier for me to feel at home here."

269

"I hope you will feel at home here, Anna. You should because you already know all the people living in the compound."

"It is hard for me to believe that I am really safe here. We have lived for so many years with the threat of going back into slavery. I think it will take awhile for me to really understand that this is a sanctuary."

Zephaniah stopped the buggy and looked at Anna. "I promised you safety, Anna. I would not rest until I had obtained that goal for you and for our children. This...all this," he gestured around the plantation, "is so that I can keep that promise to you. Do you understand, now, how important you have been to me?"

Anna sat silently a moment, touched deeply by his words.

"Yes, I understand."

Zephaniah smiled and clicked at the horse.

They approached a grouping of houses, some wooden and some made of tabby bricks. Each home had a neat garden beside it. Anna's eyes scanned the area for Sophie.

"Where is Sophie's house?"

"Sophie and Abraham chose to build their place next to Flora's. Would you like me to take you there?"

"Please." Anna's enthusiasm to see her old friend could not be denied.

Zephaniah chuckled. "We are on our way."

Their horse and buggy arrived in a swirl of dust at a small wooden house. Anna jumped down at the same time that Sophie rushed through the doorway. They embraced, tears streaming down both their faces. They stood back, hands still holding, looked into each other's eyes, then hugged again. Abraham ambled out and leaned on the doorframe, grinning. Zephaniah remained in the buggy but nodded, smiling, at Abraham. "Anna, I will go say hello to Flora and the children. You have a little visit with Sophie."

Anna glanced back, grateful for his understanding of her need. "Yes." She and Sophie turned, arms around each other, and headed inside.

As Sophie spoke to her in the familiar Wolof dialect, Anna felt that she had come home.

* * *

The weeks slipped into months, then into years as Anna nestled into the life of Mayorasgo de Koka. She began wearing loose, brightly colored cotton dresses that reminded her of the *bukina* of Senegal. Rather than the head rags that many of the free black women still wore, Anna used colorful scarves to wrap turban-style around her head.

* * *

Anna woke early and gazed out the window at the rain. She sighed deeply. *I should be used to this rainy season after five years here. I know it is necessary for all the plant growth, but knowing it will continue until fall makes me tired.* She rose slowly, stretching out joints that ached now that she was in her fifties. Walking to the large armoire in her room, she flicked through the outfits hanging there. She smiled, disregarded the gowns, and chose instead a loose-fitting dress with a pattern of blue and red swirls that resembled the style of Senegal. She took her favorite powder-blue scarf and wound it around her head. She regally made her way down the stairs to have her breakfast.

Although there was a study designed in the house, Anna preferred to take care of her correspondence at the mahogany desk in her bedroom. She delighted in using the quill and crystal inkwell that Zephaniah had given her. On sunny days, she loved the way the sun's rays would pierce it, sending rainbow colored rays around the room.

Dear Susan,
I know it has been months since my last letter. I hope you will forgive me for that. Spring is so busy here. As

you have surmised, I still insist on being in charge of planting the huge vegetable gardens. These vegetables we use to feed everyone at Mayorasgo de Koka, and I have enough planted so that we have extra to sell in town. Over sixty freed slaves live here now. Some have already married among the local population and started their families. Mayorasgo de Koka is very profitable, supporting all of us, not only with the cotton and sugarcane crops, but with the timber forests of mahogany, pine, and cedar.

I enjoy being involved with George and Anatoile's children. John Maxwell is growing up so fast. He seems like quite a young man already at almost nineteen years old. George has really taken him under his wing and is teaching him to manage the plantation. They work well together.

Zephaniah is due for a visit any day. Just between us, I will say I don't think we will see him too many more times as this is his seventy-eighth year. The thought makes me sad, He has been the most powerful force in my life since I was thirteen years old."

Anna paused in her writing and stared vacantly out the window. She laid the quill down. *Is this rainy weather making me melancholy? No, it is my age and knowing that things are changing. John Maxwell will soon find a wife, and they will build a house of their own, and I will be all alone. When Zephaniah comes for this visit, that it probably will be his last. How did life change so much...and so quickly?*

Anna picked up the quill and finished her letter. She went downstairs and called Florence to have someone bring her the buggy.

"But the rain, Ma'am Anna," protested Florence.

"It looks as though it will be ending soon. I want to go into town and post my letter. I will be fine."

As Anna started down the drive, she was glad that she had been correct in her weather prediction. The sun burst through openings in the dark clouds, and the wind was chasing away the rain. She felt her spirits lifting. As she urged the bay gelding along the drive, she noted the growth of the palms she had planted almost five years ago. They reminded her of the ones along the drive at Kingsley Plantation, and it pleased her to see how they were thriving.

Anna seldom left the compound, so she was always surprised by the noise of Cabaret Village. People seemed to be hurrying, and vendors were always shouting about their wares, "Buy my fresh fish." "Mangoes, papayas, onions, potatoes."

Anna pulled back on the reins to stop the bay by the hitching rail. She wrapped the reins around the sturdy log rail. As she turned toward the shop where she could mail her letter, she suddenly felt shaky. She grabbed at the wooden post to steady herself, but that didn't help.

*Am I having a weak spell of some kind?* The horse snorted frantically, and Anna could see the whites of his eyes. He reared as a frightened squeal came from his rolled back lips. It seemed that everything was shimmering and sliding. People were screaming. *It's not me, but what is it?* Her mind could not grasp what was happening.

The post did not support her, and she found herself tossed on the ground. The noise of the people roared around her. Anna felt as frightened as she had been the night of the tyeddo raid. *What is it? What was happening?* Her heart raced, and her mouth was dry with fear. Anna screamed as she saw the hooves of the bay pawing the air over her head.

# Chapter Thirty-Four

Mayorasgo de Koka
1843

Without warning, everything stopped shaking. Anna got to her feet and looked around. The bay stood trembling in front of her. People were picking up things that had been strewn around the ground from the vendors stalls. Everyone was talking at once.

"Earthquake!" Anna heard the word above the babble of excited voices and understood what had happened. She had read that earthquakes were possible in this country, but she never expected to experience one. *I must get home,* she thought. *I must see how everyone at Mayorasgo de Koka has fared.*

She rubbed the horse's neck, murmuring soothing words. The gelding's trembling stopped, and Anna climbed into the buggy. She headed for home.

She wanted to whip the horse into a fast run, but she didn't dare. Any more agitation might send him completely out of control. *What has happened to the family? Is my house still standing firm? Oh, God, where is the safety you held out to me? Is there no place in the world for sanctuary?*

Anna arrived to a scene of chaos. Everyone was milling around the center area, children and women crying, men shouting to each other, horses and mules running loose. John Maxwell grabbed the gelding and tied him to the rail in front of Anna's house. Anna jumped from the buggy and embraced her son.

"Mama, are you all right? I was so worried when I couldn't find you."

"Yes. Yes, I am fine, but what of you? Where is George? Where are the children?" She searched the throng of people.

"Everyone here is fine. They say it was an earthquake. Mama, it was so scary."

"I know, son. I was...." Anna caught sight of her older son making his way to the center of the group. George mounted a wagon in the center of the area, and his words interrupted Anna's sentence. "Attention, everyone. Quiet, please." He held up his hands in a calming motion. The noise ceased, and everyone gathered around him.

"We must remain calm. Everything is all right here. It was an earthquake, but we were just on the edge of it. The effects could have been much worse. There may be some more of what they call 'aftershocks.' They won't be as severe, so do not be frightened if they occur." The murmur of voices began again.

George held his hand up for quiet and continued. "I will come around and check all your houses and our common structures to be sure there is no damage. Now, we do not need to be frightened. There is no longer a problem. We might as well all get back to work." He hopped off the wagon, hurried to his mother, and drew her into his arms for comfort.

"Where were you? We were so worried."

Anna smiled and patted his arm. "I had gone to town to post a letter. I was worried about you all out here, but I see now what good hands we are in with you in charge. You are a fine leader, calm and strong, my son. You learned well from your father."

George put his arm around Anna's shoulders. "And from you, Mother. Especially from you."

Anna could not answer. *Have I really taught these children of mine the strength I wanted them to have?*

As Anna read about the earthquake in the newspapers

she realized how fortunate they were. The main earthquake had struck to the northwest. Port-de-Paix and Fort Liberte were leveled. Cap Haitian had ten thousand people lost, buried by the quake's destruction. All the cities were looted. Anna shivered, thinking of what might have happened to them if the earthquake had been closer.

"There is no safe place," she murmured.

\* \* \*

His ship had docked at Puerto Plata the day before and Anna noticed that Zephaniah still seemed tired from his journey although he had slept through the night. His color was not good, she thought, and he had a cough.

"Zephaniah, you should stay awhile and let this tropical paradise you found for us restore you."

"I am fine, my dear, just older."

"We are all getting older."

"And because I am older, I have made some arrangements, some final arrangements to be certain you, John Maxwell, and the others are cared for after my death."

"Zephaniah, please, don't..."

"Now, Anna, hear me out. This is important. I have gone over all this with George, and with Mary's husband, John." He coughed, took a deep breath and went on. "John Sammis is a good man, and, fortunately for us all, he has become a very rich and influential man in Florida. It was good luck for Mary that they married. He will look out for your interests there. I have worked out all the details with my attorney in New York"

Anna sat very still as Zephaniah spoke. *I know I must pay attention to this, but I do not want to hear talk of "final plans." I am afraid of a world without Zephaniah to protect me.*

"George will act as guardian for all the minor children. He is level-headed and intelligent. You can be guided by his decisions."

Anna thought back to George's calming influence after the earthquake and knew that what Zephaniah said was true.

"You and all my co-wives will be able to live the rest of your lives on the profits from Mayorasgo de Koka and all the properties I own. I am making a stipulation, though, which I want you to understand and help the others to understand. This is the only safe place for you, Anna. If you return to Florida you will not be safe. So, to insure that you and Flora, Sarah, Munsilna, and all the children remain protected, I am stipulating that any who leave here will forfeit any support from Mayorasgo de Koka."

Anna looked at him, puzzled. "That seems like an extreme condition."

Zephaniah shook his head and coughed deeply. "No. It is absolutely necessary, Anna. Life is good for you here, comfortable and secure. I must see that those conditions continue, even after I am gone."

Tears came to Anna's eyes. "Please. No more talk about that. It makes me too sad. Come, let's walk through the citrus grove." She stood and reached for his hand.

The weeks of Zephaniah's visit were melancholy to Anna. They sat often on the terrace, overlooking the beauty of the plantation. Zephaniah's conversation was full of nostalgia.

"Remember, Anna...?" he often began. "Remember when I was teaching you the English language? What an eager student you were. I knew right away how bright you were.... Remember, Anna, when you had to burn down Laurel Grove and your own house? How brave you were, Anna, dear.... Remember when we first arrived at Kingsley Plantation? There was so much rebuilding to be done, but you knew what must be done and you saw to it. You were such a partner to me, Anna.....Remember, Anna? Remember?"

Anna did remember. She remembered it all with a poignancy that surprised her. She sat across from this man who had controlled her life for the past thirty-seven years as they

sipped their chilled fruit drinks in the summer heat of Haiti
and wondered how she could say good-bye to him. His slight
frame had grown even more frail; his hair was now white, the
strength in his hands reduced to a tremor.

On their last evening together, they walked arm in arm
among the orange groves. Anna inhaled the gentle citrus
aroma that always reminded her of Zephaniah and his love of
the Mandarin orange trees. They walked in silence, as if both
knew that any words spoken should be important ones. This
was the time for complete truth between them.

Anna broke the silence. "I have always wondered why you
never had a white wife."

Zephaniah's laugh rang with almost its old gustiness.
"Anna, I never met any white woman who could hold a candle
to you in running my plantations. Why would I want to
marry one?"

Anna smiled at the compliment. "I just thought...perhaps
one of your own kind...."

"Remember, in those days in Spanish East Florida it was
not unusual to have mixed marriages, relationships."

They walked in silence for a few more moments.

"Zephaniah, all these years you have looked out for me,
protected me...."

"Yes, that has been my goal."

"Why...." Could she finally, should she dare, put the
question into words?

"Why, what?"

"You always introduced me as your wife. Why did you
never marry me?"

Zephaniah stopped and looked at Anna. She could see
the puzzlement on his face in the deepening twilight.

"Anna, we could not have been more married. You were
my helpmate, my partner in everything. I always looked out
for you. I felt that we were married."

"But, the Frasers,...You wanted my safety and that of our

children." She paused and asked again. "Why didn't we marry?"

"There is no explanation that could satisfy either of us. Please be content with what we have...with what we shared."

Anna looked up in the growing darkness at the ripening fruit hanging against the deep green leaves. She began to accept what she had never been able to accept before. He had done the best for her that he could do. Whatever intangible something she had needed from him, she would never have, could never have gotten. He had given her the most that he could give.

As the rose-colored clouds of evening gave way to a deeper purple, Anna leaned toward this man that had shaped her life and kissed him gently on the cheek. She really felt that she was his wife...and that was enough.

The next day everyone at Mayorasgo de Koka turned out to see Zephaniah off. His face became wet with tears as he bid a final farewell to his wives and his children. As he walked up the gangplank to his ship, he stopped and looked over all the faces. He raised his hand, a wave of good bye, a blessing, turned and boarded the ship. He stood at the railing as the dock workers untied the ropes and the schooner slipped away from the pier.

Anna stood there, long after the others had left. She watched until the ship was a tiny speck on the horizon. The sea breeze flapped her long gown, and the sound of the water splashing against the pier was a melody.

*Zephaniah, how I will miss you.* A lump stayed in her throat, and her arms tingled with the desire to hold him once again. Still she stood silently, looking out to the vast emptiness of the ocean.

# Chapter Thirty-Five

*Mayorasgo de Koka*
*1843 – 1846*

When George appeared in her sitting room six weeks later, Anna knew immediately from the expression on his face. Her heart froze.

"Tell me," she said.

"He died in New York City on September 13." His own voice was choked with emotion. "Mama....What are we....?" He was her little boy again, in need of assurance. He was looking to her for strength, for help, but that was what she needed from him. A moment passed. Anna could almost see the struggle between boy and man. Another moment. George squared his shoulders and squeezed Anna's hands, and she knew the man had won. Her son would be what he had become, the head of the family.

Anna nodded. There were no words to say. She turned and walked out to the orange groves and tried to absorb George's words, her heart breaking with the finality of the news. She felt a loneliness and a vulnerability settle in her heart. A baobab tree with swirls of smoke flashed through her mind.

\* \* \*

Anna found herself visiting Sophie more often in the year

following Zephaniah's death.  Her old friend usually sat in an old wooden chair in front of the home she and Abraham shared by Flora's, her face to the warming sun.  Her short, stocky body had grown quite heavy, and sitting was what she wanted to do.

Anna and Sophie slipped comfortably into the Wolof language, sometimes humming old songs from Senegal.  Today, they were remembering the trees of their childhood, the baobab, of course, and the acacia gum tree.

"I remember my mother would grind up the Nere pods that hung from trees into a sweet, sticky powder and cook up treats.  Did your mother make those, too?" Sophie asked.

Anna laughed.  "Oh, yes.  I had forgotten.  And, remember...."

She stopped as she saw George riding up.
*Something has happened to John Maxwell or one of the children.* She walked the few step to meet him.  "What's wrong?"

George dismounted and nodded a greeting to Sophie.  "I've just gotten a packet of mail.  There was a letter from the lawyer.  Father's sister, Martha McNeill, has contested Father's will.  It must go through the courts before anything can be divided."

"But that should not affect us here," Anna replied.  "You have title to this land.  Those profits are what support us."

"That is true, Mother, but there is a large inheritance from the Florida properties also.  Father was extremely wealthy.  That wealth is to be distributed also."

"Why is she contesting the will?"

"She is a widow now.  Perhaps she is concerned about her financial security."

"Do you think she will win?" Anna felt her indignation rising, more because of the insult than from concerns about the inheritance. She remembered how Martha had treated her when they visited, as if Anna were a slave to be ordered about. *When Zephaniah let Martha's son, Charles, live at Kingsley*

*Plantation to teach him how to be a manager, I was good to him. Is this how she repays me?*

"She could win, Mother. Her argument is that you, and the others, are 'negresses or mulattos,' and the law states that you cannot move into Florida, so you could not inherit any property there."

"What should we do?"

"Leave it to me, and to John Sammis. We will work it out."

"Very well. I do not want to have to worry about all that." Anna went back to sit with Sophie. She was content to let her son and son-in-law take care of matters. It would not directly affect her life here in Haiti. Florida was a lifetime away and no longer concerned her.

* * *

For the next two years, the dispute in the courts of Florida did not mean anything to Anna. Her days were filled with family and activities within the compound. John Maxwell married a young woman from town, and they moved into a large house next to Anna's. Anna was glad to let George and John Maxwell oversee all that went on at Mayorasgo de Koka. Not much occurred, however, that she was not aware of.

In the summer of 1845, one of Flora's sons banged on Anna's door.

"It's my grandmother," he gasped, tears on his face. "Mama says she's dying! Come, please. She's calling for you." Anna hurried to Flora's home. Sophie was on a bed, the family gathered around.

"Sophie. Please, Sophie, don't you leave me, too."

Sophie's eyes remained closed a moment, then fluttered open. "Anna," she whispered. "Anta Majigeen."

"I'm here, Sophie." Anna held Sophie's hand close to her heart.

Sophie slipped into the dialect that warmed Anna's heart. "Do not be afraid, little Anta....You always want...more....but you...you have everything you ...need."

"I know. Life is good here."

Sophie shook her head slightly. "No....I mean....what Bella taught you....Everything ...you need...is...inside you, Anta.... Inside you."

"Oh, Sophie, I need you, too!" Tears coursed down Anna's face.

Sophie smiled. "You...have me...in your heart. Now, it's time....I can go home...home to Senegal."

Anna looked around at Sophie's family. Abraham, gray-headed and stooped, and Flora. Her expression begged them to change things, to make it a lie that Sophie was dying. She saw only agony in their eyes.

"Let me...rest now," Sophie whispered. *"Be beneen yon... good bye..."*

"Good-bye to you, dear friend." Anna kissed Sophie gently on the cheek and smoothed the coverlet over her. She hurried from the room, unable to see any more.

Anna's tears were so plentiful that she could barely see her way back to her room. She sat on the edge of the bed, rocking back and forth. *Sophie, Sophie. What will I do without you? I am so tired of loss. I need you, Sophie. Do not leave me, too. I will never hear anyone call me by my real name again, my African name. I will lose my roots, my true self. Anta Majigeen Ndiaya will die with you, and only Anna Kingsley will remain.*

The afternoon sun became lost behind growing clouds. The air cooled, and the wind increased as sheets of rain slapped against the house. Anna was startled by a loud clap of thunder as she looked out the window. She wondered if she were seeing rain or tears pouring from her own eyes. Finally, Anna had no more tears. *Sometimes, I feel that I am spending my whole life grieving the losses I've endured. God, if you're really there, please help me fill the emptiness inside.*

They buried Sophie in the cemetery of Mayorasgo de Koka. Anna could not seem to shake her feelings of gloom. The summer sun was relentless, the air sticky and oppressive. Anna was glad when the humidity of the rainy season ended in November, and the activities of Christmas filled her mind.

Since the death of her dear friend, Anna had avoided the part of the compound where Sophie and Abraham had lived until she found herself not far from their house on an aimless walk. *I should go see Abraham.* She walked the short distance to their front door and called softly. There was no answer. Anna called louder. "Abraham. Abraham, are you in there?"

She heard the scratching sound of a chair pushed against the wooden floor and slow footsteps making their way toward her.

Anna was shocked at Abraham's appearance. His face was gaunt, skin stretched over a skull. His eyes were sunken deep in his head, and they were dull and cloudy, as if a strange kind of blindness had struck him.

"Abraham." She hugged him, trying to bring some warmth and life back to his body. As she pulled away, he turned and padded back inside to the chair. Anna followed him, wondering what she could do to help him. *Sophie, what should I do? What can I say to him?*

Anna knelt in front of the old man and took his hands in hers. "Abraham, I miss her, too. Let's talk about her, share our memories. Maybe we can keep her close that way." She paused and watched his face. Did she just imagine it, or was there a flicker of light in his eyes? She went on.

"Remember the time Flora and George were little and they sat in the ant hill? Remember how Sophie grabbed one up in each arm and carried them into the river? She plopped them down in that water and sat right down with them. Remember?"

Abraham nodded, and a low chuckle came up from some-place deep inside him.

"And remember," Anna pulled a chair close to Abraham's, and took his hands in hers again. "When that storm came up so fast and strong and everyone in the slaves' quarters might have lost all their garden produce, but Sophie got all the children and house slaves and everyone working so hard to pick it all, and she saved enough. Remember?"

Abraham looked straight at Anna, and her heart lurched when he smiled. "Dat Sophie were somethin', weren't she?"

"She was. She was really something." Anna knew that Sophie would be proud of her and grateful. That made Anna feel good. She vowed to visit Abraham often. *I want to keep Sophie close to me, too.*

* * *

Anna's family, especially the children, were the bright spots amidst her grief. She had enjoyed dining with George and Anatoile on this sultry July evening. She loved hearing the chatter of children, but something in George's serious expression disturbed her.

After the family finished their meal and the children left to play outside, Anna asked, "What is it George? Something's troubling you, I can tell."

George smiled. "You know me too well, Mother. Yes, I am somewhat troubled tonight."

"Well, out with it."

"The state of unrest in this country is what troubles me. I had hoped that when Boyer got pushed out and sailed away for Jamaica, the country would begin to move toward economic stability, but I see no signs of that."

"Your father thought Boyer would be good for the country."

"We hoped that would be the case. He wasn't a cruel despot, but there was so much corruption and nepotism in his government. The economy kept spiraling downward, the rate of illiteracy went up, the demarcation between blacks and mulattos kept escalating....There were just too many problems."

"I read about the violent clashes in the south. Do you think we will have problems here?"

George shook his head. "I don't think so. Even if there were problems in this area, we are a self-contained free colony here. Mayorasgo de Koka will be safe."

"Then what is it that concerns you so?"

"Simply the economics of it all. We do well here financially, but our income is still connected to the affluence of the country. If there is going to be constant strife and civil unrest combined with intense poverty, eventually we will feel some effects."

"George, where is security for our family? Why can I never find it?"

"I don't want to be the voice of gloom. We will always manage with what we have here. This land can support all the families on it, but I had hopes of increasing our wealth here. That has been possible so far, but I'm not sure that will continue."

"What do you think we should do?"

"Nothing yet. Let's see what happens under Boyer's successor. Riviere-Herard has set up a government of military rule. Let's see how Haiti prospers under him."

That night Anna dreamt of Yang Yang, of her mother and father, of Bolanile and Urbi, of carefree days and childhood games. When she woke in the silvery-gray of dawn and realized those happy days were long gone, she turned over, pulled the soft white sheet over her head, and willed herself back to sleep. *Waking up and facing the worries of the day sometimes is simply too hard.*

# Chapter Thirty-Six

*Mayorasgo de Koka, Haiti*
*1846*

As she got older, a full night of sleep was rarely possible. She was no stranger to the blue-black skies and sparkling stars of the night, and she found some comfort in them. She often rose in the darkness, wrapped a shawl around her, and went walking around the compound. When she stayed in her bungalow at Cabaret Beach, she walked the beach at night, finding solace in the lapping noise of the rippling tide against the sandy shore. She never feared walking alone.

On such a night in August, she headed along the beach-front, savoring the salty tang in the air, the beauty of the night, the breathy whisper of the breeze through the feathery needles of a Casuarina tree. She heard drums and singing and saw a bonfire some distance down the shore. A large group was gathered there. Anna thought a lone woman walking by would not be noticed.

As she got closer, the rhythmic drum beat and the swaying of the dancing bodies silhouetted by the fire reverberated within her in a strangely powerful way. She became caught up in the sound, feeling some long-absent connection, as if the music were a physical thing, curling around her, bringing her closer and closer to the crowd.

She stood at the edge of the group, listening, swaying, feeling... something, something like the peace she used to feel when speaking in Wolof to Sophie, feeling as though an ancient longing was going to be eased... *Was Sophie here in this gathering?.. No, of course not... Why did she feel her presence?* Anna shook her head to clear her thoughts. No one noticed her.

The drums spoke faster and faster. She could feel them inside her, as if the drums were her heart. Suddenly, the sound stopped. Anna felt as though she had been jolted awake. Someone in the center of the group was speaking. As she pushed forward to try and hear the words, Anna noticed Florence, one of the girls who helped in her house, standing to her right. She made her way over to the young woman.

"Florence! What are you doing here? What is going on?" Florence jumped when Anna spoke to her, and Anna couldn't help but notice a flash of fear when Florence recognized her.

"It's all right, girl. You're free to come and go as you want. I only wanted to know what this was all about."

Florence looked around, then pulled Anna a short distance from the crowd.

"It's a voodoo ceremony," she whispered. "It's a celebration for renewed health for the woman there in the center. The *houngan*, the man next to her, was in a trance and a *loua*, a family spirit, entered his soul. He's telling what the *loua* is saying."

Anna drew back. She did not want to be part of a voodoo rite, but she was shocked at how strongly she had felt involved.

"Florence, you are a Catholic like me. You don't believe in this witchcraft, do you?"

"It's not witchcraft!" Florence said vehemently. "There's nothing in voodoo that says you can't still be a Catholic. It just takes you in a little different direction." Florence kept looking back at the group, wanting to return.

Anna backed away. "Good night, Florence." She turned and hurried back the way she had come before the drums could cast their spell over her again. Anna's bare feet moved swiftly along the hard-packed sand of the beach. All the way back to her home, she kept glancing over her shoulder toward the bonfire, feeling an uneasiness that someone...or something...might follow her.

Back in her bungalow, Anna sat for a long time on the edge of her bed, her head in her hands. *What happened to me back there? I will not let myself get caught up in voodoo. There was something there; something called to me. No. It was just the power of the music, the rhythm of those drums.* These thoughts tumbled over in her mind like a shell in the ocean's tide. Finally, before the dawn would pull her fully awake for the day, Anna lay down and tried to sleep.

* * *

Anna was able to put the lure of the voodoo ritual out of her thoughts over time. She kept busy with activities within the compound, especially spending time with her family. She knew it was necessary to have distractions so that she didn't dwell on all her losses. Writing to Susan helped, too.

January, 1846

Dear Susan,

I am so glad I have you to write to. I miss knowing that Zephaniah is in the world. His death has made such a void in my life. Losing Sophie, too, has made it worse. I miss having someone to talk to, especially someone who connects me to life long ago. I try to think about what she said to me, that all I need is inside myself. That seems to be a lesson I've heard over and over in my life. Do I dare believe it? I look over my life and I see that I have survived a lot, so maybe that strength is inside me. I hope so.

At least I don't have to worry about the legal issues. George has gone to New York to meet with our lawyer.

He should be back soon and we will learn what the courts say now."

Anna looked up from her letter as John Maxwell appeared at the door. His face was ashen, his hands holding a letter, trembling. "Mama." His voice was hoarse with strain.

"Mama," John Maxwell began again. "George's ship....the ship has wrecked....George....he drowned, Mama."

"No!" Anna screamed. She jumped up, scattering the papers, and ran to John Maxwell. Her hands gripped his shoulders, shaking him, willing him to deny what he said. "No! Not George, too!"

John Maxwell could only look at her, his eyes dulled with shock.

"No." Anna pulled John Maxwell close to her, hugging the only son she had left. The two stood together, rocking in their grief, sobbing.

Florence and Hannah ran in, looking at each other in confusion.

"Ma'am Anna?" Florence finally spoke. Anna gave no response, but continued holding John Maxwell and weeping.

"Ma'am Anna?" She placed her hands on Anna's shoulders. "What you want me to do?"

Anna stood back from her son but kept holding on to him as if she could not stand on her own. Her face was swollen and blotched from tears, her eyes wild with grief. She looked at Florence as if trying to figure out who she was.

John Maxwell tried to pull himself together. "Let's sit down. We must think what to do."

Anna nodded, and they made their way to the two chairs by the desk. Anna sank into one and buried her face in her hands. Racing through her mind was the vision of the vast, cruel ocean, of Madu, the sharks following the slave ship, her own precious George....

"Get some water for my mother," John Maxwell instructed the girls. They scurried from the room.

John Maxwell took his mother's hands, pulled them from her face and sat facing her.

"Mama, I must go tell Anatoile. Will you be all right with Florence and Hannah?"

Anna seemed to come back from some place far away. "Anatoile? Yes, we must tell her. I will go with you."

"You don't have to do that. I will go. I am the man of the family now. I can do it." His voice caught in his throat, but Anna could see he was making an effort to be strong.

She looked at her son for a long moment. "I know you can, but I must be strong, too, for Anatoile and the children. Give me a moment, and I will go with you."

She shook her head as if she could not believe the news. "George....George gone. It just can't be. How could God take away my son, my first-born son? It just can't be."

"Send someone for the doctor," John Maxwell turned and instructed Florence. "Have him come to us at my brother's house."

Florence nodded and ran.

John Maxwell rose. "We need to get to Anatoile. Do you want to come?"

Anna numbly looked up at him. From that well of strength inside herself that had sustained her over and over in her life, Anna reached deep and found the will to reply. "Yes. I will come with you."

\* \* \*

The weeks after were a blur to Anna. John Maxwell stepped into his brother's role of plantation manager. She perceived on some level of consciousness that the property continued to be self-sufficient, and Anatoile and the children were surviving. She had received several letters from Susan, begging Anna to respond and to use the reservoir of strength that had always been hers. Anna tried. She started letters, but they ended up on the desk, unfinished, until she threw them out.

Anna also received a number of letters from the attorney about Zephaniah's estate and the need for a family member to respond so he could take action in the courts. She sent the letters on to her son-in-law, John Sammis, without reading them. She spent many hours sitting by the window, watching the light change over the distant mountains as the day drifted into evening. Sometimes, she would jump up, as if the need for activity were crucial, grab a walking stick, and walk for hours through the forests and hills adjoining the plantation, then down to the beach at Cabaret.

John Maxwell visited her every day as did all the grand-children. She smiled blandly at them and responded to their comments, but she had the strange sensation that no conversation really touched her. Her heart remained cold and still, as if it, too, had died on that January day when George's ship was wrecked.

# Chapter Thirty-Seven

*Mayorasgo de Koka*
*1846 – 1847*

"Mama, we need to talk." John Maxwell was firm.

"We talk every day, son."

"Something must be done to insure our share of Father's Florida holdings. Mayorasgo de Koka has to support a large number of people, and it will, but the timber is diminishing, and we cannot count on as much as we have been getting."

"What are you saying, John Maxwell? Are we in jeopardy?"

"No, but John and I believe we must look at the long term. I should go back to Florida and fight in the courts for what Father wanted us to have."

"No. I will not have you take that risk." His suggestion terrified Anna. "Don't you realize what that would mean? No free black is allowed to enter Florida. You would be sold into slavery, John Maxwell. Slavery. No, you cannot consider going."

"But, we must do something."

Anna felt frantic. "There is no way you can even think of going to Florida. In fact, I could not bear it if you went anywhere by ship. I have lost enough, I tell you. Enough!" Anna felt a rage filling her and spilling out. A terrifying sense of danger and helplessness surrounded her, crushing her, just as it had that night of the tyeddo raid. That horror lay just under the surface, ready to jump out at her when her defenses were down. The chance that John Maxwell might end up as a slave was too painful to think of. Loss was surrounding her, pushing her from all sides, and she could not bear it.

"Mama, calm yourself, please." He took her slender hand in his large one and gently began rubbing it. "I'm sorry. I didn't mean to upset you."

Anna felt the grief inside become an overwhelming force. She could no longer contain it. She could not control the wracking sobs. They had a power of their own. She ran to her room, slamming and locking the door. She heard John Maxwell beating on it and pleading with her, but she could not respond to him. She wept. She sobbed. She wailed her grief. She called for her mother and father, for Madu, for Bella, for Sophie. She cried Zephaniah's name, begging him to come back. Finally, she could speak George's name, the precious name of her son, lost to her forever. *Forever.* It was too much, too painful.

"Oh, George, my son. My son." She said his name over and over, a litany of grieving she could no longer hold back.

"Mama. Please. Open the door. I have the doctor here. He will give you something to help you. Mama." John Maxwell's voice penetrated her consciousness.

Anna's sobs subsided. She was spent, exhausted beyond any fatigue she had ever felt before. Slowly, using every ounce of strength she had left, she walked to the door and opened it.

John Maxwell wrapped his arms around her. She leaned against him. He lifted her and carried her to the bed, placing her on the quilt.

"Mama, the doctor will give you something to help."

Anna could barely open her eyes, she was so tired. "No, I don't need anything. I just need to sleep. Just promise me you won't leave Haiti. Promise me."

John Maxwell paused and looked into her worn face. "I promise, Mama. Now rest."

As he turned to leave her, Anna said, "I'll think of something. After I rest, I'll think of something."

\* \* \*

Reluctantly, Anna came awake the next morning. She had dreamed that George was sailing home, that he would be with them soon. She struggled against the reality that tore her heart apart. As her eyes opened and the dream faded, she moaned. The pain of losing George was as physical as it was emotional.

Some days, Anna was able to get up and stumble through her daily life. Others, she could not bear it and escaped to the stupor of sleep.

Anatoile came to Anna's bedside one morning. George's widow had lost weight, her face thin and strained. "Mama Anna," she said, taking Anna's hand in her own trembling one. "George was... so full of life... We must live life for him now. Will you help me?" She paused. "Please...." Her eyes were brimming with tears.

Anna sat up in bed and leaned forward to hold her daughter-in-law in her arms. "Yes," she whispered. She leaned back into the pillows, but she kept Anatoile's hand in her own. "I know about loss and...." She shook her head. "We will find our strength together."

Anna looked down at their clasped hands, her own ebony skin against the creamy peach tone of Anatoile's. *Heartbreak does not care about race or color. The only requirement is love. If we can find the courage inside to love, I guess we can find the courage to go on.*

Anna got up and dressed that day. She looked in the mirror as she wound her worn powder-blue turban around her head. Her eyes were clear under her highly arched eyebrows, her skin still smooth over her cheekbones, her lips generous and full. Behind the face in the mirror, she could see the face of a frightened girl of thirteen wearing the yoke of a captured slave. She could see the young mother of twenty dumping coals on draperies to burn Laurel Grove and brandishing a torch to do the same to her own property. She was able to visualize the face of a competent manager of Kingsley Plantation as she smiled at Zephaniah. She tucked in the last edge of the turban. *I will go on from this day and do whatever it takes to look after my family*

\* \* \*

A month later, Anna looked at the faces of John Maxwell, his wife, and Anatoile as they sat at her dining table. She waited until the meal was served and Florence was back in the kitchen before she smiled at them. "I have asked you to dine with me tonight because I have made a decision that affects all of you. I have been in touch with John Sammis, and today I have heard from Judge Bethune in Florida. The Superior Court has ruled against Martha McNeill's case. That means the case is going back to the Duval County Circuit Court."

"That is good news, Mama." John Maxwell smiled broadly.

"Things are still not cleared up, however. I have decided to go back to Florida and fight for what is due us."

"Go back to Florida?" Anatoile and John Maxwell spoke at the same time.

Anna sat serenely before them. "Yes."

"But, Mama," John Maxwell sputtered, "you said that if I went I might be sold into slavery. What about you?"

"Ah, there is a big difference, son. I was a free person before Florida became part of the United States. I am protected by a treaty, remember? You are not. And the fact that the Superior Court ruled in our favor on this case shows that they consider me to have full citizenship. John feels that it is safe for me to return, even with racial mistrust higher than ever. I do not care what people think, but I do want some legal protection, and now I think I have it."

Anatoile's eyes were spilling silent tears. "You would do this for us?"

Anna looked at her daughter-in-law and resisted the urge to go to her and put her arms around the young woman. If she did, Anna knew they would both dissolve in tears. Their wounds were still too raw. Anna wanted to convey the sureness of her decision, the confidence she had in her plan. Once she had allowed her grief to be expressed weeks ago, she was able to think clearly, to make decisions. She was excited about this decision.

"It is what I want to do, and it makes the most sense. John has looked out for our interests well, but he has his own plantations and business to tend to. Now, someone will need to oversee all of Zephaniah's holdings. I am familiar with them, and... and," her voice caught for the first time. "I need something to do, something to take my mind off of... the... grief."

There was silence around the table.

John Maxwell cleared his throat. "I see the wisdom of your plan. But, what about Father's stipulation that any who leave here lose their support from Mayorasgo de Koka?"

"I have considered that. John assures me that there is more than enough value in the Florida properties to support me the rest of my life. I am willing to take the chance in order to secure the inheritance for all of us. Besides, things are changing in Haiti. We must be assured of the inheritance from Florida."

"When do you plan to leave?"

Anna smiled at him, grateful for his understanding. "As soon as I can get things organized. We do not want anything to happen in the Circuit Court without my being there to protect our interests."

# Chapter Thirty-Eight

*Strawberry Mills, Florida*
*1846 – 1848*

Anna stood at the railing of the ship John Sammis had sent
to bring her back to Florida, leaning into the March breezes.
Every palm, every live oak hanging with Spanish moss was so
dearly familiar.  She felt that she was soaking in the beauty of
the land as they passed by.

They entered the mouth of the St. Johns River, and Anna
wept as they sailed past the south end of Fort George Island.
She could just catch a glimpse of the rooftop of the white
two-story house that had been her home for twenty-four years.
Anna's eyes looked up to the highest point, her favorite, the
observation deck.  She could almost feel the wind on her face
as she stood up there, surveying the entire plantation. The
Mandarin orange trees were in full bloom.  Anna imagined
that she could smell the heavy citrus scent as she sailed by.
The slaves were preparing the land for new crops, and her
heart ached to be part of it.  The plantation belonged to
Zephaniah's nephew now.  She had no place there.
Tears slid down her ebony cheeks.  No one was there to
comfort her, but she sensed Zephaniah's presence beside her.
She lifted her shoulders straighter as she guessed what he
would have said.

"Anna, this is a new beginning.  Think of all you can do."
She smiled. "Zephaniah,  you are with me still."  The

wind carried the words to Fort George Island. She wiped her tears with the back of her hand, and looked ahead toward the dock of Strawberry Mills, the Sammis plantation.

As the swift schooner nipped into the dock, Anna saw a small group waiting there. Soon she could make out Mary and Martha... the grandchildren...both sons-in-law, John Sammis and Oren Baxter... and was that?... It was... Susan.

Anna rushed off the ship into the arms of her daughters. She tried to hug the grandchildren one by one, but they all crowded around her: Martha's children– Isabella, Anna, Julia, Osmond, and Emma –and Mary's flock, George, Edward, Albert, and Egbert. John and Oren came forward and kissed her on the cheek. Susan came last and took Anna's hands in hers.

"Welcome home, dear friend." The lump in Anna's throat made speaking impossible. She squeezed Susan's hands.

They all clung about Anna as they walked to the Big House. Inside, the noise was louder as they all chattered at once.

"Mama," Mary's voice rose above the racket, "Don't you want me to show you to your room? You can freshen up then we'll all have dinner together."

"Yes, that would be good." She took Mary's arm and they went up the center staircase together.

"This is your room, Mama."

Anna stepped into the room. It had clean white walls, large windows with white sheer curtains to soften the sun-light, and heavy blue damask drapes. Beautiful mahogany furnishings and a powder-blue coverlet on the bed made Anna feel welcome and warm.

"It is lovely, Mary." She ran her hand along the coverlet. "Your father gave me a scarf this color once."

"I remember it. You wore it often."

"Yes. I still have it." So many memories.

"Mama, I'm glad you're home. This will be your room for

as long as you can stay. I don't want you to leave us again."
"Thank you, darling. I will need to be here awhile until I can
get everything organized, but I intend to have my own place
again. I do have title to land here already, and I still have my
own slaves. But, it will take me some time to get it all sorted
out."

Mary kissed her cheek. "Well, just come down when
you're ready."

Anna drew aside the sheer curtain. The river glittered in
the afternoon sun. *How many times have I looked out on this same
river, from Laurel Grove, from my own place, from Kingsley Plantation?*
She inhaled, savoring the scent of sea and marsh. A pelican
dove down and swooped back up with a fish. Anna smiled, went
to the wash basin and pitcher, and began to wash her hands.
She was looking forward to hearing the chatter of her grandchildren. After dinner she and Susan could walk by the river.

* * *

Within the week, Anna sat across the desk from Mr. Frederick
Scott Phillips, attorney-at-law. She wasn't sure yet whether
or not she liked him, but John said he was the best, and that
was what mattered. She was determined that no one would
cheat her or her family out of anything. She looked over the
attorney reading through a legal paper. His hair was thick
and graying, but his eyes were still a deep blue. His large,
bulbous nose had little rivulets of red running over it. *Was he
a drinking man?* His mouth was generous, his smile apparently
sincere. He occasionally lifted a hand to stroke a large mole
with two sprouting hairs near the corner of his mouth.

"Well, well," his voice boomed out, almost making Anna
jump. "This looks good, very good." He smiled at Anna. "It
appears that after this action was dismissed by the Superior
Court, Mrs. McNeill has decided not to go forward with her
petition."

Anna sat up straighter. "You mean everything is safe now? My family is free to inherit Zephaniah's properties?"

"That is precisely what I mean. Of course, there is a lot of work to do to straighten out who has title to which properties, and in the meantime, someone must see that they continue to run profitably."

"Mr. Phillips." Anna squeezed her hands tightly in her lap. "Can I get the court to appoint me to be in charge of Zephaniah's properties?"

"You?"

"Yes. No one except..." Her voice faltered for a moment. "Our son George knew, but now, no one knows the properties better than I. Zephaniah left me in complete charge of Kingsley Plantation, and he always discussed his other business dealings with me. I am the logical choice."

"My dear Anna....May I call you Anna?" Her nod was slight.

"You have been away for several years. I do not think you realize the depth of racial...antipathy that exists in Florida today."

"My daughters have kept me informed of the feelings here, Mr. Phillips."

"Hmm." He stroked his mole again. "I have heard of your abilities. Perhaps this might work, but only under certain conditions."

"And what are those conditions?"

"First, you know already, I'm sure, that every free black in Florida must have a white guardian?"

"Yes, and my son-in-law, John Sammis, has agreed to act in that capacity."

"Very good. Very good. I assumed that he would. He is a powerful man. You will need his influence. The second thing is that you must not appear to be in charge."

Anna bristled.

Mr. Phillips put out his hand. "Now, settle down and

listen to me. You can be behind the scenes running things, but if you let it appear that it is Mr. Sammis making the decisions, people will not protest. That is the only way you can get anything done."

Anna sighed. "I understand. Do you think the court will appoint me?"

"That is hard to say, but we can try. I will file the necessary papers, and I will talk to John about using his influence to call in favors."

Anna smiled. She decided that she did, indeed, like Mr. Frederick Scott Phillips.

\* \* \*

As Anna and Mr. Phillips continued to meet and work together to protect Zephaniah's assets, she liked him more and more. Of even greater importance, she trusted him completely.

"I'm glad you came in today. The court has taken under consideration your request to distribute all of Zephaniah's assets. You realize, of course, that this process will take several years. In the meantime, you are managing the properties well. In this day and age, it is getting harder and harder to show profit on these large plantations."

"That is why I've come to see you. I have studied the books and talked with other planters in the area. I believe we would make a greater profit if we rented out the slaves and equipment from the San Jose plantation rather than using them to work that land. It would help future growth if we left the fields fallow for a time."

Mr. Phillips studied Anna intently. "Anna." He paused as if searching for the right words. "That makes good sense economically, but you, of all people...." He shook his head. "You, a former slave yourself. How can you think of renting or selling your slaves without regard to family units. Any action like that would not take into consideration the structure of a family."

Anna sat up straighter and drew her mouth into a tight, straight line. "I am thinking of my family. **My** family! I will do what is best, what provides the most for my family. I am here for one reason only, to fight for them, for what Zephaniah wanted them to have."

"I understand, really I do. But I must ask you to reconsider. While our government and courts will do all they can to continue the practice of slavery, they have also become sensitive to the maintenance of the family unit. I do not think you will win in court."

Anna spoke sharply. "I am instructing you to file the request to go ahead with my plans. It is for the best."

"Very well."

Anna had left her African-style clothing in Haiti, and she was unaccustomed to the horsehair and linen petticoat. It made the full skirt of her gray silk dress swish against the chair as she turned to leave. She tugged at her fitted matching jacket as she bid good-bye to Mr. Phillips.

Walking to the buggy to take her back to Strawberry Mills, Anna felt a twinge of discomfort. *I don't want to separate the families of the slaves. Hopefully, that won't happen. I have continued Zephaniah's practices of allowing families to live together and letting slaves buy their freedom. I free those who have earned it by their service. I am not a cruel mistress.* Her mouth became a taut line again. *But, if it comes down to a choice between making money for my family or some slave family staying together, I must do the best for my family. They are all I have left.* She climbed into the buggy and nodded at the driver to proceed, her mind full of conflict.

# Chapter Thirty-Nine

*Chesterfield, Florida*
*1848 – 1861*

Anna helped herself to a second biscuit to go with the remainder of the ham slice on her dinner plate. Her appetite, lost after George's death, had come back.

"Mama, you don't need to buy your own place. You can stay here as long as you live."

"I know, Mary." Anna laid down her fork. "But I will be close. Chesterfield is right next door to you, and I'll have Martha's place on the other side. It will be perfect."

"But, Mama..."

John interrupted, "Now, Mary, it is all settled. Mr. Phillips and I have closed on the property for your mother." He turned toward Anna and winked. "You know what an independent woman your mother is."

"Oh, yes, I do know that."

*And I am proud of it.*

Anna settled in at her farm, Chesterfield, soon after.

A year later, Anna and Susan Fatio L'Engle spent the afternoon strolling around the twenty-two acres of Chesterfield. Anna delighted that her friend had hardly changed over the years. Susan was still the stylish, lovely woman she had always been. Susan's children were almost grown, and she seemed content to have them go off into their independent lives. They settled on the porch to relax. Anna had come to love this property. The house was a two-story, white frame with wide verandas on three sides. Anna liked the floor plan with downstairs kitchen, dining room, parlor and study. Upstairs were the bedrooms.

"Your farm is flourishing, but, then, I am not surprised. You have always been a good manager." Susan accepted a glass of lemonade from the servant.

"The land is small enough that the few slaves I still have can tend it. This is the perfect location, halfway between Mary's and Martha's plantations. You know how I've always liked managing things. It feels good to be involved again." Susan stared at the fields. "Anna, I have something to say, and it is difficult for me."

"What is it?"

"Your home here, Chesterfield, is the center of a community of free blacks."

"Yes, that is true."

"Most free black communities are declining, but for some reason, your area is growing."

"That is also true."

"Well, things are getting more and more tense between the races. My husband is not comfortable with my coming here any more. This will have to be my last visit."

Anna sat in stunned silence. "I never thought it was a problem for you to come here, a lone white woman."

"Nor did I, because I never think about the race issue between us. I am sorry, dear friend. I understand my husband's concerns, though. Fears of a slave uprising are greater than ever here."

"I will miss our visits. I have lost all my friends, it seems."

"Perhaps we can still meet at Mary's or Martha's plantations. I know you used to feel so lonely because you didn't fit in with either black or white cultures, but, Anna, I see a different life for you here. You are the matriarch of this free black community."

"I had not thought about it, but my position here does seem that way. Of all the places I have lived, this is probably the most comfortable for me." She smiled. "It is a good feeling." Anna stood and leaned against the porch railing. "Growing old is not easy, though. Everything changes."

"Not everything. You are still the same, strong person you have always been. Look at you. You're fifty-seven years old; you've lost everything over and over; you've lost people dear to you; but here you stand, not only free but also in control of all you see."

"Free? I have a paper that declares that I am legally free, but that freedom is bound as tightly as my rolled-up manumission papers are with its blue ribbon. Zephaniah bought me forty-four years ago, and to this day he is the force that controls me. Free? I wonder."

Susan's laughter still sounded like tinkling crystal. "And who of us is really free, dear friend?"

\* \* \*

Anna's contentment with her home and her busy family highlighted her life. Still, she was aware of the ominous cloud covering the country, the antagonism between north and south, the threat of war. In 1847 a dark cloud appeared over her family again. Oran Baxter, her son-in-law died, leaving Martha a widow with children still at home.

A year after Oran's death, Anna heard Martha's voice. "Mama, where are you?"

"In the study." Anna replaced the quill in the crystal inkwell.

Anna hugged her daughter, gestured her to a seat, and pulled a chair close.

"How are you doing?"

"Oh, Mama, our finances are even worse than I feared. I've just come from the lawyers. During Oren's illness, he wasn't able to pay our bills. We have so many debts."

"I'm not surprised."

"Oren took care of all our business. I didn't even know what we had until today. Will you help me? You have managed things so well for so long. Tell me what to do."

"Of course, I'll help you. I know this is a difficult time for you, but you're not alone. Now, tell me, what are your assets? What do you still own?"

"We have St. Isabel Plantation that Father gave us. There are some investments. A few years ago, Oren bought part interest in a mill."

"All those are good security. How many slaves?"

"Thirty-six."

"Here is what I suggest. Rent out your slaves to work for the places Oren owed money. There is more money in that than in using them on your own plantation. The courts wouldn't let me do it, but you can. Keep a minimum number to work your fields and use the rest to cancel out what you owe."

"That's a wonderful idea, Mama."

Anna sat back at her desk and took up her quill again. She paused, quill in hand, her eyes focused somewhere in the future. *Martha has her father's calmness and shrewdness. I believe she will do all right.*

\* \* \*

Mr. Frederick Scott Phillips continued as Anna's lawyer and adviser over the next decade. Anna looked forward to their meetings because he seemed to respect her mind the way that Zephaniah had.

A spring day in 1860, she sat across the desk from him in his office. His features had softened over the years, his hair thinner and grayer, his eyes more watery blue. The red that highlighted his nose now spread across his round cheeks, making them perpetually flushed. The mole still stood out with two large hairs protruding from it.

"Everything is in order, Anna, as always. You have done well with Chesterfield."

"Thank you."

"Martha seems to be following in your footsteps. She has not only paid her debts, but she has increased her wealth significantly."

"I am proud of her."

"As well you should be. She is one of the ten wealthiest individuals in the county. I believe she inherited wisdom from both her parents."

Anna nodded her acceptance of the accolade before a slight frown crossed her face.

"I am concerned, though. It's not our family's personal affairs that concern me, but those of our nation. I have sensed John and Mary's tension, and Martha's, too. I'm feeling more and more uneasy about the threat of war over the slave issue. What do you think?"

Mr. Phillips formed a tent with his fingers. "You are right to be more concerned. I believe that the matter of states' rights is coming to a head. I think we will have a war within a year."

Anna felt an icy hand of fear close around her heart. *What will that mean for my family? Where is the security Zephaniah tried to build for us?*

\* \* \*

By fall, as the harvest was concluding, Anna knew the time for action had arrived. The nation would soon be divided. Her family could no longer ignore the threat. Newspapers were full of dire predictions that if Abraham Lincoln became president, South Carolina will lead the move to establish a Southern Confederacy. Anna was sure that war would soon follow. In February of 1861, Mary sent word for Anna to join them for dinner.

After dinner, the family all gathered in the living room at Strawberry Mills. John Sammis closed the sliding doors and stood in front of them. Anna sat in the middle of the sofa, surrounded by her grandchildren. Mary and Martha sat on the other sofa with more of the children.

"You all know that I have just returned from the "People's Convention," he began. "I am concerned. Very concerned. I have acted as adviser for all of you, so I wanted to let you know my feelings and what Mary and I have decided to do." He looked around at the faces of his family. The ticking of the grandfather clock could be heard in the silence.

"There is no doubt that Florida will secede. There will be a Confederate States of America organizing, and soon. As Union sympathizers, we are all in grave danger. Mary and I are going to convert all our slave holdings into cash, and I suggest you all do the same. I can send them over to New Orleans to the slave market there. It would be best if we sold our large plantations and moved north, but I fear that will not be possible. Large cotton plantations require many slaves, so nobody will be foolish enough to purchase them now. I fear we will have to write them off."

Anna sat as if she were carved in stone, but her mind and her heart were racing. *I am almost seventy years old. Must I lose it all again? Zephaniah, where is the protection you promised me?*

"What about your mercantile store, Father?" asked Albert.

John Sammis shrugged. "I will try to secure the store and warehouse when we leave, hope that the Union forces will take over this area. They will try to get Fernandina, and if they do, they will be in a better position to come and control Jacksonville. If that happens, we are safe. But if the Confederates gain control, we must flee."

"Where will we go?" one of the younger children asked.

"Only to Fernandina at first, in case we can return sooner than I expect."

"It's not far to Fernandina," said Albert.

"That won't be our final destination, however. If the Union forces do not secure northern Florida, we will sail on to New York. I have friends in the north who will help us."

"I think I will not go," Anna said.

"What do you mean, not go?" John's question sounded sharp to Anna.

"I am old now. I am tired. I had to flee when I burned Laurel Grove and my place. I had to flee from Kingsley Plantation to Haiti. I had to return here to save our family's inheritance. I do not want to run any more. No one is going to bother an old woman. Just let me be." Talking about it made her tired.

"Mama, listen to me," Mary said. "You are not an old woman. You have property and influence here in northern Florida. Everyone knows you are the most respected leader of the free black community. The Confederates will not 'just let you be.' I could not rest easy if we left you behind when we go north." Mary got up and came to her mother, kneeled in front of her and took her hands. "We will take care of you. You won't have to be the one looking out for everyone else this time. We are going to look out for you."

Anna looked into her younger daughter's face. *How can I be separated from my family again? I still have no choices in life. I must go with them.*

"Very well, I will go north with you. But I promise you, this is the last time I will flee anywhere." Anna leaned against the tufted back of the sofa. She felt weary in every bone of her body. She closed her eyes and let the plans they were making swirl around her like the dust on the walk from Yang Yang to Rufisque.

# Chapter Forty

*New York City, New York*
*Jacksonville, Florida*
*1861 – 1870*

She followed the war news closely, reading with chagrin of the first battle outside the city of Washington in July of 1861. Spectators from that city had gone out in their buggies with picnic baskets to watch at Manassas, Virginia, expecting a quick and easy defeat of the rebel Southerners. At first, it looked like that might happen, but the Virginians stood firm. Just before he was mortally wounded, Gen. Barnard Bee rallied his troops by pointing out General Jackson's solid stance. He called to his men, "There is Jackson, standing like a stone wall." That so encouraged the rebels that they pushed on, causing the Union forces and all the spectators to flee back to Washington in complete chaos. *This is going to be a long war. When will I ever get back to my home?*

In Fernandina, it appeared that the Jacksonville area of northern Florida would be safe for Union sympathizers. Of course, there was a lot of harassment. Many of the wealthy whites were required to sign loyalty oaths to the Confederacy or asked to make donations to the rebel cause. The free blacks were treated like slaves. Early in 1862, Anna began to feel a little encouraged when General Grant won the Kentucky forts for the Union. A fierce sea battle in March ended inconclusively between the warships *Merrimack* and

*Monitor.* In March of 1862, Anna began to believe that they might be able to return home soon. Gen. Thomas Sherman was sent to Jacksonville to establish a Union base. That was not to be. Anti-Union sympathies became even stronger.

"I have been receiving an increasing number of threats. I think it is time to go on to New York," John Sammis announced to the family in early April. Within a week, Anna found herself on one of his ships as the extended family sailed for New York harbor. She felt the salty sea breeze on her face. *It is always a sea journey that takes me to a new place, a new unknown. I am so tired. I long for the peacefulness of life along the river, but it is forever snatched away from me.*

New York City overwhelmed Anna. So many people. So much noise. Anna felt closed in by all the buildings. If she had been young, she might have enjoyed the city. Mary and Martha delighted in the many stores, the afternoon teas, the concerts, and plays. Anna rarely went out.

Anna complained when she did accompany the girls out for a buggy ride. "It's so different up here. Look at the men. They no longer wear the distinguished top hat your father wore. They plop those little round hats with their narrow brim on their heads when they go about."

"Mama, those are called bowler hats. They're the latest style."

"Well, they are certainly less dignified."

"And look at the women," Anna continued. "Their skirts are so full that two women can't pass each other on the sidewalk."

Anna didn't miss the look that passed between Mary and Martha. She knew she was being difficult, but she couldn't help it. She was too old to be uprooted and taken to a strange place. She didn't like the situation at all.

She spent her days reading the several newspapers available and longing to walk along the St. Johns River again. Mary had taken her for a buggy ride to see the East River and the Hudson River, but they seemed dirty and congested to Anna. With barges and ships of all sizes, the rivers were not restful to her like the St. Johns was. She was content to stay in the large brownstone house that John had rented for them.

John Sammis kept up with what was going on in northern Florida, and Anna was eager for news when he returned from a trip there. "Fernandina is securely in Union hands. I think it is safe for us to return, at least that far."

Anna rejoiced. For the first time in months, she lost the listlessness that had been pressing on her. She was packed and ready the next day.

During the next months at Fernandina, Anna often walked to the St. Mary's River. She loved hearing the gentle lapping of the water against the shore. Her eyesight was growing dimmer, and it was easy for her to imagine that she was back at Chesterfield or Kingsley Plantation and that the river in front of her was her own St. Johns or Fort George. The croak of a heron or the squawk of a gull transported her back in time. She lived more in her memories, and she found that was more pleasant.

In the first months of 1864, the situation in Jacksonville became stable for Union sympathizers. John Sammis returned to his merchant businesses there as the Union occupation became secure. He was a member of the Florida delegation that nominated Abraham Lincoln at the Baltimore convention in June.

The family went home to Jacksonville, not to the plantation or to Anna's farm, but to a house on the edge of the growing city. The war raged on, but they were safe as Union forces controlled that area of northern Florida.

Anna stopped reading the newspapers in the latter months of 1864 and 1865. She was tired of the tragedy that the war had brought; the devastation; the destroyed lives. Even so, she was keenly aware when a peace agreement was signed at Appomattox, Virginia, in April of 1865, and only days later, of the tragic loss of President Lincoln.

*What a waste. What a waste of lives, and years, and time when I could be seeing to the planting of crops, or watching the river. The war has finally ended, the slaves are free, but what good was the effort? I must talk to Sophie about it.... I forgot. Sophie died. It's so hard to keep it all straight....*

Anna was confused about the war. She had trouble remembering why it had happened. She was very aware of the outcome, however. She knew that she no longer had any slaves or any property. She knew that she no longer had any choices. She had to live with Mary or Martha. She wanted to talk to Zephaniah about it, but, of course, he was gone too. He had promised her safety. *I guess I am safe here with Mary. Maybe my safety was Zephaniah's doing after all. He gave me these children who are taking care of me, and he gave them the properties that began their wealth.*

She often thought about Zephaniah as she rocked on Mary's porch. She saw him as he was in their earlier years, remembered his strength and vitality, thought about all he had taught her. *It was really Zephaniah who made it possible for me to live up to Bella's words, to be the strong person I could be. I was a strong person. No matter what happened to me on the outside, none of it destroyed me. Bella was right.* Anna closed her eyes and hummed a song her mother used to sing in Senegal.

It seemed to Anna that the days flowed without any pattern. She often was surprised to be called to dinner when she thought they had just finished breakfast. Where had the day gone? She remembered nothing of it.

Anna shuffled to the porch on the front of Mary and John Sammis' house in Jacksonville to enjoy the spring breeze. She held the arms of the white wicker rocker and rocked gently. She couldn't seem to ease the pain in her chest. The giant magnolia was in bloom, the white blossoms nestled on shiny green leaves. Two live oaks shaded the porch. Anna watched the sun ease into the horizon. She knew it was casting a net of silver on the river, but the St. John's was too far away to see from the house. *I miss the river. I never thought I would spend my last days away from its beauty. I never thought I'd spend my last days dependent on my daughter, without anything of my own.*

"What are you doin', Mama?" Mary came and sat by her mother.

"Just sitting."

"Are you feeling all right?"

Anna rocked in silence a moment. "I feel a little poorly, but I'll be all right."

"What are you thinking about?"

Anna looked at her daughter and smiled wanly. "I'm thinking about the river, you know, the way the water sparkles when the sunlight hits its surface, the sound the ripples make against the shore. I miss the river."

"It's only a mile away, Mama. We can drive there in the buggy any time you want."

"I know, honey." She patted Mary's arm. "It's just not the same, though. The river was always part of our life, running by our land. Now, when I see the flowing water when we go to town, I feel like I am seeing someone I used to know, and I just can't place who. Makes me kind of sad."

"Well, things are different now. The war changed so much. It has been over only five years, but almost nobody has plantations anymore."

"Yes, everything is different now."

"At least we've been able to move back to Jacksonville."

"It's been good to have the family all around, too. There's nothing like family."

Mary and Anna continued to rock, their silence a comfortable robe around them, not separating them as silence can do, but holding them close together.

"I believe I'll go lie down awhile, Mary. I feel a little spent." Anna pushed herself up and shuffled off to her room.

She pulled aside the powder-blue coverlet that Mary had kept for her and climbed onto the bed, pulling the cover over her bony shoulders. She'd had a pain in her head all day, too. The rumbling sound that pulsated in her ears reminded her of the surf. *Was it the ocean's edge as they pushed toward Gorée Island in the canoes? No...that was long ago.* She blinked her eyes several times trying to bring the room into focus. She gave up and shut her eyes.

She was a young girl, running through the savannah grass. She could smell her mother's bread frying. Bolanile and Urbi called to her to come play. She was happy, feeling strong and secure. *Was that long ago, too?* Her thoughts swirled around in confusion.

A feeling of terror began somewhere deep inside. It was night time but her father was calling to her.

"Anta. Get up. Run."

She knew she had to get away, but there was darkness and chaos all around. Smoke filled the air. Anna's throat was raw. She was choking on dust and smoke. If only she could get to the baobab tree, she would be safe. Safe. What could she do to be safe?

The baobab tree was just in front of her. The smoke swirled around, making the tree's bare branches seem more grotesque. She ran toward it as fast as she could.

She thought she heard someone calling her. *Anta. Anta Majigeen Ndiaye.* Suddenly, the smoke cleared as if a giant wind had blown it away. There, behind the old tree, was.... *Mama. Papa.*

"Come, little one." Her mother held out her arms to her. *Bolanile. Urbi. Madu.*

"Come join us." *Bella. Sophie.*

"You have been strong on your own long enough. Come." *Zephaniah.*

"Anna, my dear one. Come and be safe. Safe, Anna."

*George. My son.*

"Mama."

The roaring noise stopped. The baobab tree faded into blackness. There was silence. A mile away, the river lapped against the shore. The sun beams through the window sent rainbow-colored light across the figure lying still on the bed. They shimmered through the prism of the crystal inkwell on the desk.

For Anta Majigeen Ndiaye, there was, finally... freedom.

# EPILOGUE

Anna Kingsley's life was an example of inner strength, determination, and courage. Because she was buried in an unmarked grave, probably in the Sammis family cemetery in Jacksonville, Florida, the memorial to her life must be in the sharing of her story.

The facts of Anna's life are recorded in Dr. Daniel Schafer's account, *Anna Madgigine Jai Kingsley: African Princess, Florida Slave, Plantation Slaveowner.* His book ends with pictures of Anna's descendants through her younger son, John Maxwell, who reside in the Dominican Republic. Mayorasgo de Koka fell within the Dominican Republic when Haiti divided. The home which John and Mary Sammis built in Jacksonville, Florida is now listed on the National Register of Historic Places.

Part of Anna's story has been told by Susan Fatio L'Engle's great granddaughter, the author Madeline L'Engle, in her book *The Summer of the Great-Grandmother.* Besides the legacy of strength that Anna leaves behind, there remains one unanswered question. How can someone whose motivating force in life was to be free and to keep her family free, reconcile the paradox of owning slaves herself? When Anna's will was read after her death in 1870, the four slaves she owned in 1860 are named with instructions to sell them. No consideration is mentioned about maintaining any familial ties those slaves had. Of course, by the time Anna died, she no longer held any slaves, so the instruction was moot. When we consider the life of Anna Kingsley, the question lingers... like the wisps of smoke over Yang Yang on that long ago night in 1806.

The End

# QUESTIONS FOR
# BOOK CLUB DISCUSSION

1.  What does the image of the baobab tree convey through-out the book?
2.  Discuss the relationship between Anna and Zephaniah Kingsley.
3.  How did African slaves keep their culture alive in their new surroundings?
4.  How did Anna react to Zephaniah's other wives? Why do you think this was her reaction?
5.  What lessons for women in general can be gleaned from Anna's story?
6.  Would Anna's life have been different if Zephaniah Kingsley had taken her to the states instead of to Spanish East Florida? What might have been different?
7.  Is the story of Anna and Zephaniah a love story?
8.  What was it that enabled Anna to find the inner strength she needed each of the five times she had to start anew?
9.  One day, Susan L'Engle laughs and comments, "And who of us is really free, dear friend?" Discuss the ways Anna was still bound. What ways are each of us bound?